High drama. Hea[...]
Legendary fa[...]

TEXAS SHEIKHS

Texas was the only home the
Coleman brothers had ever known.
But secrets of their past have been unveiled
to reveal the truth: royal blood flows through
their veins. To forge a new destiny, they will
need to draw upon their deep familial bonds
and find loves that legends are made of.

Don't miss any of the exciting stories in this
brand-new series!

HIS INNOCENT TEMPTRESS
by *New York Times* bestselling author
Kasey Michaels
April 2001

HIS ARRANGED MARRIAGE
by Tina Leonard
May 2001

HIS SHOTGUN PROPOSAL
by Karen Toller Whittenburg
June 2001

HIS ROYAL PRIZE
by Debbi Rawlins
July 2001

Dear Reader,

Spring is the perfect time to celebrate the joy of romance. So get set to fall in love as Harlequin American Romance brings you four new spectacular books.

First, we're happy to welcome *New York Times* bestselling author Kasey Michaels to the Harlequin American Romance family. She inaugurates TEXAS SHEIKHS, our newest in-line continuity, with *His Innocent Temptress*. This four-book series focuses on a Texas family with royal Arabian blood who must fight to reunite their family and reclaim their rightful throne.

Also, available this month, *The Virgin Bride Said, "Wow!"* by Cathy Gillen Thacker, a delightful marriage-of-convenience story and the latest installment in THE LOCKHARTS OF TEXAS miniseries. Kara Lennox provides fireworks as a beautiful young woman who's looking for Mr. Right sets out to *Tame an Older Man* following the advice of 2001 WAYS TO WED, a book guaranteed to provide satisfaction! And *Have Baby, Need Beau* says it all in Rita Herron's continuation of her wonderful THE HARTWELL HOPE CHESTS series.

Enjoy April's selections and come back next month for more love stories filled with heart, home and happiness from Harlequin American Romance.

Wishing you happy reading,

Melissa Jeglinski
Associate Senior Editor
Harlequin American Romance

Kasey Michaels

TEXAS SHEIKHS:
His Innocent Temptress

HARLEQUIN®

TORONTO • NEW YORK • LONDON
AMSTERDAM • PARIS • SYDNEY • HAMBURG
STOCKHOLM • ATHENS • TOKYO • MILAN • MADRID
PRAGUE • WARSAW • BUDAPEST • AUCKLAND

Special thanks and acknowledgment are given to Kasey Michaels for her contribution to the TEXAS SHEIKHS series.

To Tina Colombo, just because.

ISBN 0-373-16869-1

HIS INNOCENT TEMPTRESS

ABOUT THE AUTHOR

Kasey Michaels, a *New York Times* bestselling author of more than thirty books, divides her creative time between writing contemporary romances and Regency novels. Married and the mother of four, Kasey has garnered the Romance Writers of America's Golden Medallion Award and the *Romantic Times Magazine* Best Regency Trophy for her writing.

Books by Kasey Michaels

HARLEQUIN AMERICAN ROMANCE
869—HIS INNOCENT TEMPTRESS

TEXAS SHEIKHS

Habib Bin Mohammed El Jeved (King of Sorajhee)

Azzam m. Layla

Badia Fayza Jamila
(Twins)

Ibrahim m. Rose Coleman

① Alim
(aka Alex Coleman)

③ Makin
(aka Mac Coleman)

② Kadar
(aka Cade Coleman)

④ Child Born
(Whereabouts Unknown)

① HIS INNOCENT TEMPTRESS 4/01
② HIS ARRANGED MARRIAGE 5/01
③ HIS SHOTGUN PROPOSAL 6/01
④ HIS ROYAL PRIZE 7/01

Legend:
— Twins

the Moroccan presents

Prologue

If it weren't for Layla, Rose was certain she and her children would be dead.

Four days earlier, Rose's Ibrahim Bin Habib El Jeved had been husband and father, and ruler of Sorajhee. Loved, adored, a benevolent ruler who always remembered that he served at the favor of his people.

To protect his people, Ibrahim had been negotiating a very public political alliance with a neighboring kingdom on the edge of Saudi Arabia, planning for Sorajhee and Balahar to become allies in the troubled Middle East. He'd even gone so far as to secretly pledge that one of his three young sons would one day marry a daughter of King Zakariyya Al Farid, ruler of Balahar.

Layla's husband, Ibrahim's brother, had been very much against the idea. Yes, Azzam was very much against the idea.

And four days ago, during a well-orchestrated demonstration against the proposed political alliance of Sorajhee and Balahar, Ibrahim had been assassinated.

Rose had gone into shock at the terrible news, barely able to function. She had come to Sorajhee as a young bride, leaving her American roots behind her to follow the man she loved with all her heart and mind. Now she was alone, and with three young, vulnerable princes to protect.

Layla had come to her the same day Ibrahim was buried, warning her that Azzam planned to take over the kingdom, first ridding himself of "Ibrahim's half-breed whelps and their bitch."

"He said this? He would kill us? Kill my *babies?*" Rose asked her sister-in-law, her shock giving way to panic and anger. "Ibrahim had considered this, but I never believed him. You and Azzam have been our friends. Our family."

"Azzam wants his brother's throne, my sister," Layla told her, "and if he has to crawl over the bodies of his brother and his nephews, he will do it gladly. Sister, he has already begun. I have learned that it was Azzam's order, if not his hand, that marked the end of Ibrahim."

Rose pressed her hands to her cheeks, willing herself past the horror, the anger. She had to set aside her sorrow and pain. She had to consider her children.

Drying her tears, she sat down to think. Small and blond, and looking very much the American that she was, she knew that Azzam and many others believed her to be young and witless. An easy pawn.

An easy target, now that her beloved Ibrahim was gone.

How wrong they were.

She was queen of Sorajhee, mother of the heirs, widow of the sheikh.

But even a wise queen knows when preservation means leaving the field, regrouping, gathering her strength. Protecting her young, as a mother lioness would protect her cubs.

Rose stood and ran to the corner of the room and a small locked chest Ibrahim had shown her months ago, when he had first begun his public negotiations with Balahar. She pulled the slim golden chain from her neck and used the key attached to it to open the chest and retrieve its contents.

"What is this, sister of my heart?" Layla asked, standing behind her, watching.

Rose turned, clutching the wrapped package to her. "The last gift of my husband, Layla. A Swiss bank account with enough funds in it to care for my children, the entire trust fund from my parents, and more. Passports for the four of us."

"Passports? Sister, consider. Azzam will stop you at the border. Unless…no, it couldn't work. Azzam would find out and kill me, too. He is my husband, Rose, but I fear him. We must all fear him. Remember, I had been promised to Ibrahim before he met you. Azzam would see me as a traitor who favored the widow of his brother and enemy."

"Don't worry, Layla. Most of the work has already been done. These are American passports in my maiden name, Coleman. And very American first names for my boys, names no one will recognize unless they have been warned to look for them. I've just got to get the boys across the border and we can fly to safety. I know a way—it has already been planned—but I'll need your help to get Azzam to let me leave the palace."

She put her hand on Layla's cheek. "Sister of my heart, you have warned me. Now help me. Please, help my children."

THREE DAYS LATER, Rose and her boys were on their way to the summer palace, taking with them a carefully chosen retinue of servants loyal to Ibrahim.

It had been announced in the newspapers that Rose and her sons had voluntarily moved from the palace to retire to the privacy of the country, where they would mourn their husband and father.

The number to the Swiss bank account and the four passports traveled with them, as did a young colt, Jabbar, Ibrahim's beloved Arabian stallion. No one would expect Rose to flee, not when she was taking a horse with her. Azzam let them go.

They never reached the summer palace. Ten miles outside of the city, Rose and her children stopped at a small house owned by relatives of her maid. They changed clothes and changed transport.

Three hours later, they were across the border to Balahar; five hours later, they were airborne, on their way to England and safety. The servants, well paid, were also on their way to safety from Azzam's revenge. Jabbar was on another airplane, already winging toward Boston and the necessary quarantine for animals coming into the United States.

Rose held Makin, the oldest of the twins, on her lap as his brother Kadar slept in the aisle seat. Barely more than babies, only three years old, they had no idea what had happened to them, but they could sense the nervousness of their mother and had been fractious and demanding until at last sleep had claimed them.

Their older brother, and heir to the throne of Sorajhee, Alim, was only a year older than the twins, but he had a wisdom and demeanor beyond his four years. He sat beside Rose now, holding her hand, stroking it. "I will protect you, Mama," he told her solemnly. "It is what my father would want."

Rose felt tears stinging her eyes as she smiled at her oldest son. How like his father he was, with a thick thatch of night-black hair, a handsome but serious face, and already showing signs of being as tall as Ibrahim. They had named him Alim, which meant "wise and learned," and Alim seemed to know what was expected of him, even in such a terrible time.

"You will be a little boy, my son," Rose told him, carefully cradling Makin as she bent to kiss her oldest son's cheek. "And, one day, you will take your father's place on the throne of Sorajhee."

They landed at Heathrow airport, to be met by Rose's brother, Randy Coleman, who had flown out from his home in Boston the moment he got the wire Layla had sent alerting him that a "precious cargo" would be needing his assistance.

That message had hit Randy square in his stomach, as it was the same one Ibrahim had sent him months ago, another precaution he had taken to protect his family. If Randy received such a message, he was to go directly to Heathrow to pick up his sister and the boys, who would be traveling under the name Coleman. Within minutes of receiving the wire speaking of "precious cargo," Randy had rented a private jet to take him to England, just as his brother-in-law had requested.

Ibrahim, much as he loved his family and wished to protect them, had known that his duty to his subjects was more important, even more sacred, than his own life. But that didn't mean he would sacrifice his family, and he had planned well. There had never been more than four passports, for Ibrahim would never leave his people, no matter how desperate the danger.

An hour after arriving at Heathrow, Rose was hugging her boys goodbye in another terminal. She had just given them each a different precious gold ring from Ibrahim's collection, proof of their royalty. Hung around each small neck on slim golden chains, they were the only tangible memory each would carry of their father until Rose could reclaim their destiny.

"My sweet darlings, don't cry," she begged the twins, who clung to her neck as she knelt before them. "Mama will join you soon, and Uncle Randy will take such good care of you, I promise. Alim,'' she said, reaching past the twins to gather him close. ''You know that I must go back and work to uncover the treachery behind your papa's death. I cannot do that if I am worrying about you and Kadar and Makin.''

''Aunt Layla will help you?'' Alim asked, fighting back tears. ''I could help you, Mama.''

''And you will, my darling. You will help me by watching over your brothers and obeying your uncle. And you must tell Uncle Randy all about Jabbar, as your papa has already taught you, help raise him to be the champion your papa knew he would become. Now kiss me, and know I love you. I'll be with you again soon, I promise.''

Randy, already aware that it would be no use to try to talk his sister out of returning to Sorajhee to rally those loyal to Ibrahim, lifted both twins into his strong arms. He kissed his sister and followed Alim into the passageway leading to the plane, as Rose stood with her hands pressed to her mouth, fighting sobs.

Within days she had lost her husband, and now her sons were leaving her. Pain, real physical pain racked her body, and an emptiness such as she had never felt threatened to swallow her, body and soul. She staggered blindly away, down a narrow side hallway, then dropped to her knees and sobbed as if her heart would break.

''I'll come back for you, my babies, with your father's murder avenged and your rights restored to you. I promise you that. But now you must be safe, and there is no safety where I'm going.''

THE DAYS PASSED, the months…and then the news came from Layla. Rose was dead, killed while breaking into Azzam's chambers armed with a knife, clearly out of her head with grief, planning to murder the new ruler of Sorajhee. Layla warned Randy to hide the children, for they were still in danger from her husband, who was now bent on destroying everyone who could be linked to his dead brother.

Randy had already made sure the boys were both legal and hidden as his wards in Boston, using the names on their passports while gaining them the American citizenship that was their right due to their mother. But it wasn't enough. The press would soon be hounding him, he knew it. Worse, Layla knew where he was, and Layla was with Azzam.

Clearly he needed to do something to make Rose's sons disappear.

At Layla's suggestion, Randy returned the three rings to Azzam, telling the man that his nephews were lost in a boating accident off the coast of Cape Cod. There were no bodies to return to Sorajhee to lie with their mother and father. Azzam accepted Randy's word and returned the rings to him. Randy put the three rings away until the boys were older, to give to them when they could truly understand their heritage and their loss.

As far as the world knew, and the press was avid in following the fate of the martyred Ibrahim's widow and children, Rose and her children had retired from public life and wanted nothing more than their privacy. Azzam had declared it, therefore it was so. Sorajhee sighed and accepted the word of a Jeved, as it always had, and Azzam closed the borders, declaring that the Fates had spoken. Sorajhee would not ally itself with Balahar.

Randy moved to a ranch near Austin, Texas, just outside a small town called Bridle. Alex, Cade and Mac Coleman moved with him, as did Jabbar, already growing toward the champion Ibrahim had declared he would someday be. Alim and Kadar and Makin were no more.

With his new wife, Vivian, by his side, acting as surrogate mother to the three boys, and with the birth of their own daughter, Jessica, Randy Coleman's ranch, The Desert Rose, grew to be one of the finest Arabian horse farms in Texas.

Randy brought a partner into the family's Boston-founded business with him, to help conceal the Coleman name, and Texan Jared Grayson ran the extensive family businesses while Randy and his nephews worked the Arabians. The three boys grew into manhood as Americans, barely remembering their roots in Sorajhee.

But they never forgot Rose, or her promise to return to them....

Chapter One

"Damn it!" Alex Coleman hastily wiped his hands on a towel, then threw it to the ground as he went racing out of the stall and toward the phone hanging on the wall at the far end of the stable. "Damn it, damn it, damn it!"

This couldn't happen. It just couldn't. He hadn't been expecting the birth this soon, or even considered the possibility of complications.

Hell, he hadn't expected the pregnancy. Jabbar hadn't been put to stud in years, having earned his retirement from both the stud and the showring, where he'd been a perennial champion. It was Jabbar who had made The Desert Rose a top breeding farm for world-class Arabians, and his offspring numbered a multitude.

Plus one, if Alex could get Dr. Clark to the ranch in time.

Why had he put his new breeding mare in the pasture with Jabbar? He had thought Khalahari would be safe, be slowly introduced to the ranch, and that Jabbar, in his old age, would ignore the retired showring horse whose injury had taken her from the ring. Alex had bought the mare for almost nothing, but she had such good lines that he hoped one day to breed her. Just not now, and not with Jabbar.

"Somebody must have slipped the old boy some Viagra

or something," his brother Mac had joked when Alex confirmed that Khalahari was unexpectedly carrying Jabbar's foal.

Consternation had changed to excitement as Alex decided that this could be a fantastic union, producing a true champion to take Jabbar's place in the ring, in the stud. He didn't know precisely why he felt that way, but it seemed as if fate, and Jabbar, had decreed it.

Now Khalahari was in trouble, the foal twisted inside her, and Alex knew he could lose them both.

"Come on, come on," he chanted as he listened to the phone ring, willing Dr. Clark to answer, to be there, to come do his magic as he had done in the past.

"Hello? Dr. Clark's office."

Alex began speaking even before the woman had finished her greeting. "This is Alex Coleman out at The Desert Rose. I need the doctor, *now*."

"I'll be right there," the woman answered.

"What?" Alex held the phone away from his ear for a moment, then realized what was going on. It wasn't old Doc Clark. He was speaking with the daughter. Hannah? Yeah, Hannah. And fresh from veterinary school. "Not you, woman—your father. I've got a prize mare down, foaling, and she's in big trouble."

"I understand, Mr. Coleman," Hannah answered, and he could hear her moving around, probably on a portable phone, gathering supplies or keys or whatever. "My father isn't available, but I can be there in twenty minutes."

"Look, sweetheart, I don't think I'm getting through to you. This is an important foal. Get your hands-on experience somewhere else. With kittens, or something. But get me your dad, now."

"He's in Dallas attending a conference, Mr. Coleman, and won't be home until very late tonight. I don't think your mare can wait for him. As I said, I'll be right there. Beggars can't be choosers, Mr. Coleman. I'm a vet. You need a vet. Now we're wasting time, aren't we?''

"But—but I don't—"

He was talking to the dial tone.

HANNAH MADE IT in fifteen minutes, pushing her four-wheel drive all the way, skidding to a halt in the stable yard as Alex Coleman ran into the yard, waving his arms at her.

Hopping out of the driver's seat, her bag already in her hand, she got caught in the seat belt and landed on all fours in the stable yard. She quickly got up, brushed herself off, then followed him into the stable at a trot. "Where?" she said, as the man obviously wasn't going to waste time saying hello.

"The big stall, down at the end, if you can get there without falling on your face again," Alex told her, leading the way. "It's a breech. Her first foal, and probably her last."

"Gee, that pumped me right up, makes me all chock-full of confidence," Hannah grumbled under her breath as she turned into the stall, tripping over a towel lying on the straw. Some entrance she'd made, pratfalls all the way. But she couldn't think about that now. Not with the mare lying there, her single visible eye wide and wild with pain.

Hannah's well-known klutziness, a symptom of her life-long shyness and her father's belief that she could never really please him, disappeared in a blink of the mare's eye, and Hannah became all business.

"Grab her head, and hold it firm while I take a look, see where we are," she ordered Alex. She was already throwing her fleece-lined jacket into a corner of the stall and rolling up her flannel sleeves. It was early March, and cold as hell outside, and the weatherman had actually promised there'd be an ice storm by nightfall, not that the weatherman was ever right. "Talk to her, let her know everything's going to be all right."

"Is it?" Alex asked, his tone caught somewhere between concern and sarcasm. "Oh, all right," he said, dropping to his knees at the mare's head. "It's not like I have a choice, do I?"

Hannah looked at him. Tall, dark and handsome is as tall, dark and handsome does, and at the moment Alex Coleman wasn't doing it for her at all. Which was strange, because she'd spent the past sixteen years of her life dragging around a crush on the man that probably matched the size of Texas and parts of Oklahoma. Not that he ever noticed. Not that he ever would notice.

Shaking herself back to attention, Hannah pulled on tight latex gloves and examined the mare, being careful to avoid the animal's sharp hooves as she confirmed Alex's own conclusion. "Breech, and too late to turn her," she said, gathering her instruments for what would be a difficult birth.

There were alternatives. Cesarean, for one, but even that was risky, as one of the foal's legs was already partly out of the birth canal. There was nothing else to do but reach in, find the other leg and pull like hell. Not exactly fancy, but the last resort usually isn't.

"Can you do it?" Alex asked, obviously figuring out what she planned to do.

"I can do it," she muttered from between her clenched teeth as she literally reached inside the mare, all the way up past her elbows. "Got it!" she said after long moments of fruitless searching, grabbing onto the foal's legs, praying the birth canal had softened and widened enough to allow a safe passage for the foal.

"Small foal, thank God," she said, pressing her head against the mare's flank as she eased the second leg beside the first and waited for the next contraction. "Probably early?"

"Yes, early," Alex said, soothing the mare. "She's rolling her eyes again."

"Contraction coming. Hold on, here we go," Hannah said, then took a deep breath. She felt as if her arms were being crushed in a vise, as the mare tried to expel the foal and her arms from its body. She had a moment to rethink the gloves, as she was afraid she might end up losing one of them inside the mare.

"Watch the spine," Alex warned.

"I...know...that," Hannah gasped, for the first time worried that her strength wouldn't be enough. But she'd gotten both back legs clear of the birth canal, and that was the biggest trick. One more contraction ought to do it. "Come on, little lady," she crooned. "Come on and give us another push. You can do it."

Her hands and arms still inside the horse, Hannah closed her eyes and visualized the drawings in one of her textbooks. Hands here. Position the foal, trying to turn it so the spine isn't against the mother's spine. Be careful of the cord. Wait for the contraction. Pull. *Pull.*

"Here it comes!" she shouted as the mare's womb convulsed again and the animal screamed in pain. Half cradling, half turning and pulling, Hannah breathed a silent prayer and, moments later, felt the foal slip into the world. Ass backwards, but here just the same.

"Keep holding her head while I check both her and the foal," Hannah ordered Alex, deftly dealing with the aftermath of the violent birth.

"What is it? Is it a mare?"

Hannah sneaked a quick look as the foal, typically light,

as an Arabian destined to be coal-black looked at birth. "Nope. You've got yourself a new stud, Mr. Coleman, and he's a beauty. Small, but a beauty. Oh, just look at that face! A perfect dish shape. A real champion!"

Within minutes, Khalahari was tending to her foal, both of them standing in the stall, the foal wobbly on his legs but already trying to nurse, and Hannah was stripping off her gloves, trying not to shake. It had been her first breech birth, not that she'd admit as much to Alex Coleman.

"Thank you," he said as they left the stall, on their way to the large washtub at the other end of the stable. "I'm sorry I was so rough on you, but...well..."

"You thought how could klutzy Hannah Clark know anything about birthing a baby," she completed for him as he turned on the water and handed her the soap, which she dropped, so that it clunked heavily in the bottom of the metal washtub.

Crisis over, klutziness back. It figured.

"Yeah, something like that," Alex said, picking up the bar of soap and handing it to her again. "Anyway, I apologize. You did a terrific job."

"I heard about this foal from my dad," she told him, concentrating on soaping her hands. "It's Jabbar's, isn't it? The original unplanned pedigree, registered pregnancy."

"A gift from the Fates," Alex said, handing Hannah a clean towel. "Desert Rose Khalid. That means—"

"Eternal. Yes, I know. It's a lovely name."

Alex tipped his head to one side, looked at her quizzically. "Arabic is one of the classes at the veterinary school?"

"Not really," Hannah answered, avoiding his smile, which had the power to reduce her to a puddle of insecurities and unnamed desires. "Arabians are of special interest to me, because there are so many stables around the area, of course, but also personally. They're just such beautiful, graceful animals.''

And an Arabian horse never looked better than when Alex Coleman sat one in the costume class of a competition, wearing snow-white Arab costume banded in gold, with a snow-white *kaffiyeh* on his head, ropes of gold weaving forming the *agal* that held the headdress in place.

The focus of such an event should still be the mount, the decorative bridle and other trappings, the proud lift of head and tail. But not when any of the Coleman boys were in the saddle, dressed in their ceremonial costumes. Then all eyes were on the dark-haired, dark-eyed men, their uniquely kinglike posture and ease, the deep golden tan of their skin against their *kaffiyehs,* the almost sensual thrill that filled the air when one of them rode into the ring.

Yes, all three were magnificent, but it had been Alex who had caught Hannah's attention, and dreams, ever since she'd stood on the sidelines sixteen years ago, at the impressionable age of twelve, and knew that she had just lost her heart to the unattainable.

''Hannah? Hannah, are you listening to me?''

She shook herself out of her dream, rather surprised to see Alex standing in front of her in a deep brown corduroy jacket and skintight jeans. ''Huh?'' she said, and then blushed to the roots of her honey-blond hair.

''I said, I want to apologize again, and thank you. You came through like gangbusters, totally calm and professional.''

''You say that as if you still don't believe it,'' Hannah remarked, carefully stepping around a fallen rake, mentally seeing herself stepping on the tines so that the handle snapped upward and knocked her cold. Proud of herself, she turned her head to say something else to Alex—she wasn't sure quite what—and felt her flannel shirt snag on a nail, ripping the sleeve as she instinctively pulled herself free. "Oh, God."

Alex was biting his bottom lip, manfully trying not to laugh at her, she supposed.

"That's the nail where we usually hang the rake, using the hole in the handle."

"Yeah, figures," she answered, her cheeks so hot they were stinging her eyes. Her stupid deer-in-headlights, too-big baby-blue eyes. Blond hair, blue eyes, and not quite five feet and three inches of too-slender body. All in all, at the ripe old age of twenty-eight, she felt about as seductive as a three-year-old with a lap full of dolls.

Still, anyone would think she had clown feet big enough to wear the boxes instead of the shoes, and Mister Magoo eyesight, for the way she was always walking into things, falling over things, knocking things over and generally showing all the grace of a bowlegged kangaroo.

"Maybe if you were to stand still for a minute?"

"Hmm? Oh, all right, Mr. Coleman," Hannah said, wondering how she had gotten back into the stall, when she had picked up her jacket, her bag. It was like her dad always said, she just didn't pay attention. Among her other failings, like daydreaming. Boy, had she picked a bad moment to daydream.

"Ah, good. I think I feel more comfortable when you're standing still," Alex said. His grin was still gorgeous, full of white teeth and smiling eyes, but this time Hannah wanted to bop him over the head with her medical bag, because he was openly making fun of her.

"You don't have to keep thanking me, you know. You will get a bill."

"Which I'll play, gladly. However, I want to do more than just pay the bill. You can't know how much Khalid means to me, to The Desert Rose. We've put Jabbar to stud any number of times, and kept some of his offspring for ourselves, but most get sold, as you know. Khalid? Well, he's a gift, from Jabbar to me, to my brothers, my family. He's special.''

"That's nice," Hannah said sincerely. "And almost mystical.''

"Yes. Yes, it is, and so my gratitude should be larger than just saying thank you and then paying the bill. So, if there's anything else you want—anything, please just ask. I will tell everyone I know about how cool you were under fire, and that they should have no qualms about calling you in when your father isn't available. But that doesn't seem like enough.''

Hannah lowered her eyes as the most ridiculous, out-landish, *absurd* idea flashed into her mind. Boy, could she ever think of a favor Alex Coleman could do for her! But no, that was impossible. First, because she'd never have the courage to ask him, and two, because it was a stupid, per-sonally revealing request. Totally stupid.

"Hannah? How about dinner tonight? It's not much, but it's a start, and maybe by then you'll have thought of some-thing else I could do to show you my gratitude.''

"Dinner?" Hannah's head flew up so quickly, and she was standing so close to Alex—actually, he was standing so close to *her*—that she nearly clipped his chin with her head. Stepping back quickly, stumbling for a moment, of course, she looked up at him. "Dinner? Tonight?"

Alex smiled, shook his head. "But no sharp knives," he teased, taking the medical bag from her hand and walking out of the stable with her, back to her SUV. "I'll pick you up around six or so, okay?"

She slid onto the seat, praying the keys were still in the ignition, because otherwise she'd be damned if she knew where they could be, and she wouldn't be able to stick them into the ignition anyway. Her hands were shaking badly, too badly to blame on the damp, biting weather outside the warm stable. "At six. Sounds…sounds *fine.*"

"Good," Alex said, slamming the door, then stepping away, probably to make sure she didn't back up over his toes. Hannah felt his gaze on her until she'd made the turn that would cut off his sight of her, then stopped the SUV, gripped the steering wheel with both hands and tried to get her breathing under control.

He had asked her out! Not a date. Nobody in their right mind could call it a date. It was a thank-you offer. Maybe even a pity offer. But he'd made it, and she'd accepted, and he still wanted to do something else for her. "Anything," he'd said. "Anything at all."

Oh, brother. Would she ever get a chance like this again?

ALEX SPENT ANOTHER HOUR in the stable, just leaning over the top of the bottom half of the stall door, watching Khalahari and Khalid.

They would lose Jabbar soon, it was inevitable. He'd had a long, good life, and enriched their lives as much with his presence as with the foals he provided that made up the bedrock of The Desert Rose, the growing legend of The Desert Rose as a premier Arabian stud.

Jabbar. The last legacy of his parents, the only thing besides his two brothers and the golden ring he wore on his right hand, left to remind him of Sorajhee.

There were so few memories, clouded by the passage of time and the fact that he'd only been four-and-a-half years old when he was suddenly ripped from his mother's arms and put on a plane, traveling halfway across the world to a new land, a new family.

He could remember his father, but only vaguely. A tall man, who never hesitated to bend down to speak to a small child. A man whose face Alex believed he saw in his own mirror as he shaved each morning, now that he was thirty-two, already a year older than his father had been when he was murdered.

Flashes of a long white robe. A bright white smile in a swarthy, sun-kissed face. Big hands, hands that gently held those so much smaller. The soft musical murmur of Arabic, a language Alex once knew but now had almost totally forgotten.

That was a sin, and a shame. But Uncle Randy had seen no need to keep up the boys' Arabic lessons, or so he'd said, right up until the day he'd sat the three of them down and told them otherwise.

Hiding. They'd been in hiding for twenty-seven years, all of them. Hiding from their Uncle Azzam, who still ruled in Sorajhee. Alex kept up on the news about his homeland, although he didn't say anything to his brothers, his aunt or his uncle. There was no need to worry them, make them think that he might plan to one day go back, claim his rightful throne.

It was too late for that. Years and years too late. All that was in Sorajhee were the graves of his parents. He didn't know the people, didn't even know much of the language. His life, his memories, and those of his brothers, were here in Texas.

Alex knew his father had died trying to make Sorajhee strong, safe from invasion, and that his mother had died to avenge their father and reclaim the throne for her sons. Now, with the passage of years, and the borders still firmly closed, Azzam's rule was keeping Sorajhee out of the mainstream, keeping open only the ports that were the main income-making industry in the small country. Nobody save the natives of Sorajhee were allowed outside the ports, inside the country that was nearly an island, with only one strip of well-defended border touching the mainland. It was as if Azzam had built a high fence on three sides of the country and marked it "No Trespassing."

Sorajhee was the past, both because of the time Alex had spent away from the land, and because his Uncle Azzam had decreed it to be so. But Azzam had been lucky so far. Keeping his ports open had kept the greedy eyes of the Middle East turned away from him for years, concentrating them instead on oil-rich countries like the neighboring Balahar.

But nothing stands still, and Alex, from his reading, felt sure that Sorajhee and Balahar would soon have to unite, as his father had prophesied, or they would both be overrun.

No. This was no place for a son of Ibrahim Bin Habib El Jeved. Enough Jeved blood had already been spilled, enough Jeved lives had been altered forever. Let his Uncle Azzam realize his brother had been right, or let him perish. Alex sometimes wondered if he was fatalistic or if what he felt inside him was the age-old Arab belief in fate. Either way, the fate of Sorajhee was not his. That he did know.

Alex had a job, a sacred trust his mother had given him that last day. He was to take care of his brothers, of Jabbar. He was to help his uncle Randy. And that is what he'd done. He was at peace with his past and with his future.

"I just heard," Cade said, leaning on the wood beside Alex. "I got back from town a little while ago, and Mickey stopped me to give the good news. He's a beaut, Alex. A true son of his sire. He'll be black as Jabbar, too. Glorious and proud. But that will take a while."

Alex smiled at his brother. "First he has to learn to control all four legs at one time," he said. His brother, youngest of the twins by a few very important minutes as far as the succession went, was the Coleman who had chosen running the business end of The Desert Rose as his life's work.

Both Cade and Mac resembled Alex, but there was something softer, more human, about their dark handsomeness. More of Rose lived in her twins.

Alex flicked at Cade's lapel. "A suit? You're wearing a suit? Where did you say you went? And what's her name?"

"Business, big brother, I went into Austin on business," Cade corrected him, then shook his head. "Okay, and a girl."

"There's always a girl, isn't there, Cade?" Alex said, turning to walk away from the stall. He was filthy, a little bloody, and suddenly he wanted a hot shower and clean clothes. "If you weren't so damn good at your job, I'd have to call you a playboy, you know."

"Well, now I'm insulted. I'd *like* to be considered a playboy. Has a certain ring to it, you know," Cade said, obviously joking. "Not that anyone could call you a playboy, big brother. When was the last time you were out on a date? Your Bridle High School senior prom?" They walked across the stable yard together, Cade careful of his dress shoes, heading for the main house.

"Just because I don't see one girl for drinks at seven, and another at ten for a late dinner, and call that a *double date,* doesn't mean I don't have a social life. As a matter of fact," he said, knowing he was about to put his foot in his mouth, "I have a date tonight."

Cade stopped dead outside the front door of the house. "Excuse me? I couldn't have heard that right. You have a *date?* Has anyone notified the newspapers? Who is it?"

"Hannah Clark," Alex muttered under his breath as he opened the front door, gestured for Cade to enter the house ahead of him.

"Oh, Hannah Clark," Cade said, wiping his feet on the mat, his attention momentarily distracted, as he knew his Aunt Vi didn't think he was too old to be scolded for tracing stable yard dirt into her house. "Whoa! Wait a minute. Did I just say Hannah Clark?"

"Actually, I said it." Alex hung his hat on one of the hooks just inside the foyer. "She delivered the foal, a breech, and I wanted to thank her."

"Uh-huh," Cade said, watching as Alex stripped off his jacket and hung it on another peg. "Aunt Vi hates when you do that, you know. She says the rack is just for show. You weren't even supposed to come in the front door in your boots. But, then, having a date with *the* Hannah Slip-on-a-banana Clark has probably scrambled your brains. Hannah Clark, Alex? *Really?*"

"Oh, shut up," Alex said, stomping off to the wing of the house where he and his brothers all had their own rooms.

Chapter Two

Half of Hannah's wardrobe now resided on her bed, on a small chair in the corner and draped over the desk in front of the windows. And still she didn't know what she would wear.

Fourteen pairs of jeans. How had she ever accumulated fourteen pairs of jeans? Granted, some of them dated back to her high school days, as she hadn't grown as much as a quarter inch since the tenth grade. She'd lived in jeans then, as she pretty much lived in jeans now. Jeans, and flannel shirts, or tank tops in the summer.

The only dresses in her closet were the prom gown she'd worn the night Bobby Taylor stood her up for the sophomore Sweetheart dance and the navy-blue suit she'd worn on college interviews. Even the suit had slacks instead of a skirt.

Every penny she'd ever earned at summer jobs had gone toward veterinary school, and every penny she'd earn working with her father—*for* her father—would go to pay down the student loans she'd taken out when her father refused to help her. She didn't have "casual" money, go-out-and-shop money.

And she had no reason to buy dresses. Working two part-time jobs all through school had limited her social life, not that anyone had ever asked her out more than once. Shy, tongue-tied, unsure of herself, she hadn't been any young college guy's dream of a hot date, and she'd known it. Soon the whole school knew it, and Hannah had plenty of time to keep her grades at a constant 4.0.

"Project at hand, Hannah," she told herself out loud. "Ancient history is ancient history. Concentrate on the project at hand." She jammed her fingers into her hair, put her other hand on her hip and glared at her wardrobe. She had no choice. It was the blue suit or jeans, as the pink organza would definitely be too much.

Dropping the large white towel she'd wrapped around herself after her shower, she stepped into panties, located a bra that didn't have a strap held together with a safety pin, and spent ten minutes trying to remember where she'd stuffed her only pair of panty hose—bottom left desk drawer, under a copy of *Common Parasites and Their Animal Hosts*.

She couldn't face the idea of the high-necked white blouse she'd bought to go with the navy suit. It was too virginal, just like everything else about her. Virginal to the hilt. Mold had more of a sex life. Deer ticks. Any one of those common parasites. Anything had more of a sex life than did Hannah Clark.

"Therefore, you don't have to advertise that fact," she said, returning the white blouse to the closet. Which left her with a blue suit, and no blouse.

Hannah bit at her bottom lip, shifted her eyes right, as if considering something naughty. And it would be naughty. Definitely.

Still, it beat the hell out of her white blouse.

"You're twenty-eight years old, so what are you waiting for? Go for it," she told her reflection as she pushed back her blond hair and leaned toward her reflection in the old, clouded mirror above her dresser. ''Lipstick, eye shadow, the perfume sample you ripped out of the magazine in the waiting room downstairs. The whole nine yards. Knock the man off his feet. But not literally,'' she added, pointing to her reflection.

Fifteen minutes later, she'd done it. She'd decided against the eye shadow, however, because she couldn't seem to apply it so that she didn't end up looking like a raccoon. But her freshly washed hair hung bright and clean almost to her shoulders, rather than in its usual no-nonsense ponytail. Her legs were shaved and encased in silky panty hose. Her legs felt good when she walked, when the lining of her suit slacks slid against her, but not as good as the lining of her jacket felt as it caressed her from the waist up.

All the way up to the top button, which was somewhere south of the beginnings of her cleavage.

Now, if she could keep from slamming her hands against her chest every three seconds just to be sure the top button hadn't opened, she might be able to carry this off.

She slid back her left sleeve, looked at the utilitarian watch on her wrist. Six o'clock. Alex hadn't told her exactly what time he'd pick her up—just some time around six—so she wanted to be ready and waiting when he arrived.

He would arrive, wouldn't he? Hannah's stomach hit the floor as she considered the fact that the man could phone at any minute to cancel. After all, it wasn't as if this was some big hot date. He was just thanking her for her work this afternoon. He could have done that with flowers, or just the thank-you she'd already received.

No. He'd asked her to dinner, and Alex Coleman wasn't the sort who backed out of a commitment. Was he? How the heck would she know? Worshiping a guy from afar like some lovestruck teenager wasn't the same as knowing the guy. He could be a real louse with great eyes and a bone-melting smile. She may have given him every attribute possible in her fantasies, but that didn't mean he could live up to any of them.

"You're driving yourself nuts, you know," she said as she bent down and fluffed the ancient pillows on the sturdy but relentlessly ugly brown couch in the living room of the small apartment above the office.

"Hannah? Talking to yourself again? I can think of something more productive, like making my dinner."

"Dad!" Hannah exclaimed, whirling to face her father and forgetting that she was wearing her only pair of heels. Her ankle twisted beneath her and she sat down on the couch with an inelegant thump. "I—I didn't think you'd be home this early."

Dr. Hugo Clark was a big man in every way. Six feet tall, he weighed over three hundred pounds, all of which had once been composed of very impressive muscle. That muscle had gone soft a few years ago, but Hannah didn't see that. To her, Hugo Clark was still the great big man with the disapproving eyes and disappointed expression—at least it was disappointed every time he looked at Hannah, measured Hannah and found her wanting.

"Obviously not," he said, throwing his fleece-lined plaid jacket on a chair. He never hung up his coat, or anything else. That was woman's work. "What the hell is that on your mouth?"

Hannah raised a hand to her lips. "Lipstick?"

"You look like a tart. Just like your mother before you. All those years of school, just to make a dead set at some man. Total waste, educating a female, and I always said so. That's what you're doing, isn't it? That war paint couldn't be for the animals downstairs. And for God's sake, put something on. I can damn near see your breasts.''

Hannah squeezed her eyes shut even as she instinctively pressed her hands to her chest, hiding herself from her father's condemning eyes and blunt speech. *Twenty-eight,* she reminded herself silently. *You're twenty-eight. You're a trained, licensed vet. You're not little Hannah anymore. Don't let him do this to you.*

It didn't work. Pep talks weren't Hannah's forte, and her father had mastered the art of the cutting remark, the insulting put-down. Ever since her mother had run away when she was a child, Hugo Clark had worked on making sure his daughter wouldn't turn into the same flighty creature Ellen Clark had been.

Twenty-eight years also meant twenty-eight years of being told she was worth nothing, would never be worth anything; told she was stupid and clumsy and unattractive, and probably immoral thanks to her mother's blood running in her veins.

Worse, she was small like Ellen, and blond like Ellen. If Hugo Clark wanted a whipping boy to take his frustration and hate out on, he'd found it in his daughter, in spades.

Hannah stood up, one hand still pressed to her breast. ''I really thought you wouldn't be home until very late, or even tomorrow. There are…there are some cold cuts in the refrigerator,'' she said, heading for the kitchen. ''And soup. I made soup yesterday. Let me heat it up for you, make you a sandwich.''

''A sandwich? You call that a meal? Never mind, I'll go out. I should have known I couldn't count on you. Never could, never will. Just thank God I called my service and there were no emergencies while I was gone, or you would have screwed that up, too. I can't understand it. I've taught you and taught you to remember your responsibilities, and what do I get? A cold supper and my own daughter tarted up to go out barhopping.''

"There was an emergency," Hannah said, hoping to stop Hugo before he could launch into another of his long harangues about how much she reminded him of her worthless mother. "Out at The Desert Star. Jabbar's last foal, a breech birth. Alex Coleman phoned up here on our private line, so the service didn't know about it."

"Damn!" Hugo exploded, slamming one beefy fist into his palm. "Lost them both, I'll bet."

"No, sir," Hannah said. At times like these, it was always better to address her father as "sir."

Her father looked at her curiously. "They handled it on their own?"

"No, sir. I did it. Alex Coleman phoned and I went out, delivered the foal. A beautiful little animal, and probably the next Desert Rose stud."

"You…*you* handled it?" Hugo's black-bean eyes widened in disbelief.

She hadn't pleased him. Hannah could tell by the look in his eyes, by the set of his body as he stood in front of her, that she had done the very opposite of pleasing him. "I'll get the soup started," she said, turning for the kitchen once more.

"The hell you will. I'm going out," he said, grabbing his jacket and heading for the door. "And you'd better be home by midnight, girlie-girl, or I'm throwing the dead bolt. You hear me?"

"I hear you, sir," Hannah said, subsiding onto the couch once more, flinching only slightly as the door slammed and she could hear her father's heavy tread on the stairs.

She shouldn't have come back. She should have graduated and taken one of the dozen positions offered her, from

Texas to Maine. She'd graduated at the top of her class; her options had been almost limitless.

Yet she had come home to work with her father, to help him. To prove to her father that she wasn't worthless, that she was a good veterinarian, a competent doctor. To face him as an adult, maybe even as an equal, and prove to him—and to herself—that his lifelong assessment of her had been wrong.

"I could probably give a shrink enough ammunition to have me on the couch for the next five years," she told herself as she stood up, sighed and walked back to her bedroom to put on the white blouse.

ALEX PARKED HIS four-wheel drive next to the SUV Hannah had driven out to The Desert Rose, noticing that she'd had it washed since that afternoon. An odd thing to do, considering it wasn't quite spring yet, and cold, complete with rainy weather and muddy roads. His own vehicle had a crust of mud nearly up to the bottom of the windows, and he doubted he would do much more about it for the next few weeks than let nature give it an occasional bath.

Then again, Hannah was Hugo Clark's daughter, and the man was a stickler for some things. Obviously a clean vehicle was one of them, although the man's personal appearance wasn't exactly out of *GQ*. Big and strong had softened to large and sloppy the past seven to ten years, about the same length of time Hannah had been away at school and he'd been left alone, his wife having taken off many years before that, heading for brighter lights and a bigger city.

"And away from Hugo," Alex added out loud, shaking his head. Hugo Clark was one hell of a vet, the best around, but he had all the personality of a bear with a thorn in his paw.

Alex had never thought about it before, but now he found himself wondering what it must have been like for Hannah to grow up, motherless, with Hugo Clark for a father. It couldn't have been much fun.

He knew that he and his brothers had been lucky. Uncle Randy and Aunt Vi had raised them as if they were their own, and even as they all missed their biological parents, none of them could ever say they were neglected or left hungry for love.

Alex looked at the dark two-story building in front of him; the boxlike veterinary office and the small apartment on the second floor. Quite a difference from The Desert Rose. Cheerless, with no grass, no flowers or trees. Just a cement area for parking and a double string of animal pens running the length of the cemented rear yard. Banded by streets at the front and on one side, there was a vacant gas station across the side street, while the other side of the building lined up closely with a small manufacturing plant, and the rear butted up against a small tire yard and automobile graveyard.

Hugo Clark served as vet for large animals for the most part, servicing his clients and patients on ranches more often than in his own office, which he reserved for treating dogs and cats and rabbits and, probably, the occasional armadillo. It wasn't as if he needed a fancy office.

He certainly could afford a separate home for himself and his daughter, though, that was for sure, as he was the most prominent vet in the Bridle area. Alex wondered, just for a moment, why Hugo hadn't taken more care about where he raised his daughter, then forgot about it as he remembered that he was here to take that daughter out to dinner.

Cade had teased the hell out of him before he left the ranch, warning him to wear steel-tipped shoes if he planned to take Hannah dancing, and reminding him of the day Hannah had come to the ranch with her father and fallen headfirst into a pile of manure.

Poor kid. She sure was a nervous sort. High-strung, like a young filly. Awkward, like a foal just finding its legs. Raw, unschooled, and yet with an air of promise about her, as if, with the right trainer, she could be a real champion.

Not that he would be volunteering for the job. He was here to thank her for the splendid job she'd done that afternoon. She'd saved the mare, he was sure of that, and probably the foal, as well. She'd been calm, focused, secure in her knowledge and not at all afraid to give him orders, take charge, take action.

And then, once the foal had been delivered, she'd reverted to type, turning back into Hannah Slip-on-a-banana, tripping over her own feet, stumbling over her own words, and generally reverting to the klutz he'd known and mostly ignored ever since he could remember.

But did he know her at all, beneath the shy, almost nerdy outside that she showed the world while trying to hide herself from it? Obviously not, because he hadn't believed she could handle the mare, hadn't even suspected the strength in her slim body, the calm purpose she could exhibit, the self-confidence that had practically oozed from her pores as she did the job she had been trained to do.

Hannah Clark wasn't quite Jekyll and Hyde, but it was rather like there were two of her—the competent doctor, and the insecure, stumbling girl who'd always stood very much in her father's shadow.

Not that Alex planned to look any more deeply into Hannah's life, the hows and the whys of it. He was here to take her out to dinner, thank her again and then forget about her until the next time they needed a vet at The Desert Rose.

He'd knocked on the door twice, with no answer, and

finally tried the knob, which turned easily, opening onto a set of narrow, steep wooden steps. No wonder she didn't hear his knock. He'd thought there might be one or two rooms downstairs, and the bedrooms upstairs, but it would seem that the entire first floor had been turned into offices, leaving the second floor for all of their living purposes.

Talk about your cramped quarters. Alex already could tell, from looking at the building, that there couldn't be more than four rooms upstairs, none of them very large. Hugo Clark probably filled up each of them every time he entered a room, leaving very little space for his shy, easily spooked, motherless child.

Damn, now he was getting melodramatic. Alex smiled, blaming his more imaginative and passionate side on his Arab roots, but also pleased to know that he was, even in Texas, very much his father's son.

He climbed the steps in the dark, having checked the light switch and finding the bulb burned out at the top of the stairs, and knocked on the door, which opened almost immediately.

He blinked twice, adjusting to the light spilling out into the stairway, then smiled at Hannah, who seemed to be blocking his way into the apartment.

"I'll get my purse and be right with you," she said without preamble, turning away from the door. Alex stepped back just in time, as the door closed in his face. He grinned, shook his head and headed back down the stairs, figuring it safer than standing on the top step to wait for Hannah to come barreling through the doorway and knock him down those same steps.

He stood in the small dark hallway, listening as at least three locks were turned, then looked up when Hannah, holding tightly to the railing, came toward him. Her legs were long, for such a petite woman, and her slacks were slim, allowing him to imagine how straight her legs could be underneath them.

But that was about all he could imagine. She wore a dark jacket, fully buttoned, and a white blouse that, by all rights, should have been cutting off circulation to her brain. The entire effect, minus the slacks and her sweep of blond hair, was like one big No Trespassing sign.

Not that the woman had anything to worry about on that head. It wasn't as if Alex had a death wish, and trying to get close enough to clumsy, nervous, klutzy Hannah Clark to kiss her wasn't something a guy would think about without first reviewing his health insurance. The only other time Alex could remember kissing as a sport not without potential mishap was the time he'd kissed Melody Pritchert when they'd both had teeth braces, and they'd gotten their hardware stuck together.

Kissing Hannah Clark would probably start with him putting his arm out to hold her and having her react like a startled mare, rearing up, and end with his arm in a cast.

"You look very nice tonight," he said almost automatically as Hannah hesitated on the bottom step, looking at him as if she had no idea what came next and hoped to hell he had a clue or they were both in big trouble.

"Thank you," she said formally, then pressed her lips together as if she didn't trust herself to say anything more without giving away nuclear secrets or some such thing.

"You're welcome," he said, taking her hand so that she'd come with him out of this dark, confining hallway. Otherwise, he believed they might end up standing there all night. "I made reservations for six-thirty, so we'd better get a move on, all right?"

After a false start that called a halt until Hannah bent down to replace her left shoe, they actually made it out the door and into Alex's vehicle without further mishap. He sighed as he closed the passenger door, hoping Hannah would put on her seat belt without incident, and wondered if he should be offering up the rest of the evening for some poor souls somewhere.

NERVOUS WAS SUCH A LAME WORD for the feeling that had invaded Hannah when she'd heard Alex's knock. There should be a bigger word, one that sounded the way it felt— a real *bam* of a word. A *ka-pow-ee* sort of word that gave true meaning to the slam-in-the-gut sort of terror Hannah had felt, was still reeling from as she sat across the table from the man of her dreams and wondered, not for the first time, what had possessed her to order linguine with clam sauce.

With garlic.

But the garlic wasn't the worst of it, especially since she certainly wasn't counting on a good-night kiss.

It was the linguine that had proved a challenge too great for her and her trembling hands. Linguine twirling, to Hannah's mind, could qualify as an Olympic sport, with degree-of-difficulty scores for picking the right amount to put on the fork, for twirling, for getting the slippery noodles into your mouth without dribbling the ends onto your chin.

She'd seen the grin twitching at the corners of Alex's mouth when she'd finally figuratively thrown in the towel and cut the linguine into pieces. But anything was better than having to rescue another forkful of the stuff from her lap.

"So," Alex said as the waiter cleared the plates, "what made you decide to come back to Bridle after veterinary school? I would have thought you'd get as far from here as possible." As he said the words, he winced, adding, "Sorry. I shouldn't have said that."

"You're talking about my father," Hannah said, believing she knew what he meant. "Dad's getting on, and I thought he needed me. He married late in life, you understand, and I was born when he was nearly forty. Besides, I want to work with horses, and this is horse country with a vengeance. Your stables alone keep us pretty busy."

"True enough," Alex said, picking two slices of chocolate cake from the serving cart the waiter had pushed up to the table and handing one to Hannah. "Coffee?"

She nodded and the waiter poured cups for each of them.

"You know, Hannah, I stood in front of your apartment tonight and realized that you might have had it pretty tough, growing up there without a mother."

"And with my father," Hannah said, feeling disloyal, but she couldn't seem to help herself. Something about the look in Alex's eye had kept her talking all through dinner, and telling the truth more often than not. In fact, the only flat-out lie she'd told was to say that college had been a lot of "fun." College had been work, which she had liked, but it certainly hadn't been fun.

"He's very...direct."

"Blunt," Hannah translated.

"Maybe a little stern."

"Rigid," Hannah amended.

Alex grinned. "Opinionated?"

"If that's your opinion," she shot back, then almost gasped when Alex laughed. What was she doing? She was teasing with him, bantering back and forth. And it was fun. "Want to go for the gold?" she heard herself ask. "And number one of the top ten reasons Hugo Clark is not exactly a barrel of laughs is...?"

Alex's grin faded as he sat forward, propped his chin on his hands and looked at her. Through her.

She waited, trembling, wishing she'd kept her big mouth shut.

"He doesn't appreciate what he has?" Alex asked at last, his voice low, intimate.

Hannah bowed her head, concentrated on pleating her napkin in her lap, then mentally slapped herself for fidgeting and folded her hands on the edge of the table. "I shouldn't have said anything."

"Wrong. Somebody should have noticed sooner," Alex told her sincerely, then rocked her to her core by adding, "I should have noticed sooner. Life with Hugo hasn't been a picnic, has it, Hannah-banana?"

He reached across the table, took her hands in his. "I'm glad you came home, Hannah. And I'm glad we're here tonight, as adults, rather than as the sometimes rotten kids some of us used to be. Not you, but me. Let me make it up to you."

"Make it up to me?" Hannah's mouth was so dry she was surprised she could even form words. "I don't understand."

"Neither do I, exactly," Alex said, releasing her hands and handing her a fork so that she could eat the cake in front of her. "And I don't want you to think I'm some kind of do-gooder, or a penitent making up for past sins. Still, I do remember the way you were pretty much on the outside of things growing up, even if you were younger than I, and Cade and Mac as well. I remember you coming to The Desert Rose with your dad just about once a week, and I remember the way we used to tease you."

Hannah poked the fork into the cake, breaking off a piece but not daring to lift it to her mouth just yet. "It wasn't so bad. Except maybe the day Mac tossed me into the watering trough. It was hot, and he said I looked like I needed some cooling off. He was just having fun, and I couldn't have been more than ten or twelve at the time. I think I thought it was fun, too, until everybody else started to point and laugh.''

Alex winced. ''Where was your dad?''

''Standing there, laughing,'' Hannah told him, remembering how her father had laughed with the boys, as if it had all been a very funny joke, until she'd stood up in the trough and everyone could see that her white T-shirt had become pretty close to transparent after her dunking. Then he'd grabbed her by the elbow, dragged her to the truck and lectured her all the way home about how *real* ladies don't show everyone ''their wares'' like common sluts.

Hannah frowned now and decided maybe she'd been closer to thirteen the day of the dunking. She wasn't sure, but she did know she woke up the next morning to see a training bra lying on the bottom of the bed. She'd looked at it, then cried for hours, wishing her mother would please come home and tell her what to do with it.

Some time after that, she'd wished her mother home again to explain what was happening to her body, why she was bleeding and feeling so sore and sick. She couldn't ask her father, she already knew that. So she had searched his bookshelves until she found one that explained what ''going into heat'' meant. Until tenth-grade biology class, she'd actually feared that each time she ''went into heat'' the boys in her class would know and try to go after her like stallions.

What a fear-ridden childhood she'd had. Alone, lonely and filled with fear. And all the time made very well aware that she was as worthless and shiftless and potentially wanton as her mother.

''Hannah? Hannah, what are you thinking? You have such a strange look on your face.''

''Hmm?'' she said, coming out of her private thoughts, to realize she'd finished her cake, and to become aware that she'd been lost in those private thoughts while Alex sat there, ignored. "Oh, I'm so sorry," she said quickly, reaching for her water glass and knocking it over on the table. "Oh! Look what I've done!"

Alex calmly patted the wet spot with his napkin, telling her, "It's all right, Hannah. Look—" he said, knocking over his own water glass "—we might just be starting a new after-dinner ritual, washing the tablecloth while it's still on the table."

Hannah's eyes were wide as she looked at what he'd done. "Well, that's just plain silly."

"Yes, it is, isn't it?" Alex agreed, and then he smiled. He smiled so completely and happily that Hannah smiled with him, and a part of her that never seemed to relax slowly warmed, defrosted and allowed her to laugh in real enjoyment.

Alex laughed with her, laughed even louder when the waiter came rushing over to the table with a pile of dry napkins to blot the spills. "We've started a new tradition," he told the waiter. "After-dinner spills. What do you think? Will it ever catch on?"

"I really couldn't say, sir," the waiter said sternly. "I'll get your check."

"He's not very happy," Hannah said, watching the waiter walk off, his spine rigid. "I guess that means you'll have to leave him a big tip."

"Oh, yeah," Alex said, nodding. "A really big tip. But it was worth it to see you smile, hear you laugh. You do both much too seldom, Hannah."

She dropped her gaze, then dared to look up at him again. "Don't do that or I'll get all nervous again, and I don't think there's a tip large enough to cover me knocking over the entire table when I stand up. And that's possible, you know, knowing my history."

"Hannah Slip-on-a-banana," Alex said, also sober once more. "I wonder—how much do you think that name had to do with your little mishaps? It's got to be really difficult to be graceful when everyone's waiting for your next misstep. After a while, you'd have to start believing everyone's right, and just plain give up trying."

Hannah melted. Right there in the restaurant, with the waiter placing a burgundy leather folder in front of Alex and waiting until he'd produced a credit card to pay the check, Hannah Clark melted. He knew, Alex Coleman *knew*. For the first time in her life, she felt as if someone understood her, even cared about her, cared enough to consider how she got to be the local joke, the clumsy child, the awkward adolescent, the shy teenager. The oldest virgin in Texas, perhaps in all of the United States.

"Do…did you really mean it earlier when you said you'd like to make it up to me—you know, for that stuff we talked about?"

Alex pulled back her chair and helped her to her feet, then led her out of the restaurant. "Yes, Hannah, I did," he said as he fished in his pocket for his keys, then opened the door into the night. "Why? Have you thought of a way I could begin repaying you? Tipping over my water glass seems somehow inadequate."

How would she say it? *Could* she say it? She couldn't believe she was even *thinking* it.

"Well," she said at last, once they were in the car, "there is *something*…"

Chapter Three

The last time Alex had nearly run his own car off a road had been when he had just turned sixteen and decided that driving and smoking menthol cigarettes "went together." He'd taken his first drag, choked, dropped the cigarette between his legs and nearly taken out Mrs. Rafferty's hand-painted mailbox.

This time it was a U.S. mailbox at the corner of Fifth and Main that nearly bit the dust. But then, he was older now, and the shock had been bigger. Therefore, the mailbox should be bigger, too.

"You...you want me to *what?*" he said as he recovered, slowed the vehicle to look over at Hannah in the darkness.

She had sunk down in the seat, sitting on her spine, her head on her chest. "You did ask," she said in a small voice.

"Well, hell, *yeah*—but what kind of answer was that? I mean, you could give a guy a little warning. You know, something like, 'Hey, Alex, I'm going to drop a bomb now. Maybe you'll want to duck and cover.'"

"Never mind, okay?" Hannah said, pushing herself upright once more. "Forget it. Just—forget it."

"Forget it? How am I suppose to forget it? You just asked me to rid you of your...to...you want me to—oh, hell, Hannah. You can't still be a virgin. You're what—twenty-six, twenty-seven?''

"Twenty-eight," she told him, her high-buttoned blouse choking her, half from sliding down in the seat and partly because she may just have swallowed her tongue. She wasn't quite sure. But if she choked to death in the next five seconds, she really didn't think that would be a bad thing. "I'm twenty-eight and never been more than kissed. It's embarrassing."

"How? Nobody knows but you. And now me," Alex added, shaking his head. "And that's another thing, Hannah. Why me?"

"Good question," Hannah mumbled, mortified. What had gotten into her? She hadn't had any wine, so she couldn't use drunken stupidity as an excuse. "It's just that...well, you did *ask* what you could do for me. And you said I could ask anything, anything at all, and I...well, I really would like your help."

Alex pulled up in the small cement parking lot beside the veterinary office and cut the engine. "My help. Hannah, it isn't as if you asked me to change a tire or help you move—which I think you ought to consider, not that it's any of my business. But asking me to...to—"

"Make me a woman is how I think I said it," Hannah said, helping him and cringing at the same time. The only thing worse than saying the words again would be to hear him say them.

"Yes, that," Alex said, pushing his fingers through his hair. "Is it really so necessary to you?"

Hannah nodded. "Maybe it's stupid, but yes, I do think it's necessary." She turned toward him, trying to explain. "It's time I grew up—all the way up. I thought I had, but then I came home, and I'm right back where I started. Unsure of myself, wondering who and what I am. Falling back into old patterns, probably unhealthy patterns. I still feel like a girl. A young, clumsy little girl. I'm twenty-eight, Alex. Twenty-eight! It's time I grew up."

"Having sex doesn't make you a grown-up, Hannah. Just ask all the teenage mothers, if you don't believe me."

"You…you'd be careful," she said, averting her gaze once more, grateful for the relative dark inside the vehicle, even with the streetlight shining at the corner. "You wouldn't let that happen to me."

"No, of course I wouldn't let anything like that happen to—what the *hell* am I saying? Hannah, no. It's a crazy idea. I'm sorry, but it just is."

"Okay," she said quietly. "Just forget I asked. And you're right, it is a crazy idea."

"So you're not going to go out hunting for someone else to…to make you a woman?"

Hannah bowed her head, bit her lips. She'd been right. It was worse when he said it.

"Hannah? Answer me. You *are* going to give up the idea, right?"

She looked over at him in the darkness. He couldn't know, must never know. She'd rather go to her grave a repressed virgin than give herself to anyone but this man she'd dreamed of all her life. All she'd wanted was this one time, this one memory, before she went back to her unfulfilled and unfulfilling life. Was that too much to ask? Apparently it was.

"Hannah? Would you please answer me?"

"Good night, Alex," she said, opening the door and quickly hopping out of the vehicle. "I had a wonderful time."

"Hannah!" he called after her as she ran toward the door. Then he sat back in his seat and slammed his fists against the steering wheel. "Damn it! *Now* what do I do?"

THE THRONE ROOM in the great palace of Sorajhee, located in the capital city of Jeved, had always been one of the most beautiful chambers, its simple Moorish architecture accented with golf leaf, its tall, ornamental windows looking out over the perfect blue of the Persian Gulf.

From this room, from the jewel-encrusted throne set at the top of a pedestal surrounded by steps on which the guilty, the penitent and the hopeful petitioner had all prostrated themselves, the Jeved family had ruled for generations.

Today the air in the throne room was tense, almost trembling, as Azzam, ruler of Sorajhee, looked down at his counterpart from Balahar, King Zakariyya Al Farid.

"Will you speak, my friend, or only continue to pose, impressing me with your power, which is no less or greater than mine own?" King Zakariyya Al Farid turned away from Azzam and walked to the gilt chair that had been set out for him, his white robes flowing around him as he sat, placing his forearms on each arm of the chair. "Well, Azzam? Do we talk like men or must I remind you that I am here as your invited guest?"

"More of a guest who invited himself, Zak, don't you think?" Azzam stood, motioning for one of his servants to bring another gilt chair and place it near Zakariyya's. "Very well. We will talk, old friend," he said as yet more servants brought a small table to place between them, then loaded it down with golden plates filled with figs and dates, small, rich squares of baklava and a pot of strong tea. "We will talk of what the nightingale has told me."

"How poetic. And what has the nightingale told you, my friend?"

"Whispers, my friend. Whispers of Farid planning to unite Balahar with the enemy of Sorajhee. I would slit the nightingale's throat, should I know this to be the truth, that the alliance between Balahar and Sorajhee is no more."

"What alliance would that be, Azzam? That dream was no more the day your brother died, my friend. I know that, the world knows that, and you most certainly should. Our last treaty was made more than fifty years ago, and never did have teeth," Zakariyya said, selecting a fig, turning it in his bejeweled fingers as if inspecting it, then popping it into his mouth.

He was a large man, with large appetites, but his oil-rich country was still small, just a dainty nibble for any larger country with its own appetite that wished to swallow it up. The age-old, tenuous and outmoded treaty with Sorajhee of both Azzam's and Zakariyya's fathers' time no longer kept Balahar safe, and Zakariyya knew it. Azzam knew it. The time to act had been decades ago, and had passed along with Azzam's fallen brother, that brother's fallen sons.

King Zakariyya kept his expression carefully blank as his mind became busy. There was no good, strong alliance. So why this meeting? What purpose would it serve? Or had his spies been doing more than repeating women's prattling? Was there truth to that gossip about Queen Layla, about the sons? Had he cast out his political nets on the strength of that gossip, in hope, and now stood ready to reap a great catch?

"You declared that there would be no political alliance, by deed if not by word, Azzam," he continued, "even knowing of Ibrahim's secret agreement with me that a son of Jeved would wed a daughter of mine, to insure our alliance. Now the sons of Ibrahim and both their parents are dead these many years—ask others to believe your lies that they are in seclusion, my friend, not me—and you have only daughters.''

Azzam half closed his eyes, hiding their expression behind his heavy lids. He would overlook Zakariyya's less than veiled hint that the sons of Ibrahim had been martyred along with their father. Zakariyya had delivered an even deeper insult to his manhood, or so it would seem if Zakariyya had been able to father any children of his own, which he hadn't. What was worse? Azzam's three daughters and the fact that he'd been unable to sire any children at all within his harem, let alone a son—or Zakariyya's adopted son and daughter, proof that his only wife was barren.

Children were a treasure everywhere, but here, in the Middle East, and with a succession to assure and a country to protect, often with alliances through marriage of royal children, they were essential.

Azzam's brother had fathered three sons—two at one time—and Rose had proved fruitful enough to have borne many more children, many more male babies, each birth pushing Azzam further and further from the throne he'd coveted, believed to be his right as his father's son.

"And how is your son, Zakariyya?" Azzam asked, wishing to draw attention away from himself and his daughters. Away from the badly broken alliance between Sorajhee and Balahar.

"Sharif is well, as always. Headstrong, but a good, loyal son," Zakariyya said smoothly. "We are so grateful to your Layla for bringing him to us as a newborn, gifting us with such a precious honor. My people accept him, love him, and Balahar is stronger for Sharif."

"My wife meant to assuage some of your wife's grief when her child was stillborn, and the foundling was in a need as great as your own. I rejoice that Layla showed such a generous spirit, and that your Nadirah found solace with her adopted son. Indeed, you are twice blessed by another's misfortune, as your adopted daughter came to you only because her American parents perished. She is a woman grown now. How does she fare?''

''Serena is more the Arab than those with the blood of the Middle East flowing through their veins. She is my pride, and her mother's treasure until that dear woman's death. She would have been a splendid princess of Sorajhee. But, alas, we all know this to be impossible.''

Azzam lifted a hand to his mouth and gnawed on his knuckle, knowing the moment had come for him to tell Zakariyya what he knew, or at least what he thought he knew. ''My friend, perhaps…perhaps it is not impossible for our countries to resume the alliance.''

Zakariyya spread his hands, palms up. It was time to pull in the net and inspect the catch. ''My friend, although I have not yet announced it publicly, I have already begun talks with—''

''Not this new political alliance I've been told you are considering, Zak. Such alliances are only bits of paper. I'm speaking of a blood alliance. I'm speaking of the promise made between you and my brother. You were right to question the story that Rose and her sons are hidden away in Sorajhee all these years, in seclusion, but you are wrong to believe that I had them killed.''

''Really?'' Zakariyya steepled his fingers in front of him and waited, not quite as patiently as it might seem to Azzam. He had allowed rumors of negotiations with another neighboring country, but he had done so only after hearing from his agents in Sorajhee, only in the hope that he would be sitting here today, listening to Azzam's words.

''There has been treachery, Zakariyya, but not of my making. Treachery, and many lies. I believed them all dead, much as it shames me to admit to being so gullible, so eager to accept news that benefited me. Ibrahim's American wife may still be alive, her children still alive,'' Azzam said quickly, motioning for his chief adviser, Abdul-Rahim, to step closer. "Tell him," he ordered. "And spare me nothing in the telling."

"Sire," Abdul-Rahim said, bowing. "It gives me great pain to repeat the words, knowing they may be true."

Zakariyya held up his hands, effectively silencing the advisor. He would never admit to the spies he had planted here in the palace, but he saw no reason to draw out Azzam's humiliation. "Then it is true? I have heard rumors over the years, but since half were that you had the queen and her boys killed, and half were that you keep them imprisoned somewhere, I could be sure of nothing. Ibrahim's wife, the beautiful Rose—she's alive? And the sons?"

He sat forward in his chair, no longer bothering to keep up the pretext of kingly unconcern, longing for the words that would tell him the information brought to him was correct. "What of the sons?"

Abdul-Rahim bowed, cleared his throat. "We are sure of nothing, Your Highness. But as Sorajhee comes closer to danger from our neighbors, and as word of Balahar's negotiations with those neighbors comes to our ears, negotiations that would further weaken us…"

"Yes? Speak clearly, man. You have been given permission."

The advisor folded his hands together in front of him. "It is Her Highness, you understand. Queen Layla. She has…she has become *volatile,* Your Highness. Agitated. And she has said some things within the harem…"

"Layla is losing her mind, her reason," Azzam said abruptly, and the advisor bowed again, backing away from the two royals, and quickly took his leave. "My wife is going mad, Zakariyya, and she is saying things that threaten my own sanity.''

Zakariyya popped another fig into his mouth, careful not to look at Azzam, for the man had his pride and that pride must be respected at all costs. Even as the man figuratively bared his breast and groveled before him. Zakariyya had all but invited himself here, to Sorajhee, to learn the truth. He did not feel comfortable watching his old friend fall to pieces. ''If you do not wish to continue, I understand.''

''I have to continue. Layla is distressed, and has begun to say things, disjointed fragments that, when strung together, form a necklace of treachery, betrayal and even murder. Allah forgive me, Zakariyya, but I have come to believe that Layla ordered the murder of my brother.''

Zakariyya wiped his fingertips on a damp linen napkin. Now here was something he had not suspected. Still, it was not the news he wished to hear. ''You will pardon me, old friend, if I tell you that this information only changes the culprit, not the murder itself. I have always thought Ibrahim was assassinated on your orders. The man beheaded for the crime was only the weapon, not the plan.''

''I would *never*—'' Azzam shrank in his chair, the brother now, and not the king. ''No, I won't lie. Not anymore. It is past time for truth. I organized the demonstration against Ibrahim—that much is true—as I wanted him to realize the people were against any further political alliance with Balahar. Even more, I wanted to stop your secret alliance that would have bound Ibrahim's son to your yet unborn daughter. Zakariyya, I made no secret of the fact that I, not Ibrahim's son, should have succeeded him. If his son and heir was also heir to Balahar, I could not have overcome this union to take my proper place. I needed the people on my side, rallying around me. We Jeveds rule at the pleasure of our people, as you know, and I'd hoped to make Ibrahim hear what the people wanted.''

Zakariyya relaxed, now on more comfortable ground. Speaking of political treachery, oddly, was much easier than discussing Azzam's pain over his wife. "What you *believed* they wanted, Azzam," Zakariyya pointed out silkily. "We all know what our people want, what all people want. They want peace. A strong political alliance between our two countries would have gone a long way to assure that peace. The marriage between our families would have completed the job. Now, as the years pass, that peace becomes more and more elusive. This is why I am here, Azzam. This is why you need me now, just as I still need you, since I would rather ally Balahar with Sorajhee than seek elsewhere for protection. Azzam, my Sharif has a great love of American slang. A pity at times, but I remember one phrase he uses that seems apt at this moment. Could it be possible, my old friend, that we *cut to the chase?* In other words, tell me all that you know and, together, we might see what we can do.''

"Thank you, my friend." Azzam stood, beginning to pace. "Abdul-Rahim has taken what Layla has said in her ramblings, and combined it with what he learned while interviewing Layla's servants. If we are to believe what we have heard, Rose is most definitely alive.''

"Where? Where is she?''

Azzam stopped pacing, turned to look at Zakariyya. "Rose tried to kill me, old friend. About a month after Ibrahim died, I found her in my rooms, a knife in her hand. Clearly Rose had lost her mind to grief.''

"Understandable," Zakariyya said, nodding. "She believed you murdered her husband, and must have been convinced you would murder her sons as well. Were you wounded?''

"Only in my heart," Azzam said, retaking his seat, curling his fingers around the ends of the chair arms, his knuckles going white. "I will not deny wanting the throne, Zakariyya, but I would never murder my brother or his sons in order to gain it."

"But Layla would?"

"Yes. Allah forgive us, yes. If her ramblings are to be believed, she pretended to be Rose's friend and savior, helping Rose to flee the country with her sons, then come back here to unmask me as Ibrahim's murderer, assure the throne for her sons. Layla probably gave Rose the knife she had with her that night, and helped her get through my guards, all the way to my bedside. And I was blind to it. Blind to it all."

"You didn't have Queen Rose brought to trial, executed, that I know. You said only that she and her sons had retired to a life of seclusion and mourning. What did you really do, Azzam? Whatever did you do?"

"I *ruled*, Zakariyya. I ruled my mourning, shattered country as best I could. And because I was so busy, I allowed Layla to talk me into sending Rose to an asylum for those with illness of the mind. I believed her when she told me the boys had gone to their uncle in America, then all had died in a boating accident. I have believed Layla all these years, but now I know she lied. I turned my head, preferred not to hear, and allowed Layla to make my sister-in-law a political prisoner. I cannot be entirely sure of Rose's fate anymore, but the sons are still living somewhere in America. Layla stalks the harem nightly, wringing her hands, beating at herself for not having them killed when she had the chance."

The sons. The sons were also alive. His spies had learned the truth. It was almost more than he could hope to have heard. Zakariyya's heart sang, but he kept his expression blank. "So now you question the boys' fates as well? Where is this uncle?"

"Texas," Azzam said quietly. "Randy Coleman owns a ranch called The Desert Rose there. A horse farm. Arabian horses." He looked at Zakariyya. "The first stud is retired now, but that stud's name is Jabbar."

"Ibrahim's favorite," Zakariyya whispered. "I remember. And the boys? Are they there?"

Azzam nodded, unable to speak. "Abdul-Rahim is convinced Coleman's three sons are Ibrahim's. Grown men now, all three, and one of them promised to a daughter of Balahar. Your daughter Serena, Zakariyya."

Zakariyya was quiet for some moments. "You will contact this Coleman?" he asked at last. "Ibrahim's widow is his sister."

Azzam nodded. "It will be done in good time, but not yet. I want to do more than simply tell him his sister may be alive, in an asylum somewhere in Europe. Unfortunately, I know not where as yet, but I will. It is my duty to find her, and pray that she is saner than my poor, misguided Layla, who now suffers the fate she wished upon Queen Rose."

"And if Coleman's sons are really the heirs of Ibrahim, and the true heirs to the throne of Sorajhee? What then, my old friend?"

Azzam's expression was bleak. "As it has always been for the Jeved of Sorajhee, as it has been for the Al Farid of Balahar. It will be as my people will. This I promise you, Zakariyya. If the people wish it, I will step aside. There has already been too much pain."

SHORTLY AFTER DAWN, Alex made his way to the stables to look in on Khalahari and the foal, Khalid. He stood just outside the last stall in the stable that held more than fifty splendid Arabians, and marveled at the sight of Jabbar's son.

The foal finished feeding, then shook his head and looked straight at Alex. The small animal's head lifted proudly before it turned away, disdainful of the interruption by a mere man.

"Oh, you're a prince, all right," Alex said, grinning. "But learn who is the master here, Khalid. Although I suppose you already have decided that, haven't you?"

"Morning, Alex," Mac said, walking toward him down the length of the stables. "I've come to see the new stud. Cade told me he's a beaut."

Alex turned to look at his brother. Cade's mirror image. How changed they both were from the small, whimpering, motherless babies that had traveled with him to Boston, to their new lives. The softness of their mother was still in their faces, a gentleness of feature that might be discernible only to Alex, but there just the same, always filling his heart with memories of the woman who had loved them all enough to leave them.

The twins were thirty-one now, the same age their father had been when he'd been cut down, assassinated by some madman who believed bloodshed was the way to peace. While Cade was a major force in the running of the Coleman businesses, Mac had proved himself to be a gifted trainer. It was Mac who trained the boarder horses for the ring, as well as some of The Desert Rose's own bloodline.

Cade was the playboy, Mac the relentless worker. Cade was a brilliant businessman beneath his banter, and Mac could care less about the business. To him, life was his horses and The Desert Rose. Especially now that he had been unlucky—damned unlucky—in love, and had all but given up on women. Horses could trust, or so he said.

"May I take a closer look?" Mac asked, already opening

the door to the stall and stepping inside. "Ah, Alex, he's magnificent!" Mac bent down, eye to eye with Khalid, and the foal allowed his attentions, even seemed to welcome them. There wasn't a horse in the world who didn't, not when Mac was the man who approached.

Alex smiled at his brother as he leaned on the low door and watched Khalid and Mac bond.

Uncle Randy and Aunt Vi had done a splendid job in raising the sons of Ibrahim Bin Habib El Jeved, for Alex wasn't so dedicated to his brothers that he believed he had done so well all on his own. He was only a little over a year older than Mac and Cade, but he was still the older brother. He had been given a mission by his mother, and he had always taken his responsibility seriously. Even now, with the twins grown, Alex felt responsible for them, as he had always taken on the role of big brother for Randy and Vi's daughter, Jessica. Sometimes he thought he felt responsible for the whole world.

That thought brought him back to Hannah Clark, and the mind-blowing request she had made of him last night. He did feel some responsibility for Hannah's self-conscious demeanor, her shy and awkward bumbling and stumbling. After all, she'd been at The Desert Rose weekly with her father, and if Alex had not joined in the lighthearted but— he saw now—painful teasing his brothers had indulged in, he certainly had done nothing to stop it.

He'd never looked beyond the nervous smile or the pratfalls, the stumbles, the awkward child who sometimes seemed to have her legs on backwards, and her tongue in a knot. He'd never considered her as a person, another motherless child like himself, but without the love of someone like Aunt Vi. A boy needed his mother, certainly. But a girl without a mother, and with a bombastic, sarcastic, hardheaded and bitter man like Hugo Clark for a father needed one most of all.

Could Alex absolve himself from all blame for the way Hannah Clark had turned out? He certainly hadn't helped her, not in all the years she'd hung around the fringes of The Desert Rose, watching and hoping and either teased or ignored.

Now she'd done him a favor and asked a favor in return. She didn't see that she had grown into a competent veterinarian, a woman who didn't mumble or falter or feel insecure when it came to helping a distressed mare in real danger.

Hannah had been competent and assured the entire time she'd dealt with Khalahari, only reverting to type after the job was done, the mare and foal safe. There was a part of Hannah Clark that had grown, matured. Triumphed.

But she didn't see that, obviously, and Alex highly doubted that she had heard a single word of praise from Hugo.

And yet she'd come back to Bridle, come back to her father. He was getting older, she'd said, and she'd come back to help him, be the dutiful daughter. Why was it that so often the most undeserving parents were gifted with the most loyal love? Was the need for a parent's love, a parent's acceptance, that strong?

Probably, or else Hannah would have been long gone, never returning after getting her degrees, which she'd instead carried home to Hugo who, if Alex read the man correctly, never uttered a word of praise for her accomplishment.

That wasn't Alex's fault, damn it, and he knew it. And yet...and yet he felt this *responsibility,* this need to help Hannah realize who she was, how wonderful she was all by herself.

Wonderful? Alex shook his head, wondering where that word had come from. Yes, he'd been impressed with Hannah the vet, definitely. But he had also been impressed with her conversation, the flashes of wit and humor that she tried to hide. And he'd been just about blown away by that damn top button on her blouse, spending at least half the night wondering what would happen if he reached across the table and undid it.

"Alex?" Mac said as Alex stepped back, allowing Mac to exit the stall. "Cade told me you took Hannah Clark to dinner last night."

"To thank her for saving Khalahari and Khalid, yes," Alex said, turning with his brother and walking back down the length of the stables.

"I don't think I've seen her since she got back from veterinary school. How is she?" Mac asked, stopping at the door to the stables and looking out at another cold, damp morning. "Still the klutz? Good old Hannah Slip-on-a-banana."

"She's twenty-eight and a damn good vet, Mac," Alex said angrily. "I think we can safely retire that old joke now."

"Hey, hey! Calm down, brother. I didn't mean anything by it. What happened? Did the clumsy duckling turn into a graceful swan?"

Alex felt the muscles in his jaw tensing as he bit down hard, nearly grinding his teeth. "Look, Mac, I know you've sworn off women, but take it easy, okay? Hannah's a nice kid."

"Kid? Alex, you just reminded me that she's twenty-eight now. Hardly a kid. Now, if I promise to be nice, will you tell me what she looks like all grown up? I remember blond hair in pigtails."

Alex closed his eyes, surprised at how clearly he could

picture Hannah in his mind. Her thick, naturally blond hair swinging just at her shoulders. Those huge blue eyes that were too often shadowed by some inner pain. A full mouth that smiled too seldom. Her body, petite yet strong, her slim shoulders seemingly weighted down with problems much too heavy for her to carry.

"No more pigtails," he said at last, because suddenly that was all he wanted to say about Hannah Clark. Everything else was both too personal and too confusing. "See you back at the house, Mac. And don't get caught up in anything out here, okay? You know Vi expects us all to be on time for breakfast."

"Your wish, as always, is my command, Oh big brother of mine," Mac said with a sharp salute, then smiled before turning back into the stables.

Alex shook his head. Mac would forget. He'd find a hoof he thought needed cleaning and do it himself rather than ask the ranch hands—Jan or Mickey or Hal—to do it. And Cade would eat his pancakes so they wouldn't get cold, and so that Vi wouldn't fret, worried that Mac, a big strong man, would fade away into nothing because he forgot to eat.

Just another day at The Desert Rose. Another dawn, another challenge, another day.

Except that today, everywhere Alex looked, he saw a skinny little kid in pigtails, hiding behind a post, peering at his brothers and himself, her big blue eyes filled with longing.

Chapter Four

Hannah sat in the front seat of her father's SUV, her head in her hands, sobbing.

The storm raged both inside and outside, a storm of weeping from the gray skies and the flood of tears Hannah no longer fought to control. She was cold, wet, covered in mud and heartbroken.

She was also stranded on the side of the road, her front left tire shredded and flat because she had failed to clear the edge of the cow-catcher on the road leading from the Bates ranch. Instead of using the main road, she'd opted for a shortcut, knowing her SUV was capable of going off the road to avoid the cow-catcher, but her tears had blinded her, and her mind hadn't been concentrating on her driving.

Now she was stuck, unable to go farther, even limping the SUV along slowly, not without damaging the wheel, her father's precious SUV itself.

She'd have to change the tire. That wasn't impossible, and Lord knows she'd done it before, but she hadn't been cold and muddy and heartbroken, and the weather hadn't been raining and blowing and miserable.

Why didn't she just give up? Give up, cut her losses and leave Bridle, leave Texas...leave her father? He was going to run the rough side of his tongue up one side of her and down the other over the ruined tire, and then dock her meager pay for its replacement. That much was a given.

And the lecture he'd give her? Also a given, definitely, but could Hannah face another tongue-lashing on her shortcomings, her failings, her utter disregard for his property. On and on and on. She could also give herself the lecture, being careful not to leave out the bits about her irresponsibility, so like her mother's, and how both she and her mother had been the worst fates that could befall a man, any man.

How she longed to tell him to shut up, to go to hell, to take his veterinary business and shove it somewhere he could keep it safe from his worthless daughter. Because that's what her father believed—that she had planned to come home and *rob* him of his business, the practice he had built up with his hard work and sweat all these years.

Hugo didn't believe she'd come home *for* him, to be with him, to prove to him and to herself that she was no longer scaredy-cat little Hannah, but a grown woman, a person in her own right.

And now here she was, stranded in the middle of nowhere, wet and muddy and crying over a dead horse, a distant, disapproving father, and the memory of the most wonderful yet embarrassing night in her life.

"Oh, Hannah, you're such a *mess*," she told herself, her sobs, which had been subsiding, starting up again, only to be cut short by a knock on the driver's side window.

"Hannah? Hannah, are you all right?"

This was good. Now she was hallucinating. What next? Would she look at the rain on the windshield and believe she saw the outline of Elvis? Maybe carbon monoxide was somehow coming into the cab of the SUV—she had probably damaged the undercarriage as well as shredded the tire—and she was actually slipping into a coma, hearing the most beloved voice in her life as she slid silently toward death?

"For God's sake, Hannah, *open the door!*"

She raised her head and turned toward the window. There was a man standing there, dressed in a dark green rain poncho, his broad-brimmed cowboy hat collecting water like a rain gutter and spilling it off the narrowed front of the brim. "Alex? Is that really you?"

"Who were you expecting?" he growled as she rolled down the window.

Elvis, she thought, wincing, but stopped herself in time, so that she didn't say the word. Instead, she unlocked the door, then scooted over to the passenger seat when Alex yanked the door open and climbed into the driver's seat. "What...what are you doing out here?" she asked.

"Looking for you," he said, pulling off his hat and running a hand through his wet, matted black hair. He was *so* wet. His long, thick eyelashes clumped wetly, water droplets still sluicing down his cheeks, his hat and poncho dripping everywhere. "Your dad said he sent you out here, and Joe Bates told me you left an hour ago, taking the back road. Since you weren't home, I decided to drive out this way and check, make sure you were all right."

"Because Hannah Slip-on-a-banana very easily could be upside down in a ditch," Hannah said, sighing. "Well, not quite. But close."

Alex ignored her response, reaching down and picking up the revolver that lay at Hannah's feet. "What's this?" he asked, looking at her strangely.

"Oh, God—no! You can't believe I was out here thinking about *doing* something to myself?"

Alex looked at her a moment longer, then flipped open the revolver, checking the chambers. "One bullet missing,'' he said, then lifted the barrel to his nose. ''And recently fired. What happened, Hannah?''

She closed her eyes, turned her head to the side window. Sighed. ''Dad knew what had to be done when he sent me out here after Mr. Bates phoned him,'' she said quietly. ''He knew, and still he sent me, not telling me anything, not warning me. But I did it.'' She turned back to look at Alex. ''I did it, Alex. One shot, clean, behind the ear and straight into the brain...while she looked at me, watched me...told me it was all right, that she understood... understood, and even thanked me.''

''Ah, jeez, Hannah...'' Alex put his arm around her, drew her close against him. ''One of Joe's mares?''

''Bashiyra,'' Hannah mumbled against the cold, wet oilcloth. ''She had the softest eyes, Alex. So trusting. But her leg was shattered, just destroyed. She'd stepped in a hole somewhere in the pasture this morning. I had to go out there and see her, then go back to the SUV and get the pistol. I walked back through that mud and rain, and I put her down. There wasn't anything else I could do. I'll...I'll never forget that walk back into the pasture, Alex, carrying the pistol. Never.''

''Your first?''

She nodded, biting her bottom lip. ''But I didn't miss. I owed it to Bashiyra not to botch it, make everything worse. Then I just...I just walked out of there with the pistol still in my hand, got in the SUV, and started to drive. I—I didn't quite miss the cattle-guard.''

Hannah belatedly realized where she was, who was holding her, the fact that she was, indeed, being held. She pushed herself away, sat back, ran a hand through her damp hair, knowing she looked terrible. Muddy, wet, tear streaked, and now her nose was running.

And worse, ashamed. Ashamed of breaking down, losing

her professionalism. "I shouldn't be reacting this way, Alex. It's my job, I know putting an animal down is part of that job."

"If you didn't react, Hannah, if you didn't feel that mare's pain, I wouldn't let you within ten miles of any of my horses," Alex told her, reaching over to squeeze her hand. "I'm only sorry you had to do it. I had a mount go down under me one day about six years ago, and had to put her out of her misery myself, because nobody else was around and I knew I couldn't let her suffer until I called your father to do what had to be done. I got drunk afterward, the first and last time I've ever touched alcohol. You're a woman. You cried. I wanted to cry, too."

Hannah relaxed, feeling as if Alex had just given her a gift, the gift of his own story, his own pain. It didn't make hers less, but it helped to know that someone else understood that pain, had shared it.

"Thank you, Alex," she said, wishing she could look at him, knowing she couldn't. "Thank you for what you said, and for coming out here and finding me. I think I would have sat here forever, wallowing in my misery. Silly, huh?"

"Understandable," Alex countered, his tone revealing his feelings.

"You're thinking about my dad, aren't you?" Hannah asked, sensing his anger. "I shouldn't have said anything. Really. I'm not even sure he knew I'd have to put Bashiyra down. Please forget what I said."

"Hannah, he—" Alex broke off, muttered something under his breath. "All right. If that's how you want to play it, Hannah."

"That's how I have to play it, Alex, how I have to think about it. Because if I thought Dad knew about Bashiyra, and deliberately set me up to fail...well, I don't want to think about that, okay?"

"Okay. Let's change a tire, then I'll follow you home to make sure there isn't any other damage to the car. And then, Miss Hannah Clark, after you've gotten into some dry clothes you and I are going back to The Desert Rose so I can change, and *then* we're going out to lunch. All right?"

Hannah suddenly felt warm and dry, and even cosseted. "Lunch? Are you sure?"

"No, frankly, I'm not. But that's what we're going to do. Now come on, this rain isn't going anywhere so we can't wait it out. Besides, I don't think either of us can get any wetter or muddier."

GETTING INTO "some dry clothes" meant, for Hannah, showering quickly and then pulling on yet another pair of jeans, another plaid flannel shirt. After gathering her freshly shampooed and still damp hair back into a ponytail, she'd dug a dry pair of sneakers out of the rear of her closet and run back outside, before her father could come upstairs from the office and ask where she might think she was going—and then tell her, no, she wasn't, because there were cages to clean and manure to be shoveled.

"Fifteen minutes," Alex said, consulting his wristwatch as Hannah climbed into the passenger seat. "That's got to be a new world's record for females. Jessica can't be showered and dressed in less than two hours. I know, because the bathrooms in our wing of the house were out of commission while we had new pipes put in and my brothers and I had to share with Jessica. Two hours is being charitable. I have no idea what takes her so long."

"Neither do I. It's certainly not as if she needs a lot of time to look as beautiful as she does," Hannah said, conjuring up a mental picture of Jessica Coleman as she'd seen her in Bridle just last week. Lush red hair, creamy, flawless skin, her eyes bright and alive and definitely alluring. Jessica wore makeup and skirts and carried herself like a princess. Never a hair out of place, her nails always painted. And she never smelled like she'd been dragged through a stable yard; she always smelled as if she'd just stepped out of a perfumed bath.

Jessica couldn't be more than twenty-four, four years younger than Hannah, but she'd never been a tomboy or an awkward teen, at least not that Hannah could remember anyway. She'd always been the princess surrounded by her adoring princes, Alex, Cade and Mac. All-girl, through and through, and friendly, popular, one of the most popular girls in Bridle.

Hannah would give her eyeteeth to be like Jessica Coleman.

"I got a call on my cell phone while I was waiting for you," Alex told Hannah as they drove out of town on Route 73, heading for The Desert Rose. "Randy needs me to look up a few things, then call him in Austin, where he's meeting with some business associates. I promise it won't take long, but I'm afraid I won't be able to be ready in fifteen minutes."

"That's all right," Hannah said, still amazed that Alex was taking her to lunch, that Alex had come looking for her in the first place. "I'll just stay down at the stables. I can check out Khalahari and Khalid for you."

"Absolutely not," Alex said sternly, or at least Hannah believed he sounded stern. "You're my guest, and you'll wait for me at the house. Aunt Vi is with Randy in Austin, but Jessica's home, and Cade and Mac."

"Really?" Hannah said, looking down at her lap, distressed to see that she was holding her folded hands so tightly her knuckles had turned white. "I haven't seen Mac or Cade for years. I doubt they even remember me."

"Relax, Hannah, they're all grown-up now. They've actually got table manners now, have stopped dragging their knuckles on the ground when they walk—and they've even grown out of teasing everybody with their own special brand of twin humor. If you can call what those two did as boys 'humor.' Mostly, they were two very inventive pains in the neck.''

"I envied them that, you know," Hannah told him honestly. "I'm sure you know it, but the way they'd finish each other's sentences, well, it amazed me. They were so very close, almost as if they were both parts of the same person."

"Leaving everyone else on the outside, looking in," Alex said as he turned left and drove between the main gates of The Desert Rose. "Even me, sometimes. Mac and Cade are only three years older than you, Hannah, right? I imagine you probably had a teenage crush on one or both of them. Most of the girls around here did, at one time or another.''

Hannah looked at Alex in astonishment. Did he really think she'd been mooning around the stables when she'd come to the ranch with her dad to check on the horses, dreaming girlish dreams about Mac and Cade? They were three years older than her, yes, but that meant that Alex was only four years older. True, the difference between fourteen and eighteen was a huge one, about as wide as the Grand Canyon, but that didn't mean she hadn't dreamed of Alex looking at her, smiling at her, actually *seeing* her.

"It's pretty difficult to have a crush on a guy, or guys, who call you Hannah Slip-on-a-banana and ask if you've taken any good *trips lately,* when they're not walking past you as if you don't even exist," Hannah said after a moment.

"Yeah," Alex said tightly. "Guess so. I've said I'm sorry for not calling them off, haven't I? I'm sure I have.

Even so, I'll say it again. We didn't make your life any easier.''

From somewhere deep inside her, Hannah felt something building, growing. Shocked, she realized it was anger. "You know what, Alex? I think I'm getting pretty tired of hearing about what an awful childhood I had. Moreover, I don't think I like hearing you apologize to me, like it's all your fault. It isn't. It never was, okay?''

"Hannah, I'm—''

"You're sorry," she interrupted. "I know, you've already said that. And if I'd known what a pity party I started by asking you to...well, you know...I'd never have said anything. I'm sorry now that I did.'' She looked at him, her knees doing that same "melting" trick they'd always done, even now, when she'd like nothing better than to bop him one. "*Boy,* am I ever sorry I did.''

Alex pulled the car into the circular driveway in front of the house and cut the engine. "Hannah," he said, taking her hand, "I'd say I'm sorry again, but you'd probably hit me. Plus, I'm not sorry, not really. I'm beginning to think I missed out on a good thing, not getting to know you better.''

"Oh." Hannah looked down at his tanned hand, those long fingers lying on top of her own. "Well, okay," she said, then turned to open the door, catching the sleeve of her shirt on Alex's watchband. Instinctively, she pulled to get her arm free, just to hear the soft old flannel tear as the material released.

Flustered, and anxious to get clear of the scene of her latest goof-up, she opened the door quickly, and just as quickly felt her right sneaker sink into a dark brown, muddy mess.

Tears sprang into her eyes, tears she blinked away as

Alex came around to the passenger side to help her. "Back to normal?" he said, grinning at her.

"Oh, yeah," she said, sighing. "Back to normal." She walked in front of him, heading for the door to the house. "But don't worry, you'll get used to it," she said, wondering where that last line had sprung from, where she'd gotten the courage to think it let alone say it.

"I think I'm already getting used to it," Alex said, holding her arm while she slipped off her right sneaker. "Now, you go inside and sit down while I make that call, then shower. I don't know about you, but I'm starving."

Hannah smiled weakly and watched him go, hungry herself. But not for food.

"RANDY? I'VE GOT THOSE FIGURES for you," Alex said, holding on to the portable phone as he walked toward his rooms, the papers his uncle needed in his other hand. "Ready?"

"Not really, Alex," Randy said across the miles, his tone somber, his voice quiet, as if he didn't wish to be overheard. "I only wanted to be sure you'd phone back. I'd like this to wait until Vi and I are back at The Desert Rose, but it can't. Not if it gets out."

"Gets out? If what gets out?" Alex asked, putting down the papers so that he could lean against the wall and use the jack built into his bathroom floor to take off his riding boots. "Randy? Is there something wrong. Something with the business?"

"No, son, nothing like that," Randy told him, and Alex breathed a sigh of relief, a relief that was cut short as another thought hit him. "Vi? Is she all right?"

"Your aunt is fine. She's napping in the other room. Like I said, I'd wait until we got home, but that isn't for another two days, as Vi wants to do some shopping and I can't say no without tipping her off that I'm more bothered than I'm letting on.''

"You know, Randy, it's not like you to be so cryptic," Alex said, half his mind still on the fact that Hannah was waiting for him. "Are you sure you really want to tell me whatever it is that has you sounding so mysterious?''

"No, Alex, I'm not sure if I want to tell you, and I don't think we should tell your brothers, at least not yet. But if it gets out, if the media were to catch a whiff of this whole thing and someone shows up there at The Desert Rose, I want at least you to be prepared.''

Alex unzipped his wet jeans and struggled out of them, still with one hand holding the phone. He was cold, shivering in fact, but he wasn't sure all the shivering came from the fact that he was wet and half-naked. "Maybe it would be better if you told me quickly," he said, walking back into his bedroom, heading for his closet and clean clothes.

"I got an express letter just before we left this morning for Austin. From Sorajhee, signed *a friend*. I stuck it in my briefcase and didn't open it until we were on our way. Alex, I'll say this fast and get it over with, okay? Your mother might be alive. My sister might be alive," Randy said all at once, the words almost tumbling over themselves. "And more. They know about you and Mac and Cade. Somehow, they know you're not dead, they know where you are. Alex? Alex, are you still there?''

Sensations slammed into Alex. A sudden memory of a soft smile, a loving embrace. The smell of jasmine. A sweet voice singing him to sleep. A worn, tired woman—oh, so beautiful but, oh, so heartbreakingly sad—telling him, "Now kiss me, and know I love you. I'll be with you again soon, I promise.''

I promise. I promise. I promise.

Alex sank down on the edge of the bed, his eyes burning

with unshed tears, his heart heavy with an old hurt. "What...what did you say? Did I hear you right, Randy? My mother? My mother could be *alive?*"

"We can't be sure, Alex, as it is an anonymous letter. But it's the first, the only communication I've had from Sorajhee since your mother's death. Almost twenty-eight years, Alex. A lifetime. Why now? Why would I get this letter now?"

"I don't know. Read it to me, Randy. Please."

Alex heard the rustling of paper and held his breath as he waited, absently twisting the gold ring around his finger. How he wanted to believe. How afraid he was to believe, just to learn that the letter was a fraud, a fake. A terrible, malicious torture from a vile and twisted mind.

"It's short, but all the important parts are here, including the fact that the writer knows who you and Mac and Cade are, Alex. Let me read it to you.

"Your Excellency, Mr. Coleman.
We are now aware that you have been acting as guardian to the sons of Ibrahim—Alim, Kadar and Makin, and we thank you for your care of them, your protection of these orphaned princes of a martyred father. It has at the same time come to our attention that Queen Rose did not, as believed, perish shortly after the death of her husband. An unforgivable treachery has come to the attention of the king, Azzam Bin Habib El Jeved, and it is his wish to correct the sins of the past, the sins of a person dear to him who acted in his interests but without his permission. We will communicate again within a few days or weeks, when more is known."

"My God," Alex said, wiping tears from his cheeks. "And it's not signed?"

"No, but it is handwritten, on Javed palace stationery. Alex, I know these people. It's Azzam who had this letter written. He's careful to absolve himself of blame, even as he hides the identity of whoever may have caused my sister's disappearance and death. Her *reported* death. God, Alex, my head is spinning. But get past the words, the ambiguity, and it means Azzam has decided he needs you, you and your brothers. I don't know how your mother fits in this, but Azzam's wife Layla must have somehow slipped, told Azzam about the three of you, that you're alive. You might be more than simply alive, Alex, you and your brothers might also be *necessary* for some reason. You have been reading the papers, haven't you? You know Sorajhee and Balahar are in the middle of some kind of talks, that King Zakariyya has been staying in Jeved for nearly a week?"

"I know," Alex said, looking toward his desk and the stack of recent newspaper clippings. "Then it's a trick? A way to get you to Sorajhee, to get all four of us to Sorajhee? Why? If my uncle knows we're in Texas, it's not something he only found out yesterday. I'm having trouble believing that part, Randy. He must have known for years, and been happy that we were gone, unknown to his people, and no threat to his throne."

"I know, Alex, and I don't have any answers for you, I really don't. I just know whoever wrote this letter is either the most evil person in the world, or someone who knows your mother really is alive. And, believe me, if there's even the slightest chance that it's true, I'll move heaven and hell to find her, bring her here. You can count on that, Alex."

ALEX WALKED BACK into the large living room more than a half hour later to see Cade sitting on the couch, reading *The Wall Street Journal.*

"Cade? Where's Hannah?"

His brother looked up, his mind clearly still on the stock market. "Hannah? Oh, right. She's off somewhere with Jessica. Something about cutting her hair, or something like that. Ella's got lunch waiting for you in the kitchen. General Motors is up three since yesterday, Alex. I told you we needed to hang on to that one."

"Jessica? Hannah's with Jessica? Cade, for crying out loud, put down that paper and talk to me."

"Talk to you? About what? Okay, sure," Cade said, folding the paper and laying it on the table beside his chair. "Do you happen to know where Hannah's other shoe is? She walked out of here with only one on. Good old Hannah Slip-on-a-banana. Some things never change, do they?"

Alex bit down his anger as Cade's last words hit him, shot through him, on so many levels. "Some things do, Cade," he said quietly. "Some things do."

Then he turned on his heels, actually grateful Hannah was with Jessica, and went back upstairs to his room. He had a lot to think about.

Chapter Five

Hannah looked around Jessica's bedroom, trying very hard not to let her jaw drop. So this was what a girl's bedroom should look like. Pretty furniture, pretty drapes, a bedspread that flowed across the mattress of a white four-poster bed like a carpet of palest pink cabbage roses.

A collection of small bottles on a skirted dressing table, a small silver ''tree'' holding at least two dozen sets of earrings, displaying them as art. A mirror with snapshots taped to it, tucked into the frame—photographs of family and friends, even one of the family dog.

A plush pink carpet beneath her feet, the lingering smell of perfume and powder. A big black-and-white stuffed panda drooped in a corner, perhaps forgotten now but still there, always there as a reminder of a happy childhood.

Three sets of mirrored bi-fold closet doors hanging half-open, and the array of skirts and blouses and sweaters and jeans, the neatly arranged shoes, sandals and boots—enough to start her own shoe store.

Amazing. Mind-boggling.

''Oh, sit down, Hannah. You can't hurt anything in here, everything's old as dirt. I want to change it, but I just haven't had time, although I did finally find time to pack away my Barbie dolls. But this pink carpeting? Ugh! What *was* I thinking! Of course, I was only fifteen the last time we redecorated in here. You know how it is, right? Organdy and pink and ruffles, and too stereotyped for words. I'll bet you did the same thing with your own room.''

''Not exactly,'' Hannah said as she gingerly sat down on a pink-and-white-striped slipper chair beside the dressing table, thinking about her small room above the office. The secondhand furniture, dark and chipped; the yellowed shade on the single window; the white chenille bedspread with all the pulls in it; the small brown-on-brown braided rag rug on the floor.

''No? Well then, you were smarter than me,'' Jessica said, pushing a lock of fiery red hair behind her ear. ''Now I'd kill for earth tones and some authentic western furniture. You know, rustic and *real*. Not this cotton-candy stuff.''

''Uh-huh,'' Hannah said, realizing that the stem of her watch had somehow gotten caught in a bit of the white eyelet skirting the dressing table. She instinctively tugged her arm away, only to watch as two of the pretty bottles on the tabletop tipped over. ''Oh, no!'' She went to grab for the bottles, forgot about her watch and, the next thing she knew, the eyelet ripped and four more bottles tumbled.

Jessica quickly rescued her, saying, ''Well, I was wondering where to start, and now I know. Thanks, Hannah. First thing I'm going to do is get rid of this froufrou skirt on here.''

''I'm so sorry, Jessica,'' Hannah said, horribly embarrassed. ''I'm like a bull in a china shop, and always was. I don't know why. Stuff like this just always seems to *happen* to me.''

Jessica smiled, patted Hannah's arm. ''Don't apologize, Hannah. Accidents happen. I once knocked over our entire Christmas tree while trying to look at one of the ornaments—and the darn thing was twelve feet high and already completely decorated. I was being *so* careful, because I knew the last thing I wanted to do was to make a mess. Sometimes we do stuff like that because we're trying so hard *not* to do stuff like that. At least that's what Mom told me as she swept up the shattered pieces of my grandmother's antique ornaments.''

Hannah picked up the last tipped bottle, thanking the gods none of them had spilled or broken, and carefully placed it where it belonged. "You might be right, Jessica," she said, relaxing just a little. "It seems the harder I try not to be a klutz, the klutzier I get. Did your cousins ever tell you about the day I was startled by one of the stallions—Desert Rose Dakar, I think—and jumped backward, landing smack in the middle of a pile of fresh manure just raked out of the stables?''

"You didn't!" Jessica exclaimed, laughing. "Oh, you poor thing. How old were you?"

"I don't know. Twelve or thirteen, something like that. Dad made me ride home in the back of the pickup truck because I smelled so horrible. And, naturally, Alex, Cade and Mac saw it all.''

"I can just imagine their reaction. You poor thing. Boys can be *so* cruel.''

Hannah blinked rapidly, not used to sympathy. "I got over it, just in time to do something else stupid. It's sort of my second career. Have medical bag, will stumble.''

Jessica laughed out loud. "I wonder if it's as bad as I have it right now, Hannah. I've done the college thing, the graduate school thing, and now I'm home and Dad expects me to take my place at Coleman-Grayson, get to know the business. But I'm not sure that's what I want. Did you always want to be a vet, or do you think you did it to please your dad?''

Hannah looked at Jessica, her head tipped to one side.

"I don't know," she said after a moment. "I love being a vet, but—I don't know. Still, it worked out just fine, since this is what I want to do now, right?"

Jessica picked up a comb and scissors and approached Hannah, pushing her back down into the pink-and-white chair, draping a large white towel around her shoulders. "But it was your decision, not his?"

Hannah rolled her eyes. "Boy, do you ever have that in one! No, it definitely wasn't my dad's idea. He wouldn't support me—figuratively or financially. I had to do it all on my own." She flinched as Jessica pulled the rubber band from her still damp hair, and because she'd said what she said. "I shouldn't talk about Dad like this. He's had a hard life."

"You know, Hannah," Jessica said, pulling the comb through Hannah's thick honey-blond hair, "I think it's all right to get *mad* once in a while."

"Mad?" Hannah asked, earning herself another wince as she tried to turn her head and Jessica gave her hair a playful yank. "I'm not mad."

"Oh, yes you are," Jessica said with conviction. "You'd have to be. You know, I took these psychology courses at school. Sometimes anger shows up in other ways. Like biting your nails. Or eating too much. Maybe even in being clumsy, falling over things. Did you ever think of that?"

"No. No, I didn't." What an odd conversation, and practically the first one she'd ever had with Jessica Coleman, who was nearly five years her junior. Hannah was still trying to figure out how she'd gotten from sitting in the Coleman living room, paging through a magazine, to being in Jessica's room, having her hair cut. She vaguely remembered something about saying she was waiting for Alex, and the next thing she knew, she was following Jessica up the stairs to her room.

"Well, if you haven't, maybe you should. When Dad starts talking about Coleman-Grayson, I head for the fridge and the butter brickle ice cream. Without fail. It just seems to work better for me than to stand toe-to-toe with Dad and tell him I'm just out of college, I don't know what I want, and would he please get off my back and let me have this year off after sixteen years of school—seventeen, if we count kindergarten. Anger, Hannah. We find different ways to deal with it.''

Hannah watched out of the corner of her eye as a lock of honey-blond hair hit the floor. "But that's different. You don't want to go into the business. I've always wanted to be a vet."

"No, I want to go into the business. I just don't want to be pushed. Just like you wanted to be a vet, but wish you'd had some support from your dad. Oh, these psychology experts! They're *so* smart! How short do you want it?"

"How short do I—oh, I don't know. When it gets in my way, I hack at it. I've never really thought about anything else."

"Well, you should. Especially if you're after Alex."

Hannah leaped out of the chair, backed away from Jessica. "I'm not after Alex!"

"Yeah, right," Jessica said, rolling her eyes. "And it was some other Hannah Clark I watched mooning over the man for the past umpteen years. My mistake."

Hannah sat down again, with a thump. "It's that obvious?"

"Well, not *that* obvious. You could have worn a sign on your back, I guess. But, yeah, Hannah. It was obvious. And now you've got him interested. He *is* interested, you know. I know Alex, and he doesn't do things out of charity or anything. He's very deliberate, has a reason for everything he does. Even if, in this case, he doesn't know it yet."

"You're wrong, Jessica," Hannah said, wishing the girl was right. "Alex took me out to dinner last night to thank me for helping with Khalid."

"That explains last night, Hannah," Jessica said, bending down in front of her to peer into her face as she snip-snipped with the scissors, carving out wispy bangs on Hannah's forehead. "Now tell me why he brought you here today."

"Well, he…that is, he just wanted to…" She took hold of Jessica's hand, stilling the snipping scissors. "Why did he come after me, bring me here today?"

"I don't know for sure, sweetie," Jessica said, grinning, "but it wasn't because he's crazy about your hair. Although he will be, once I'm through. Not that cutting your hair is enough. I think you need a total makeover. Scratch that—you need a *make*. You're virgin territory, Hannah, with *nothing* to make over because you've never done anything. Oh, this is going to be fun! Just like playing with dolls. I *loved* playing with dolls."

Virgin territory. Oh, if Jessica only knew! Hannah closed her eyes, then gave a small whimper as Jessica got busy with the scissors once more.

HANNAH, WEARING BOTH SHOES, sat in the passenger seat as Alex drove her home. He'd had lunch without her, and as she and Jessica had raided the kitchen themselves, there was nothing else for Alex to do but take her home. He kept sneaking looks at her; he couldn't help himself.

Jessica had wrought a miracle. Okay, maybe not a miracle. But the change in Hannah's hair was only a little short of astounding.

He'd thought he'd liked it last night, hanging loose nearly to her shoulders. But now…?

Now the thick honey-blond hair was chin length, and

there were these wisps of hair on her forehead. Bangs. He was pretty sure women called them bangs.

Hannah's small, heart-shaped face didn't look pinched, as it did when she scraped her hair back into a ponytail and secured it with a rubber band. She looked delicate. Feminine. Her blue eyes, blue as Texas sky, seemed to have grown in size, not filling her face but calling attention to the expression in them. The soft, sometimes confused, damn near bewitching expression in her eyes.

She'd always been there, under the pulled-back hair, the baggy flannel shirts, the definitely not designer jeans. But it was as if she'd been hiding there. He'd sensed that she was there, felt it somewhere deep inside him. But now he *saw* it; saw her.

Remarkable.

"So, did you and Jessica have a nice time?" he asked as the silence in the car began to grow a little tense.

"She's really very nice," Hannah said, twisting her hands in her lap. "She says she wants us to be friends."

"Then Lord help you," Alex said, laughing. "Jessica has lots of friends, and she always seems to make them into her own personal projects. She's a great kid, always wants everyone to be happy. I just wish she'd let up on Randy a little bit and admit that she wants what he wants. She just—and this is a quote, Hannah—wants 'to make it *my* decision, not his.'"

"You mean about going into the family business, like the rest of you?"

"No, not really. The three of us concentrate mostly on The Desert Rose, except for Cade, who seems to really have a great head for big business. The family interests are much wider than just the ranch, you know. It's the Coleman-Grayson connection, the businesses under that umbrella, that Randy wants her to learn. Randy had his fingers in a lot of pies before moving us down here from Boston, buying The Desert Rose.''

"You weren't born here?" Hannah asked, looking at him. "I don't know why I never thought of that, but I guess I just assumed you were all Texas natives.''

Alex felt his hand clamping on the steering wheel and deliberately relaxed his grip. It wasn't as if he'd ever allowed anyone into his past before today, but today was an especially bad time to begin baring any family secrets. Not after the phone call from his uncle. "We moved here from Boston when I was still quite young. Around four or five.''

Hannah sighed. "I've never been out of Texas, and doubt I ever will go anywhere else, live anywhere else. I couldn't even imagine it.''

"No, neither could I," Alex said thoughtfully, then deliberately smiled. "If you could go somewhere else, live somewhere else, where would it be?''

"As I said, I couldn't even imagine that," Hannah replied, looking out the side window as they drove along Route 73. "But, if I had to, I think I could live anywhere there are horses, and lots of open land. And heat." She turned, looked at Alex. "Snow looks pretty, on television, in the movies, but I don't think I could live in Boston, for instance. I love the heat.''

"And the humidity?" Alex teased.

"I ignore that," Hannah said, unhooking her seat belt as Alex pulled the car into the parking space beside her dad's SUV. "You can't ignore thirty inches of snow, even if you tried. Oh—there's Dad.''

Alex put the vehicle in Park and looked through the windshield as Hugo Clark approached the car. The man rarely smiled, but there was something about his narrowed eyes—not to mention the way his hands were drawn up into fists at his sides—that warned Alex that the man had a bee in his bonnet, and was about to sic it on Hannah.

"Stay here," he told her, "and wait for me to come around and open your door for you." That way, he'd quickly decided, he could act as referee, if one was needed.

"Hi, Dad," Hannah said, either ignoring or not seeing Alex's outstretched hand meant to assist her from the fairly high-riding seat in his vehicle. She didn't descend to the ground as much as just slip and land there, staggering slightly as she tried to find her footing.

It was sad to watch, even sadder now that Alex had seen Hannah laughing, smiling. Confident. But just put her with Hugo, and she reverted to the clumsy duckling.

"Don't you *hi, Dad* me, girlie-girl. Where the hell were you? I needed to go out to Tom Harrison's place and couldn't find the keys to the SUV."

Hannah frowned. Shrank another inch. "You couldn't? But I—oh, wait. I think I left them in my bedroom. I was in a hurry, and—"

"You were in a *hurry*. Well, isn't that just ducky for you. And what was I supposed to tell Tom Harrison, huh? Sorry about your colt, Tom, but my *daughter* was in a hurry."

As Hannah shrank, Hugo grew. His large body seemed to loom over her, his booming voice became the terrifying roll of thunder.

"Don't you have an extra set of keys, Hugo?" Alex asked, physically stepping closer to Hannah.

Her head, bowed in yet another defeat, raised, and she looked at her father. "There is a second set, Dad. In a drawer in the kitchen."

"That doesn't matter, though it's lucky for you that I finally found them," Hugo responded, twin spots of white appearing on his red cheeks. "What matters, girl, is that, once again, you've proved yourself to be irresponsible. The keys are supposed to be on the hook right inside the door. Always were there. Always knew where to find them. Then *you* came back, and the whole place is going to hell in a handbasket. Big degree from that big school, and you can't even remember to hang up the damn keys!''

''Is Tom's colt all right?'' Alex asked, forming a mental picture of the saying, ''put a sock in it'' and picturing himself stuffing a big white cotton one straight into Hugo Clark's nasty mouth.

''Of course she's all right,'' Hugo said, turning to Alex for a moment. His expression eased from outrage to concern in a heartbeat. ''Just a bad sprain, not a real break. Tom thought he'd lose the animal, but she's all right. Lucky for you,'' he ended, wheeling back to glare at Hannah.

''You know, Hugo, it's my fault,'' Alex said, stepping even closer to Hannah. ''I asked Hannah to have lunch with me, but I also had something to do back at The Desert Rose, so I may have hurried her along a little too much. I apologize.''

Hugo looked at Alex. Alex Coleman, who represented his largest account, his biggest caseload. The greatest chunk of his practice, his income. ''Oh,'' he said, deflating like an old, sad balloon. ''Well, she still should have put the keys on the hook. That's females for you. Irresponsible, every one of them, thinking of nobody but themselves and their own pleasure. Not that—''

''Not that I could have invited Hannah to lunch for *my* own pleasure?'' Alex said, amazed that he could still smile. ''On the contrary, Hugo, the invitation was very much for my own pleasure. As a matter of fact, I was just about to ask Hannah to be my companion this Saturday night. We're having a small, informal dance at the country club, nothing too fancy.''

Alex heard Hannah, who now stood half behind him, give a small gasp of...surprise? Dismay? He turned to her, winked. "Don't worry about getting all dressed up, Hannah, it's no big deal. Just the customary simple black dress should do it, I'm sure."

"But I—"

"You know what?" Alex went on quickly, before Hannah could stumble and stutter her way into another mess. "Jessica is going shopping in Austin tomorrow for the dance. I mean, she'd rather die—or so she says—than wear anything anyone has ever seen before at the club. How about I have her pick you up, take you along?"

He looked at Hugo, his eyes narrowed, speaking volumes even this thickheaded man couldn't help but intercept, understand. "That's all right with you, isn't it, Hugo? You can spare Hannah for one day?"

"Never needed her in the first—oh, all right," Hugo amended as Alex continued to stare at him. "Fine. Fine. But now you'd better get inside. Walk-in hours start in twenty minutes."

"Yes, sir," Hannah said, then collapsed against the side of Alex's vehicle when her father turned on his heels and slammed back into the office. "Oh, God..."

"His bark is worse than his bite, Hannah," Alex told her, reaching out a hand and running his index finger down the side of her pale cheek. "Isn't it?"

She slipped her tongue between her palest pink lips and moistened them. "If you're asking if Dad ever hit me, no, he never has. He never had to."

"There are all sorts of abuse, Hannah," Alex told her softly, wishing he could somehow erase the sad, bruised look in those huge blue eyes. "But you're not a little girl anymore, Hannah. You don't have to take everything Hugo dishes out when he's in a bad mood."

She smiled weakly. "That wasn't a bad mood, Alex," she said, pushing herself away from the vehicle. "My mother didn't come into the conversation even once. When he starts on her, starts comparing me to her—*that's* a bad mood. I'm just sorry you had to listen to him. I apologize."

"Don't apologize for Hugo, Hannah, he's not your responsibility."

"Okay," she answered, nodding. "And don't think you really have to take me to that dance at the club. I'm not *your* responsibility."

Alex bent down, kissed the tip of her nose. He didn't know why he did that. He just did. It just felt right somehow. "You are my pleasure, Hannah, not my responsibility. I'll have Jessica pick you up tomorrow. Around eight? Jessica will want to get on the road early so that she has time to hit every store in Austin."

Hannah nodded, opened her mouth as if to say something, then seemed to change her mind as she lifted a hand in a small wave and left Alex standing alone on the cement parking lot, wondering what the hell he'd just done.

HANNAH SAT ON THE RAG RUG in her room, the small hammer still in her hand, the big pink piggy bank shattered in front of her.

She'd been saving loose change on and off for years, sticking it in the big plaster-of-paris pig she'd won at a fair in tenth grade when a carny couldn't guess her weight within five pounds.

All through school she hadn't touched the pig, because there were certainly emergencies over the years—like that root canal she'd needed her second year of college—but there had never been an emergency large enough to make smashing the pig a reasonable option.

Until tonight.

Tonight Hannah had paid her bills, her student loans that would probably not be paid off until she was sixty, and then looked at the balance in her checkbook: twenty-six dollars and nine cents. Her paycheck wasn't due for another two weeks, as her father paid her only once a month, and then deducted room and board before handing over her check.

She'd rather do an appendectomy on an angry armadillo than ask her father for an advance on her paycheck.

Which left Piggy—left her in pieces on the floor.

Hannah stacked quarters and nickels and dimes, smiled over the few paper bills she'd forgotten she'd folded and stuck through the slot, and mentally divided the money into payments for shoes, hose, a dress and maybe some makeup.

No, *definitely* some makeup. And a bottle of perfume. Maybe the same perfume she'd sniffed in that pretty blue bottle on Jessica Coleman's dressing table.

After all, Saturday night dances at the club were no place to show up smelling of strong soap and a lingering eau de stable.

Two hundred and forty-three dollars, and sixteen cents. Not a bad haul, not a bad haul at all. She headed down to the office to pick up a handful of coin wrappers, planning to leave the wrapped coins there and exchange them for bills kept in the office drawer. She'd still have time to take the coins to the bank when she got back from Austin, and her father wouldn't even know about the exchange.

She smiled as she sat on the floor of her room and counted out coins to put in the wrappers. She could certainly buy a little black dress with two hundred and forty-three dollars.

Or maybe a red one. Alex might like a red one.

Chapter Six

Alex called out a goodbye to Jessica, who was driving into Bridle to pick up Hannah, and walked across the room to answer the ringing phone. "The Desert Rose," he said absently, wondering just how far Jessica would be able to get Hannah to "let go," and then said, "Excuse me? I didn't quite get that."

"Coleman. This call is for Mr. Randolph Coleman. You would please to put him on the line."

Alex shook his head, flinched. Flashback city! The heavily accented English was so suddenly familiar, that same careful speech of his memory, spoken by his father's people when they tried out their English on him or his mother.

"This is Randy Coleman," he said, looking around to make sure no one was within earshot, to hear his lie. He quickly walked to the door with the cordless phone in his hand and stepped outside the house into the cool morning. "And you would be…?"

"You are please to hold the line for his excellency, King Zakariyya Al Farid," the disembodied voice told him before the line went dead. No, not dead. He'd been put on hold. On hold, and with Arabic music playing in the background.

Well, what had he expected? Balahar wasn't only an oil-rich country. It had come out of the Dark Ages long ago. Hell, Balahar had been an admirable civilization long before Columbus had set sail. Still, hearing the Arabic version of elevator music made Alex smile.

His uncle would return to The Desert Rose later today, and he could have—should have—said as much to the caller. But the news his uncle had handed him yesterday still sang through his veins, giving him hope where, before, there had been nothing but dreams. He couldn't do anything but accept the call. He had to know and, for some reason he couldn't explain at the moment, he was pretty sure this call from the king of Balahar wasn't because the man wished to buy a few Arabian horses.

Still on hold, Alex paced in front of the house, looking out over The Desert Rose, looking to his left, toward the stables and riding ring, toward the large outdoor arena they'd had built a few years ago. Familiar territory yet always pleasant to look at, he thought, feeling the pride of ownership.

He couldn't see into the pastures behind the stables, but he knew the horses were already out there, gamboling in the sweet grass, sticking their proud heads over the fence in hopes of a crisp, crunchy carrot.

This was his home, the only home he could remember with any real clarity. Everything else seemed a dream of white walls and sometimes white-hot heat. Even the smiles of his father were no longer clear, the rumble of his voice against Alex's ear as he'd been carried high against the man's chest. Even his mother. She was also a series of memories: scents and the music of her voice, feelings of comfort and safety. Not a woman at all, not a mother at all, not in any way he could remember, trying to put a face on her, pull any individual memory out of his mind to run it past him, relive it.

Except for that last day. He'd never forget that last day. Kadar and Makin fretting and crying. Their mother's eyes dark and bruised with sorrow, her slim body seemingly bent under the weight of worries too large for him to understand. The roar of jet engines.

Kicking his uncle, kicking him hard, when the plane took off, leaving Mama behind, all alone.

Kadar and Makin. Had he really just thought of Cade and Mac with their Arabic names? Names he had been told not to speak, told to forget, just as he'd been encouraged to forget Sorajhee and his father.

And he'd done it. He'd promised his mother he would watch over the boys, and his uncle had convinced him that protecting the twins included banishing Sorajhee from his mind and heart.

Alex had built a world for himself, for his brothers. Thanks to their aunt and uncle, they were here in Texas, they were safe. They had been safe for decades. They were Americans and had no reason to want to be anything or anyone else.

Ibrahim Bin Habib El Jeved was gone, murdered. The queen was dead, the whys and hows of her death not to be contemplated. The princes of Sorajhee had vanished, never to return.

That's how it was, how fate had played out for all of them.

But now? Now, after his uncle's revelation? After that revelation had planted the seeds of hope in Alex, or perhaps just finally watered and cultivated that seed of hope that had lain dormant in him since his childhood?

What would happen now?

There was a click on the phone, bringing Alex out of his

thoughts, followed by a new voice on the line. A deep voice speaking unaccented English. A voice that clearly expected to be listened to when its owner spoke.

"My apologies, Mr. Coleman, for keeping you waiting. There always seems to be someone else who needs my attention, or believes they do."

"No problem, Your Highness," Alex said, just to say something, to let the man know he was still on the line. Because the king did not sound the least apologetic. "I am delighted to receive your call."

There was a bark of laughter on the other end of the line. Clearly the king did not have a lot of time for exchanging pleasantries or the formal dancing about that supposedly was so necessary in the Middle East. "No, you're not, Mr. Coleman. What you're doing is wondering if I am the person behind the anonymous letter you received concerning the dear queen, Rose. That was a well-meant letter but, now that I've had time to think about it, I have reconsidered. The purpose of my call is to tell you that the letter you received, although anonymously sent, is to be taken quite seriously. Ibrahim's queen might well be alive. This does not, however, mean she will stay safe, or alive. A madness runs free in the throne room of Sorajhee, and my old friend Azzam has yet to harness that madness, break it to the saddle, as it were, so that it can lead him to Ibrahim's widow before it is too late."

Alex rocked his jaw from side to side. His hand tightened around the phone. "I'm a Texan, Your Highness, and we usually just say what's on our minds. Are you telling me someone in the Sorajhee palace knows where my…my sister is? Are you telling me she's not only alive but in danger? And something else, Your Highness. *Why* are you telling me any of this? Or are you planning to use this information, and my sister, to bring down the royal family of Sorajhee?''

''Ah, you Americans. So eager to cut to the chase, correct? My adopted and well-loved son, Sharif, spent a year in your country, and came home enamored of both your slang and your freedoms. Very well, Mr. Coleman. Here is what I am saying, and all I will say. I am here, in Sorajhee, and this means you have a friend in Sorajhee. Enough said? Your sister may be alive, and this is important to me because I had a fondness for her and I have a dislike of treachery. But your sister is also important because only she has the power to come to Texas, to speak to her sons, to explain their destiny to them, their duty. Balahar does not wish to see the end of Sorajhee. On the contrary, Mr. Coleman. Balahar very much needs Sorajhee.''

''And my...my sister can help? How?''

King Zakariyya ignored Alex's question. ''Please ease your mind and, at the same time, please do nothing, say nothing, that could jeopardize your sister's well-being. I should not have ordered the letter sent to you, but now that it is done, I needed to speak to you, make this clear. I will speak to you again, hopefully within a few weeks, if Allah is kind. Perhaps one day we will even meet, and rejoice, with your sister among us once more. Good afternoon, Mr. Coleman and, as you say in America—have a nice day.''

Alex took the buzzing phone away from his ear and stared at it.

Had that conversation really happened, or had he dreamed it?

He looked around at the sound of a car all but skidding to a halt in the circular driveway. A moment later Jessica was running toward the house. ''Forgot my credit cards,'' she called over her shoulder to Alex. ''Can't shop till you drop without credit cards.''

Alex shook his head, watching as Jessica bounded into the house, bounding back out again mere seconds later. "Hey," he shouted after her as Jessica sprinted toward the car, its motor still running. "Try to remember you haven't qualified for the Indy Five Hundred yet, and make sure Hannah wears her seat belt."

Jessica stopped, her hand on the door handle, and grinned at him. "Is that your way of telling me I'm carrying precious cargo today, Alex? How...*interesting.*"

Keeping the smile on his face, Alex shook his head, waved and turned back for the house. Hannah. What was he going to do about Hannah? Why did he think he had to do anything about Hannah? What was it about her that reached out to him, touched him? Why was it so important to him to see her smile?

"Forget it," he mumbled under his breath. "You've got enough on your mind. Hannah Clark should be the least of your concerns."

But she wasn't. Alex didn't know why, especially since he'd seriously begun to believe his mother might be alive and out there somewhere. Yet he could not forget Hannah.

He was even pretty sure he didn't want to forget her.

"TURN AROUND," Jessica ordered, motioning with her hands as she sat cross-legged on the floor of the dressing room. "Perfect! Hannah, I tell you, if I had your body I'd give up clothes entirely, and just go naked. Think of the money I'd save."

Hannah fought the urge to cover herself, even though she wore her sensible white cotton bra and cotton panties. "You'd need that money, Jessica," Hannah said, "to cover all those indecent exposure fines you'd be paying."

"Hey! Good one! Now come on, start trying this stuff on. I've never shopped in the petite department before. The stock is pretty much the same, but sort of shrunken, you know. I mean, those gorgeous emerald-green slacks wouldn't come down past my shins, but they ought to look great on you. Start with them…and that pretty pale yellow sweater with the cowl neck.''

Hannah did as she'd been told. She'd been doing as she'd been told ever since Jessica picked her up this morning, tossed a white bag of doughnuts onto her lap, and told her that ''carbs are necessary for marathon shopping, trust me on this.''

The drive to Austin had been a revelation. It was true. It *was* possible to have a good time without saying a word, but just listening and laughing and wondering how anyone could be so happy. Jessica had kept up a nonstop monologue about life in general, her cousins, college, her future, the benefits of shopping the clearance racks. Name the subject, and Jessica could give you ten quick minutes on it, hardly stopping to take an occasional breath.

Hannah adored her. She thought she'd envy her. She'd most certainly done so as a child, recognizing the younger child as having so much that she, Hannah, couldn't have. Like a happy home. Like people who loved her. Like a mother.

But it was impossible to do anything except enjoy Jessica Coleman, and impossible not to relax and have a good time herself. Although that good time might change once Hannah dared to peek at any of the price tags on the armload of clothes Jessica had dragged into the dressing room.

Hannah took the thin wool slacks off the hanger and stepped into them. They were lined with a silky, whispery material, and the zipper closed neatly against her flat stomach. The button eased into place as if the slacks had been made to order for her measurements.

Then the sweater. Palest yellow, and soft as the belly fur

of a Persian kitten, the sweater nipped at her waist and wrists, softened across her bodice, and the cowl neckline showed her neckline to great advantage.

At least that's what Jessica said. In fact, she exclaimed, "Oh, that neckline! So demure and all, but any guy would be just *dying* to push it to one side, do a little investigating, if you know what I mean. Oh, come on, Hannah, don't blush. You're twenty-eight years old. You *have* to know what I mean."

Looking at her reflection in the mirror as Jessica hopped to her feet, to deftly arrange the cowl neckline, Hannah wondered what her new friend would say if she responded, "No, I don't know what you mean. Oh, I know what you *mean,* but nothing like that has ever happened to me."

Rather than admit any such thing, Hannah just watched Jessica work, then asked, "What color lipstick is worn with yellow?"

"Ah, so glad you asked," Jessica said, motioning for Hannah to undress, try on another outfit. "You've got great skin, Hannah, but you're pretty much a virgin when it comes to makeup, aren't you?"

"I'm pretty much a virgin when it comes to a lot of things," Hannah murmured under her breath, but she caught a glimpse of Jessica's delighted grin in the mirror and knew she hadn't said the words quietly enough.

"I know the gal at one of the makeup counters downstairs. She's a marvel. Not only does she pick the right colors, but she can check your skin tone, suggest soaps and lotions and that stuff, and even put the makeup on for you, show you how to do it for yourself."

"I think I know how to put on lipstick," Hannah said, pushing her head free as she pulled on a sleeveless silk beige top that was to be worn beneath the chocolate-brown jacket of a pants suit.

"Of course you do, Hannah," Jessica told her, handing her the matching chocolate-brown slacks. "But it takes more than lipstick to have that natural look everyone craves today. I can't tell you how much it takes to look like you're not wearing makeup at all. And hair! I wore my hair up for last New Year's Eve, and it took my hairdresser about forty-five minutes to make it look as if I'd just casually stuck all my hair on top of my head."

"Speaking of heads," Hannah said, sighing as she looked at the price tag on the jacket of the suit. And that was just the jacket! "I think I'm getting a headache. Jessica, I don't have a lot to spend, you know. I like the sweater and slacks, but this suit is way out of line."

"End of season clearance, Hannah," Jessica told her, grinning. "Deduct fifty percent. Didn't you see the sign on the rack?"

Hannah looked at Jessica, looked at the price tag again. Then she peeked at the price tags on the sweater and slacks. "These too? Fifty percent off on these?"

"Actually, no. Sixty percent on those. Didn't I tell you I'm a great shopper? Now close your mouth and try on the black dress. Isn't Alex expecting a black dress Saturday night?"

After all her worries about the small amount of money in her purse, Hannah finally smiled, relaxed. "Jessica, could you do me a favor? Go back out there and see if there are any red dresses on sale?"

"Hot damn, *now* she's cooking!" Jessica said, already on her way back to the sales floor.

Hannah kept right on "cooking" for the next hour, trying on everything from the simple red sheath to a pair of heels she'd have to practice in if she ever hoped to walk without stumbling Saturday night.

At last even a diehard like Jessica, who'd made her own

share of purchases, had to cry uncle and beg Hannah to break for club sandwiches and French fries in the store's café.

A French fry in her hand, waving it in front of her like a baton as she rested her elbows on the small table, Jessica said, "So tell me why you came back to Bridle. I mean, I'm here, too, and I know why I came back, even if my dad thinks it was only to drive him crazy. But why did you come back?"

"I'm a vet specializing in large animals, cattle and horses. This is horse country, cattle country," Hannah explained, although she kept her eyes on her plate as she drowned a French fry in ketchup. "I didn't think my practice would take off if I moved to Manhattan, for instance."

"Har-har," Jessica said around a mouthful of French fry. "Now, come on. We're supposed to be friends here, right? *Buds?* So why did you come back?"

"Considering that coming back here meant coming back home to my father? That is what you mean, isn't it? And that I'd have to be nuts to come back here, work for the old man? Is that what everyone thinks? What Alex thinks?"

Jessica reached an arm across the table, rested a hand on Hannah's fingers. "Oh, I'm so sorry, Hannah. Damn! Me and my big mouth! And my long nose," she added, wrinkling her pert and pretty nose.

"That's all right, Jessica, honestly. We're a pretty insular community around here, aren't we? And Dad never made it a secret to anyone that I've been a huge disappointment to him."

"I know, Hannah, and that stinks," Jessica said, both anger and sadness in her voice. "Mom and Dad worship the ground I walk on, even when I'm driving them crazy. Like now, because I refuse to promise a commitment to the family business until I'm more sure of what I want—and until I recover from all those years of school. After all, I just graduated in December. What's the big rush? But to *never* have their approval, no matter how hard I tried? I don't think I could survive that. I think you're to be congratulated, just for sheer guts.''

''If you're planning on commissioning a statue in my honor in the town square, please make sure I'm wearing clothes,'' Hannah said, squeezing Jessica's hand before she let go and picked up her sandwich.

Jessica looked at her for long moments, her eyes wide, and then sat back in her chair and laughed out loud. ''The mouse that roared! Hannah, don't ever let anyone tell you that you aren't smart and funny as all get-out. Not to mention that very nice body of yours, the fantastic haircut I gave you, and the fact that you're smart as a whip. I mean, you're a vet and everything. You know, once we get some makeup on you, and push you into opening your mouth a little more often, I think Alex is going to be shocked right down to the toes of his boots.''

''He's only being kind,'' Hannah said, wiping her hands on her napkin. She was acting like a nervous twit—a lying, nervous twit—and she'd sure picked the wrong audience to lie to by sitting across a lunch table from Jessica Coleman. ''Alex has always been kind. Well, maybe not when we were really young, but ever since he began to grow up. He's a good man.''

''Oh, yeah, the best. Definitely,'' Jessica agreed. ''And you're nuts about him.''

''I am *not*— Oh, the heck with it,'' Hannah said, slumping against the back of her chair. ''Yes, I'm nuts about him. I've *been* nuts about him since I was about twelve, and didn't even know yet what being nuts about someone meant. And now, suddenly, he's being nice to me, and I don't know what to do about it.''

Jessica propped her elbows on the table once more and dropped her chin in her hands. "What have you done about it so far? Other than buying that killer red dress, I mean."

No. She couldn't say it. No way, no how, could she tell Jessica Coleman what she'd done. What she'd so clumsily, stupidly done. But, then, she'd never had a real female friend before, someone she could confide in, trust. Her mind and heart both told her she could trust Jessica Coleman.

Hannah took a deep breath. "After I took care of the mare, and Khalid, Alex told me he'd do anything for me, to thank me for bringing them through a tough birth. *Anything.*"

"Uh-huh," Jessica said, quickly waving to the waiter who was passing by with a dessert cart loaded with goodies. "Perfect opening. So? Go on. What did you tell him? What did you ask for? I know you asked for something. I can see the guilt in your eyes. Oh, I think the gal at the makeup counter is going to go with soft, creamy eyeshadows. With that lovely shade of blue eyes? Definitely! Now I've changed the subject long enough to keep you from getting up and running out of here...so tell me what you asked Alex that has him walking around The Desert Rose in a daze these past two days."

"He—he's in a *daze?* Alex? Are you sure it isn't something else? Why would it have to be me?"

Jessica rolled her eyes. "Because *nothing* ever happens at The Desert Rose, Hannah. Nothing. The last time we saw any real excitement was when we learned Mac's fiancée was pregnant by another man and the wedding was called off. Mac's about as *off* women as a man can get, almost as much as Cade is always chasing after them. Oh! I shouldn't have said anything about any of that. Forget I told you about Mac's fiancée, okay?"

"Already forgotten," Hannah said, although she'd heard all about it from her father when she'd been home on a break from college. He'd gleefully used the story to prove to her, yet again, that all women were false, fickle and out only for themselves. Like her mother. Like Hannah would be, if Hugo gave her half a chance.

They were silent while the waiter placed thin slices of very rich chocolate pie in front of them, then Jessica prodded Hannah once more. "Okay, break time's over. What did you ask him?"

Hannah pressed the heels of her hands against her eyes, bent her head. "I told him I'm still a virgin and that I'd really like to not be one anymore. And I asked for his help."

The silence across the table was deafening and, to Hannah, seemed to go on forever.

"And what did he say?" Jessica asked at last, the slice of chocolate pie lying in front of her, forgotten. "God, Hannah, what did he say?"

"He said no," Hannah told her, dropping her hands and raising her chin. "Very politely and kindly, but he said no. Not that I blame him."

Jessica spread her hands. "I...I don't know what to say. And believe me, Hannah, I think that's the first time in my life I've ever admitted to that one. He turned you down? And yet he went hunting for you yesterday, brought you back to The Desert Rose? He asked you out to the club for Saturday night? He's been in his own world these past couple of days, not hearing people when they speak to him, looking sort of lost and confused—and edgy? Are you *sure* he said no?"

"Positive. Maybe he's worried that since he turned me down I'll put an ad in the paper, like any horse farm would advertise for a stud."

"Yes, that would upset him, I suppose," Jessica said, her lips twisting in a smile. "Probably about as much as if you went after, say, Cade or Mac, or—whoa! Wait a minute!" Her smile grew into a grin. "Hannah, I think I've just had one *wowzer* of an idea!"

Chapter Seven

Saturday came all too quickly for Hannah, who wished she could share Jessica's enthusiasm for the secret plan the girl called "possibly *the* most brilliant idea of a lifetime!"

After a day that had included removing several porcupine quills from the tender nose of a Dalmatian who'd learned one lesson about other animals the hard way, Hannah had just completed fixing a dinner of baked chicken and potato filling for her father and herself, and called into the living room that their food was on the table.

There was no dining room in the Clark's apartment above the veterinary office, so every meal was taken in the kitchen, at the same small, ancient white wooden table with the white-and-black porcelain top. The food was eaten in either a cold silence or accompanied by a lecture on any of Hannah's failings Hugo deemed most eligible for condemnation at the time.

Thursday night, over bowls of Irish stew, he'd warned her, repeatedly, that it didn't pay for people to think they were better than they should be, and that "running around" with people not of their own class, getting uppity ideas, was the best way he knew for people—Hannah, of course—to end up looking like damned fools.

Friday's fish cakes had been eaten in complete silence,

that silence was not exactly, in Hannah's opinion, a better "digestive aid." Hugo had perfected a way to make his silences even more condemning than his harangues.

So tonight it was chicken and filling. And either silence or another lecture to go along with the side dishes of romaine lettuce and canned sweet corn. Considering that her father knew Alex would be picking her up for the country club dance in another two hours, Hannah was pretty sure this was not going to be a quiet dinner.

"Dad?" she called out again, pouring dark, strong coffee into the cup her father demanded be beside his plate, and constantly refilled, during every meal. "Did you hear me? Dinner's on the table."

Nothing. No response at all. The television still blared in the living room, and Hugo did not appear in the kitchen.

Vocal or quiet, Hannah knew it wasn't going to be a pleasant meal.

Once, when she was about fourteen, and already preparing dinner every night, Hugo had not come to the table when she'd called. Hungry, Hannah had waited a few minutes, then sat down and began to eat. She'd taken no more than three bites of the tuna-noodle casserole when the plate was yanked away from her and thrown against the wall.

"Don't you *ever* start without me!" the huge, physically imposing Hugo had screamed as Hannah cowered against the back of her chair. "I pay for every bite that goes into your ungrateful mouth, and *I* will tell you when you can eat. Taking everything I have, never a word of thanks. Just like your mother!"

Hannah had never prepared or eaten tuna-noodle casserole after that night. And she doubted she ever would, not while the memory of cleaning up gobs of tuna and peas and sticky noodles that had slid down the wall and all over the floor remained so clear.

And she never sat down at the table until Hugo was already in his chair. At first, for fear of setting him off, but now just because that seemed to be the way she'd always done it.

Hannah was always careful to give outward signs of respect to this man she had never respected but only feared. Not that she feared him anymore. After all, she was a grown-up now, not a frightened, motherless little girl.

Still, it was just easier to play by Hugo's rules. Less hassle. She was in charge of her own life. At least that's what she kept telling herself as she began washing the roasting pan instead of taking her first bite of chicken.

She could have gone away, left Texas after her graduation, made a new life for herself somewhere else, anywhere else, out from under the thumb and the criticizing tongue of her father. But Hannah remained convinced that the man needed her even if he couldn't say the words.

Besides, her mother might have run away, but Hannah was not her mother. Yes, she might physically resemble her, resemble her more every year, but she was not her mother. One of these days, Hugo was going to figure that out.

Hannah's father entered the kitchen at last, still wearing his white lab coat and hitching up the beltless slacks that kept sliding down below his softening belly. "Chicken again? Didn't we just have chicken yesterday?"

"That was fish, Dad," Hannah said, sitting down and putting her paper napkin in her lap.

"Really? Well, let me tell you, it still isn't steak, now is it, girlie-girl? The Colemans eat steak, probably eat it three, four times a week. But the Clarks eat chicken. We always have to save for rainy days. Am I getting through to you, girl?"

"Yes, sir," Hannah said, keeping her head bowed, her eyes on her plate. "It's only a dance, Dad."

Wham! Hugo's knife clanked against the metal tabletop. "Only a dance, only a dance. That's what your mother said. *Only* a shared soda, *only* a little conversation. Only being nice to the man. Right up until she ran off with him, leaving me here, stuck with *you.*"

"I'm not leaving you, Dad. I came back after getting my degree, didn't I? I'm here, helping with the practice. One country club dance isn't going to change that."

There was silence in the kitchen for some moments, time enough for Hannah to realize that, to her father, she had just dared to "sass" him, talk back.

Gee. It felt good.

"Who asked you to come back?" Hugo said at last, his question more of a condemnation. "I didn't ask you to come back. Hugo Clark doesn't crawl on his belly for anyone. I don't need you. I never needed you."

Hannah closed her eyes, took a slow, steadying breath. It was now or never. "Dad, I know. I know, all right? Doc Gillman called me up at school last year, and told me. I know you may be going blind, that there's not much anyone can do to stop it. I'm here, Dad, and I'm staying. Whether you want me or not, and even if you think it's only so that I can take over the practice, rob you of a lifetime of hard work, I'm staying. I love you, Dad. I don't know why, I really don't, because you're not a very nice man, you really aren't. But I love you, I respect you as a terrific vet, and I owe you because, whether you meant to or not, you showed me that I too wanted to be a vet. Some of my fondest memories, maybe my only fond memories, are the times you let me work with you, taught me just a little of what you know. Besides, you're my father.''

She looked straight into her father's eyes and waited for the explosion, but it never came. Hugo Clark simply stood up, pushed back his chair and walked out of the room.

Hannah heard the door to her father's bedroom slam a moment later, flinched at the sound, then picked up her fork once more and began to eat her solitary dinner.

ALEX DIDN'T REALLY HAVE an opinion either way on country club dances. He wasn't crazy about them; he didn't do his best to avoid them.

But he rarely, very rarely took a date to the club dances. He didn't need the hassle.

For as long as he could remember, his life had been The Desert Rose and his brothers. His aunt and uncle, his cousin, Jessica.

Not that he was celibate.

Not that Hannah's question had made him rethink the idea of celibacy…

Alex lifted his chin as he peered into the mirror above his dresser, putting the finishing touches on tying his tie. He hated ties. He hated the constricting feeling of suits and ties and lace-up shoes.

He could happily live his life in soft cotton shirts and comfortable jeans, in riding boots and fleece-lined jackets. Big-brimmed cowboy hats.

Even better, the freedom of the *kibr,* the *kaffiyeh,* the Arabic dress he wore in competitions, when he rode into the arena atop one of The Desert Rose's finest horses, a mount holding its head and tail proudly as, wearing the silken rope bridle and fancy saddle of yesteryear, man and mount appeared like a vision riding out of the desert, all mystery and mystical beauty, all flawless form and stunning majesty.

Alex remembered an old, grainy newspaper photograph his uncle had shown him, a photograph of his father on horseback. Magnificent. Simply magnificent. At his best, and winning event after event, Alex always felt he remained a pale imitation of that man's easy, kingly grace, his firm but kind hand on the reins.

Jabbar had been the last offspring of his father's favorite stallion, had become the solid base on which the reputation of The Desert Rose had risen over the years. And now, as if history was repeating itself, Jabbar had given him Khalid.

As Hannah had given him Khalid, Alex knew, because he was certain there would have been a far different conclusion to the foal's birth if Hannah hadn't been there—calm, confident, efficient.

Thoughts of Khalid always led Alex back to Hannah, and to questions he wanted answered even if he didn't know why those answers were so important to him.

Why had Hannah come back? Why was a woman so accomplished, so well trained, so competent, reduced to a nervous, often bumbling gauche girl in any social exchange? Was it Alex who made her nervous? Or life itself? Life outside the boundaries of her profession, because inside those boundaries she *was* sure of herself.

One thing he did know was that Hannah had grown up. She might still be skittish, high-strung and nervous, but she had physically matured into a woman who, if she was not aware of her beauty, certainly possessed enough of it to turn any male head.

She had a finely attuned and self-deprecating sense of humor, a sharp wit, a caring heart…and enough love inside her to remain here, near her judgmental, ungrateful father, in order to help him with his practice. She could have gone anywhere, done anything. She was smart enough. Yet she had come home, allowed herself to be dragged back beneath Hugo Clark's thumb.

There had to be a reason.

"Good old-fashioned curiosity," Alex announced to his reflection. "That's all it is, right, Coleman? Ha! Man, lie to everybody else, but don't lie to yourself. It's a hell of a lot more than curiosity when all you can think about is that favor she asked of you and how her mouth would taste…how it would feel to hold her close.."

"Alex? May I come in?"

Alex quickly pulled a comb through his hair, checked his reflection one last time, shrugged into his suit jacket. "Sure, Randy, come on in. I was just getting dressed."

Randy Coleman entered the room, neither a large nor small man, but a trim one, the sort of man whose appearance breathed of refinement, breeding. Randy's clear blue eyes were Alex's most constant reminder of his mother, and if there was a goodly amount of silver in his uncle's hair, the color was still very like Rose's had been in her youth—a soft, pale blond.

"Vi tells me you're taking Hannah Clark to the dance tonight," Randy said, tipping his head to indicate Alex's dark blue suit. "I see she's right. How did that happen?"

"I'm still trying to figure that out myself, to tell you the truth," Alex said, smiling. "She's a nice kid."

"Kid? Alex, she's got to be close to thirty by now. Hardly a kid. And she's got her degree, is working with Hugo now, right? You know, having a vet in the family would be very cost-efficient."

"You want me to propose to Hugo?" Alex asked, opening a drawer to locate a handkerchief, then stuffing it in his back pocket. "Let me get back to you on that, okay?"

"Okay," Randy said, shaking his head. "I get the message. Hannah Clark is not a topic of discussion. But your aunt would tear a strip off my hide if I didn't ask. I think she's decided that it's time for a few wedding bells around this place. Not counting the ones we almost heard a while back, before Mac woke up and got rid of that gal."

"Hannah and I are pretty far from wedding bells, Randy," Alex said, sitting down on the edge of the bed. "About as far as you can get."

"And on to the next subject, right? With no more questions about Hannah Clark? All right, although this subject isn't going to be any easier, is it?"

"My mother," Alex said, nodding. "I know we've barely mentioned her since you got home the other day. Have you been walking around as shell-shocked as I have since you read me that letter?"

Randy pulled a straight-back chair away from a small writing desk and sat down. "Vi says not to get my hopes up over an anonymous letter, but…"

"There's more than that, Randy," Alex said. "I didn't tell you, as you'd just gotten back and you and Jared were holed up going over business reports on Coleman-Grayson. But I got a call the other day. Actually, *you* got a call the other day, but you were still gone, and I pretended to be you."

Randy looked at Alex levelly. "Go on. Who called? Some reporter who just got wind of what he hopes is a juicy story?"

Alex stood, began to pace. "No, thank God. Nobody knows about any of this, Randy, except for you and me— and Vi. The call was from King Zakariyya Al Farid in Balahar, although he's not there, but still in Sorajhee, deep in those diplomatic discussions we've been reading about in the newspapers. He says he sent the letter, then had second thoughts and felt it shouldn't have been anonymous, that we deserved to know who sent it."

"I remember that name," Randy said, rubbing a hand over his chin. "Ibrahim wanted an alliance with Balahar years ago. It's what got him killed. There is still some fairly ancient, informal alliance, but Ibrahim wanted something more concrete, something he could show his people, and the world. Rose was all for it as well. I remember her saying there were the public negotiations, and some private ones at well. Secret, behind-the-scenes plans that would go a long way toward securing the safety of both countries. Although she also told me it could be dangerous for Ibrahim to move forward with the idea. That's the only reason your mother and I were able to get you boys out of Sorajhee once your uncle took over. Because Ibrahim had planned for the worst. And the worst happened. To Ibrahim, to Rose."

"To all of us, Randy. And now, all these years later, this Zakariyya guy says my mother might still be alive—somewhere. Oh, and before you think he's just a cheerful guy trying to spread good news, it would appear that he needs her to be alive for some reason of his own. Wait, I wrote down as much as I could remember, once he'd hung up. I'll get it."

Alex opened a drawer in a small chest beside his bed and pulled out a single sheet of paper. "Okay, here it is. I think I've got this part word for word. I know the words sure made a hell of an impression on me." He looked up at his uncle, then read, "'But your sister is also important because only she has the power to come to Texas, to speak to her sons, to explain their destiny to them, their duty.'"

Randy stood, crossed to Alex and took the paper out of his hand, then reread it. "What in hell does that mean? Surely he doesn't expect you and your brothers to go over to Sorajhee, bump your uncle off the throne and sit there yourselves. Does he?''

"I don't know," Alex said. "I try to think about it, but to tell you the truth, I can't get much beyond the idea that my mother might still be alive. If she is, where has she been? *How* has she been? Was she a prisoner somewhere? Whose prisoner? And then I wonder what in hell I'm doing here, going to dances, when my mother could be out there somewhere, needing me.''

Randy folded the paper and handed it back to Alex, then laid a hand on his shoulder. "Do you think it's time we told Mac and Cade?''

Alex closed his eyes, sighed. "I don't know. It doesn't seem fair to keep this sort of news from them. But at the same time, Randy, I'm going through hell right now, and I want to spare Mac and Cade that hell if I can. Until we know more.''

"Always the protector," Randy said, giving Alex's shoulder a squeeze. "I know this is going to come as a shock to you, Alex, but those boys are only a year younger than you. They're grown men, and can handle anything you can throw at them.''

"Randy, I caught the two of them at their favorite game just last week, drawing straws to see which twin got to pull off their next prank. Oh, and in case Vi wants to know who ran the flag up the pole upside down as a distress signal because she ordered the rugs taken out of the living room and beaten—it was Mac. He drew the long straw. Cade was left with the short straw and got to beat the rugs. Enough said?''

Randy laughed out loud. "All right, point made. We'll keep this between ourselves for a while longer. Did this Zakariyya guy say anything about when he'd contact me— you—again?''

"King Zakariyya is very good at saying very little," Alex said, ripping the paper into small pieces and putting it in the trash basket. "If I could just remember the language, go over there, talk to the man face-to-face, confront my uncle..."

"You can't do that, Alex. I can't do that. Your notes included something about a madness in Azzam's palace. If your mother isn't dead, it's not because she's free to move about as she pleases. It was Layla, Azzam's queen, who told me Rose had died, was quietly buried while the world believed all four of you were in seclusion. I wonder if Layla is the madness. I've always believed Azzam to be behind anything bad that happened to any of you. Now I wonder if I was wrong. Unless it was the both of them? Rose trusted Layla with her life. Was that a mistake?"

"Careful, Randy, or you'll get the same headache I've had these past days. I think we'd both better listen to your good advice, and just stay here, keep quiet and hope for the best. Even if it kills us. To do anything else, with the eyes of at least part of the world on the negotiations going on in Sorajhee right now, could be more than dangerous. It could be deadly for my mother."

"Right," Randy said, heading for the door. "It's advice worth listening to, and I'll keep my mouth shut. Right after I report in to your aunt, although she's pretty much said the same things, even without knowing what you've just told me. In the meantime, Alex, we go on as we've been going on. Your Aunt Vi and I will stay home tonight like the old folks we are, pop popcorn and watch a video. You and your brothers and Jessica will go to the dance at the club, and pretend nothing is going on. With any luck, the Clark girl will be able to take your mind off things for a while."

"Yeah," Alex agreed, his mind brought back to Hannah,

and the way she'd smiled at him the other day, the way his gut had clenched at the sight of that smile. "That might work."

RED. SHE'D WORN RED. Now Alex knew how a bull was supposed to feel when presented with that color.

Charge!

Hannah was standing outside when Alex pulled up, the headlights of his sports car sweeping over her, catching that first, startling view of red.

He'd had trouble getting the keys out of the ignition.

"Hi," he said as he eased his long legs out of the car and walked up to her. "Am I late?"

Hannah shook her head, her hair moving with her, then settling itself again in a perfect frame for her face, those huge blue eyes. "Dad isn't feeling too well," she explained, "so I thought I'd wait out here, so you didn't have to knock."

Alex bent his head a little, trying to see Hannah's face better in the light from the street lamp. She was wearing makeup. He'd never seen her wear makeup. Nothing much, he decided. Just a little something on her eyes, a hint of color on her lips. And she looked terrific, he supposed, realizing that she didn't need makeup to look terrific to him. He'd already memorized her every feature, and believed each one to be flawless, perfect.

When had he decided that? Why had he decided that?

"Hugo's sick? How sick? Have you called Doc Gillman?"

"No, nothing like that. He's...he's just a little under the weather. Headache, I think. Shall we go?"

She was lying to him. He knew it, sensed it somehow, as if he had some sort of radar that could pick up and read

Hannah for him. Hugo didn't just have a headache. There was more here than she was telling him.

Still, it was none of his business, right?

"Your chariot awaits, my lady," Alex said, opening the passenger door. "And may I say that you look *fantastic* tonight."

"I think you just did," Hannah told him, slipping onto the front bucket seat, the hem of her simple red dress—was there anything "simple" about red, and most especially that dress?—sliding a marvelous four inches above her knees.

Her fantastic knees, that were a part of her fantastic legs.

"Yeah, well, um—you're right," Alex said, wondering when he'd become a bumbling, nervous wreck. He knew now how Hannah felt each time her tongue, or any immovable object, tripped her up. He just never expected to feel that way himself, and never had. Until tonight.

He closed the door after Hannah reached for the seat belt, then walked around the car to slip into the driver's seat and turn on the ignition once more. "Jessica's already on her way, with Mac and Cade. We'll meet them there, share a table."

"That's nice," Hannah said, shifting slightly in her seat, trying to tug on the hem of her dress.

Alex fought down the urge to ask her to please stop, that he liked the view just the way it was.

"Have you ever been to one of these dances?"

Her hand stopped tugging. "No. Never."

Stupid! Why had he asked such a stupid question? Of course she'd never been to one of the club dances. As far as he knew, Hannah had never been on a date, at least not during her years in Bridle.

"I try to stay away from them myself," he told her quickly, trying to keep the conversation light. "Let me tell you about them, okay? The teenagers disappear into the shrubbery below the patio, the young marrieds all sit together and talk kids and houses, the older ones separate into men hugging the bar and women exchanging pictures of their grandchildren. The refreshments are really lame, and the band always plays each song a half beat slower than it should.''

''Fascinating. I can see I've been really deprived, never having attended one before this, at least as a teenager,'' Hannah said, and her smile seemed to light up the dark interior of the car. ''So why did you ask me to come?''

''Oh, well, that one's easy. *Everyone* goes to the country club dances. To see and be seen. To talk and be talked about.'' He grinned at her. ''To show off their really fantastic red dresses.''

''So we couldn't just go to a movie instead? Bummer,'' Hannah quipped, her blue eyes dancing. How Alex loved it when she let down her guard, relaxed, showed him glimpses of the woman beneath Hugo Clark's frightened child.

''I suppose we could, but then Jessica would kill me. She can't wait to see you tonight, you know. I think she's put herself in the role of Henry Higgins.''

''Your cousin is a sweetheart,'' Hannah said. ''We had so much fun the other day. I've never—'' She closed her mouth, shook her head. ''Never mind.''

''You've never had a real girlfriend before?'' Alex suggested. ''Why is that, Hannah?''

She opened and closed the clasp of her small purse. ''Dad…Dad always said our apartment was too small to be clogged up with a bunch of silly, giggling girls. And, to be fair, I was always pretty busy, helping in the office, going with Dad when he made his calls on all the ranches. Like yours.''

Fair? There was nothing fair about the way Hugo Clark had raised his only child, even if his wife had taken off and left him with a job he clearly hadn't wanted or known how to do. "Well," he said, pulling through the gates to the country club, "now you get to make up for lost time. I mean, if it's silly and giggling you're looking for, you couldn't do much better than our Jess."

"She's not silly!" Hannah protested, turning on him much like a mother lion defending her cub. "She's smart and funny and I like her very much."

Alex bypassed the valet parking, pulled into a vacant spot near the door and turned to Hannah. "You're very loyal and protective of those you love, aren't you, Hannah? I like that about you. I like that very much. Now, if you're ready, let's go inside and see if the band is playing yet."

She put her hand in Alex's as he helped her out of the low-slung car. "I...I don't really know how to dance."

He looked down at her, at that so sweet and honest and slightly terrified face, and couldn't help himself. He leaned over, kissed her on the cheek. "Then you know what, Hannah-banana, it's about time you learned, and I think I'm going to enjoy teaching you."

Chapter Eight

Jessica wriggled in her chair, a redheaded, dewy vision in her artfully simple black sheath. "Do you think anyone would notice if I patted myself on the back, Hannah? I mean, you look *terrific*. I'm so proud of myself—and you, of course—that I could burst."

"Would it *burst* your bubble if I were to tell you that I'd give anything for my jeans and flannel shirts?" Hannah asked, feeling her cheeks grow hot. "This skirt is just too short. I feel naked."

"But you don't look naked, Hannah. You look like a woman of mysterious secrets a man would give his eyeteeth to learn. I read that somewhere," she ended, grinning. "Honest, you do. And Mac and Cade aren't throwing daggers at me anymore, either, for talking them into agreeing with my little plan. As a matter of fact, they're outside right now, figuring out who the lucky winner is."

Hannah shook her head, realizing that the more time she spent in Jessica's company, the less she understood her. "Your little plan? I'd forgotten about that, forgotten that you promised to tell me what that little plan is. Winner? Winner of what?"

"Not *what*, Hannah—*who*. I let my cousins in on your

little secret, that thing you asked Alex to take care of, and—''

"Jessica! You *didn't!*" Hannah leaned forward, knocking over her glass of wine. She grimaced at the spreading stain. "Oh, now that's typical."

"Don't worry about a little wine," Jessica assured her, deftly covering the stain with the floral arrangement that sat on the round table. "There, all gone."

"Not quite all gone, Jessica," Hannah said, watching as Alex, a glass of ice water in his hand, wandered toward the balcony beyond a pair of open French doors. "Are you telling me—*please* let me be wrong, here—that you told Mac and Cade about me being the last…you know."

"Yes, I know. The LLTV. That stands for Last Living Texas Virgin, in case you haven't figured that out yet. And of course I told them," Jessica said, rolling her eyes. "How else did you think I could get them to go along with my idea? Although, looking at you now, maybe I didn't have to tell them what I wanted. They'd probably have come after you anyway. At least Cade would, like a shot. Mac's still licking his romantic wounds."

"Oh, God," Hannah moaned, dropping her forehead into her palm. Being alone, unloved, and pretty much friendless suddenly became a fond memory. What was Jessica going to do next? Hire a billboard on Route 73, and announce Hannah's LLTV status to the whole world? "I don't believe this."

"Well, believe it, Hannah. Cade and Mac have agreed to romance you, chase after you, right up until Alex figures out that he doesn't want anyone else near you. It's a perfect plan. Perfect! And you *are* nuts about him, aren't you?"

Hannah slid down in her seat, awash in misery. She waved one hand rather aimlessly, let it flutter in the air.

"Nuts about Alex, just plain nuts—take your pick. Jessica, what do I do now?"

"Now? Well, I suppose you just sit up, then sit here and look ravishing and let my cousins do their thing. What could be easier?"

Hannah squeezed her eyes shut. "What could be easier? Just about anything, Jessica. Just about anything…"

ALEX BELIEVED he needed a shot of cool, calming night air. He'd danced twice with Hannah, both slow songs as she was afraid to take the floor during any of the livelier numbers, if anything this geriatric band played could be considered *lively*.

She'd fit against him perfectly, even as he could feel the tenseness in her muscles, sense the nervousness in her at-first, hesitant steps.

He liked that she was small, that the top of her head came only to his chin. He liked the way she smelled of everyday soap and a hint of something soft and floral. He liked the way she looked up at him, trusting him to lead her through the steps.

And he'd adored the comments she'd made, at his urging, about some of the other dancers on the floor.

"There goes Rafe Collins," he'd said to her, using the hand that held hers to indicate the man as he whizzed by as if the waltz were a spirited Sousa march. "Someone ought to fit his string necktie with a horn he could blow, to warn people to get out of his way."

Hannah laughed as the rancher stopped dead, executed a full turn and went charging off again across the floor, barely avoiding a head-on collision with another couple. "A horn, and turn signals. He could pull the left-side string on his tie for a left turn, the right for a right turn. Backup lights, complete with an audible beep if he presses his belt buckle.

Oh, and a portable oxygen mask for his partner. How on earth can she keep up with him?''

That had started it for them. They hadn't been mean, but they'd made other comments, observations, and before long Hannah was completely relaxed in his arms, forgetting to mind her steps and simply moving with the music. Moving with him. Flawlessly, beautifully, moving with him, as if they'd danced together, spoken together, all of their lives.

After the second dance, during which he'd begun to think, unbidden, about Hannah's request that he "make her a woman," and see it as a more feasible idea, Alex had excused himself and headed for the bar for another glass of ice water.

Now he was heading outside, putting a few more minutes of hopefully sanity-producing space between himself and his lady in red.

He stopped just outside the French doors, sipped his water and let his eyes adjust to the darkness.

Mac and Cade were out there, leaning on a section of the balcony about twenty feet away from him, their heads close together as they talked.

Alex approached them, was ready to say something, when Cade spoke.

"I don't know if we should go the straw route on this one, Mac. It's not like it's going to be some big sacrifice for either of us to romance Hannah."

Alex's greeting died in his throat and he just stood there, listening for whatever would come next. Knowing his brothers, it was bound to be something very inscrutably twinlike and, most probably, prone to give Alex a headache.

"Not just romance her, Cade. According to Jessica, Hannah's looking for someone to make her a woman. Man, that's an old-fashioned way of saying it, isn't it? Not that a twenty-eight-year-old virgin could be anything other than old-fashioned.''

''Jessica's twenty-four, Mac. Are you saying she probably isn't a virgin? I don't think I like that.''

''Oh, sure. This from the guy who wouldn't rest until he'd gotten rid of his own virginity. What were you? Seventeen?''

''That's different, and I don't think it's called *losing your virginity* with men.''

''Really? What is it called, then?''

''A lot of expectation followed by the realization that some things probably are better for waiting for them?'' Cade said, shrugging his shoulders. ''Anyway, we aren't talking about us, we're talking about Hannah. Now, are we going to draw straws or not? I picked up two from the bar, and already have them ripped and ready to go.''

''Short straw gets to romance her? Or long straw? Are we going for a winner here, or a loser? Because I'd say the short straw wins.''

Alex was beginning to see red, and it had nothing to do with Hannah's dress. But he didn't interrupt, because that would do him no good at all. His brothers would just grin at him and ask him if he wanted to be included in the straw-pulling version of flipping a coin to see who got to take Hannah Clark to bed.

''You know, for once, Mac, I think you're right. How about this? Short straw gets to romance her, and long straw gets to drive Alex nuts with daily reports on the other guy's progress. That's what Jess wants, remember. For Alex to go nuts, realize that he's attracted to Hannah himself.''

Alex closed his eyes. The twins knew? Jessica knew? Hannah had *told* them? Was the woman *insane?*

''Do you think he is? Attracted to her, I mean? Just because he brought her here tonight? That isn't a whole lot to go on, you know.''

"Brother mine, when was the last time we saw Alex at one of these dances?''

"I don't know. Six months.''

"Exactly. Jessica might be all wet, but she also might know something we don't know. And you have to admit it, Alex has been walking around in a daze these past few days. He actually left Dakar's stable door open yesterday, and you know how quick Dakar is to take advantage of something like that.''

"You've got me there, Cade. Alex never forgets anything. And he is being sort of quiet. I don't think he said more than three words at dinner tonight. Okay, let's do it. And remember, Jessica said Hannah doesn't know anything about this. That's important, because otherwise the whole idea will fall flat on its face. You know, the way Hannah falls flat on her face.''

"Pretty enough face to fall on,'' Cade reasoned. "And who's to say that clumsy can't be sexy as hell? Hannah isn't just a nice kid, she's a beautiful woman. Like you said, brother, let's do it.''

Alex stepped back into the shadows as his brother leaned back from the railing and the straws were held out. He waited until Cade drew the short straw, then stood very still as the twins made their way back to the dance floor, Mac complaining that he'd been robbed.

Wasn't this great? Wasn't this just what he needed right now? The twins and Jessica, playing games with him, with Hannah, who, thank God, wasn't in on the scheme. And Randy thought Mac and Cade should be told about their mother? Hell, they'd be on a plane in ten minutes, tops, ready to play knights in shining armor, and probably put their mother in even more danger than she might be in at the moment.

However, if nothing else, overhearing his brothers had settled one thing in his mind. He might not be able to do anything to help his mother right now, but he sure could stick close as glue to Hannah, protect her from Mac and Cade's nonsense.

That Mac and Cade's *nonsense* gave him a reason to do what he wanted to do anyway did not immediately occur to him.

MIDNIGHT HAD LONG SINCE PASSED when King Zakariyya was ushered into the small compartment behind the throne room in Jeved, capital of Sorajhee.

"Azzam, my so demanding host, who all but ordered me out of my comfortable bed at this late hour. And to bring me here, to this secret place. Are we reduced now to sneaking about like guilty children?"

"So, you would play the innocent, Zakariyya?" King Azzam shifted slightly in his seat, motioned for Zakariyya to join him in the facing chair. "Then, my friend, you would reduce me to admitting that phone conversations coming to or originating from this castle are all monitored? I doubt that. You knew I would hear of your call to Randy Coleman."

"True enough. I did not, however, believe it would take you this long to speak to me of that call. Or did you find it necessary to consult Queen Layla before confronting me? A word of advice, my friend. Be careful of women who wish to rule from the shadows."

"Even those who profess to lead in the light, Zakariyya, oftentimes find it expedient to simultaneously work in the shadows. Shall I be clearer? Very well. Your man has been spotted in Paris."

Zakariyya crossed one leg over the other, arranged his robes about him. "How indiscreet of him, I'm sure. And please forgive him if he did not stop and give greetings to your *two* men in that same city."

"Enough!" Azzam leaped to his feet and began to pace. "Can you not trust the word of Sorajhee, that you make phone calls to Texas, to alert the brother? That you send dogs to nip at our heels as we go about locating my brother's widow? Too many dogs, Zakariyya, and the always ravenous news hounds will pick up the scent." He stopped, turned to face Zakariyya. "Or is that what you want? Is that why you contacted Randy Coleman? Are you hoping to take all of this out of my hands, after I so graciously confided in you?"

"Azzam, Azzam. There was nothing gracious about what you and your Layla have done, or what you are doing now. Your brother's widow is necessary to us both. Otherwise, she would be as dead today as we were led to believe she was last week."

Azzam subsided into his chair, breathing heavily. "Layla says Paris, and then she says Brussels. Today it was Geneva. Either her mind is unclear, or she has moved my sister-in-law so many times that she has honestly misplaced her."

"After so dishonestly *placing* her," Zakariyya said, idly stroking the gold braid at his waist. "Ah, forgive me, Azzam. I know you have pain over this." He stood, ready to leave the room. "Very well, I will do nothing more, make no new contact with Texas, as long as I have your assurance that you will not allow your mind to be changed, that Queen Rose *will* be found, *will* be returned safely to her American family."

"You have my promise," Azzam said.

"As I have mine to Randy Coleman. For now, I will

have no further contact with the man. But the moment Queen Rose is safe, I intend to inform him of that fact. For it is only then that Queen Rose will be able to speak to her sons, tell them of our great need and their own duty, their father's promise. In the morning I shall return to Balahar and await the happy news you will soon send winging to me with all good speed.''

"Allies, Zakariyya," Azzam said, rising as well. "We must remember that we are allies. We must trust each other.''

"This from a man who puts little bugs in telephones. How very droll, Azzam." Zakariyya shrugged. "Very well, we are allies. But only once our two houses are united in marriage will the world, or, indeed, I, truly believe that. Good night, my friend.''

Azzam watched as Zakariyya left the room, then sank back into his chair, to gnaw at his knuckles and quietly curse his wife's ambition.

THE BAND'S FINAL NUMBER had been a medley of old standards, many of them not too seamlessly drifting into the next song, but all of them adding up to a solid twenty minutes of Hannah being held in Alex's arms.

The last strains of *Good Night Sweetheart* were just fading away when Cade walked onto the dance floor and tapped on Alex's shoulder.

"I know I'm too late to cut in, brother, but I just wanted to go on record as to wanting to." He turned and smiled at Hannah, his straight white teeth a blinding flash in his tanned, handsome face. "Very much.''

"I thought you brought Betsy Hardigan," Alex said, trying not to glare at his grinning brother.

"Don't remind me," Cade said, shaking his head. "And

it wasn't a date. I only picked Betsy up as a favor to Jessica."

"That's strange," Alex said, sliding a hand down Hannah's arm, twining her fingers in his. "I didn't think you ever went out of your way to do favors for Jessica."

"Yeah, well, you know how it is, bro," Cade said, his gaze having traveled the length of Hannah's arm along with Alex's hand, and now concentrating on the way Alex was holding her hand in his, right there, in the middle of the dance floor. "I just didn't want to call it blackmail."

"Blackmail?" Hannah looked at Cade, her complexion a little too white under the now brought-up lights hanging above the dance floor. "She blackmailed you into doing her a favor?"

"Wouldn't be the first time," Cade told her, "or the last. Actually, it was more of a favor. Betsy just broke off her engagement to some guy from Dallas, and Jessica thought she could use a night out. The fact that she threatened to tell Aunt Vi that it was me who took a slice of the pie she'd made for the church auxiliary luncheon was pure coincidence. Well, anyway, Hannah, now that I lost my chance to dance with the prettiest girl here tonight, maybe you'll agree to go riding with me tomorrow afternoon? We could pack a basket, have ourselves a small picnic if the weather cooperates. Sound good to you?"

Hannah's head jerked up as she looked at Alex, who said nothing. And why should he? It wasn't as if he would have anything to say about where she went, who she went there with. But did he have to look so unconcerned—so nearly bored—with the conversation?

"That sounds really nice, Cade," Hannah said. "I'd enjoy that. I could be ready around one, if that's all right with you."

"Perfect," Cade said, then promised to meet her at The

Desert Rose stables with two mounts saddled and ready to ride, before waving to someone across the room and heading off again.

"You didn't have to say yes, you know," Alex told her as she picked up her purse and they headed toward the cloakroom to retrieve their coats. "Cade's got a reputation around here as something of a playboy. Are you sure you're ready for a playboy, Hannah?"

"I'm certainly ready for something," Hannah said, shrugging into her coat. "Please, don't worry about me. I know what I'm doing."

"You do? Now, why don't I think so?" Alex asked, motioning her to precede him past the door being held open by one of the club's employees. "And why," he asked after an uncomfortable silence as they walked across the parking lot, his hand resting on the door handle of the car, "do I keep remembering that you think it's time someone made you a woman?"

She nearly told him then. Nearly confessed that Jessica had recruited her cousins to pretend to romance her, and that the cousins were in on the joke, she herself was reluctantly "in" on the joke.

But she didn't. She couldn't. Not when Alex looked so angry. Who was he to be angry? It wasn't as if he cared one way or the other.

Oh, how she wished he cared one way or the other.

"I'm twenty-eight years old, Alex," she told him at last, daring to tip up her chin and look directly into his dark and brooding face. "A playboy might be exactly what I need right now."

"That's disgusting," Alex muttered, slamming the door almost before Hannah was safely in her seat.

They rode back to Bridle in silence, with even the radio switched off. A silence that seemed alive, running hot and cold with each passing mile, until at last they were back outside the veterinary office, the engine cut, and standing on the cement parking lot.

"This…this is where I think I'm supposed to say thank you, I enjoyed myself very much," Hannah said, absently scuffing the toe of her shoe against the cement. "And, except for the end, that's pretty much true. I…I'm sorry if I disappointed you, Alex. I really am."

Alex stepped closer, laid his palm against her cheek. "You haven't disappointed me, Hannah," he told her, and she felt his gaze warming her, as his callused flesh warmed her cheek. "But I don't want you to disappoint yourself. You're not the sort to do anything rash, without thinking everything out, weighing the consequences."

Hannah rolled her eyes, stepped away from him. "Man, am I that boring? And here I only thought I was clumsy."

"That's not what I meant," Alex said, taking her hand and walking down the alleyway, away from the building. "Nobody gets to be a veterinarian without planning ahead. Getting the grades, earning the money for tuition, putting in the years, and all with a goal firmly in sight. You're not flighty, Hannah, that's what I meant, what I mean."

"And I didn't come to my latest conclusion after only a few moments of thought," Hannah said, stepping in front of him so that he had to stop walking, stop talking. "I did just what you said, Alex. I've spent nearly every waking moment of my life working for my goal, and now I've reached it. It's time for another goal."

"Losing your virginity? That's your new goal?"

No! Hannah cried inside her head. *Having you fall in love with me, loving me the way I've loved you for all of my life. That's my goal.*

"Hannah? Answer me, please. Do you consider losing your virginity a goal? Just the act? As if lovemaking were some sort of exam you think you need to pass in order to get your degree as a woman?''

She bent her head, rubbed at her forehead. "You make it all sound so...so juvenile."

"Only because it is, Hannah," Alex said, putting a finger under her chin, tipping up her head. "You're a beautiful woman, with or without what Jessica calls her *magic*. You're intelligent, accomplished—"

"Accident prone," Hannah inserted, trying to smile.

"Adorably so," Alex said, smiling at her. Breaking her heart as he smiled at her. "And only when you're nervous, unsure of yourself."

"When I'm nervous? In that case," Hannah said, trying to protect herself from Alex's too-on-target observations, "I suggest you head for the nearest foxhole, soldier, because my next *accident* might be thermonuclear."

"Oh, Hannah," Alex said, putting his hands on her shoulders, "I didn't mean to make you nervous."

"No, you just wanted to lecture me," she said, bending her knees so that she could sort of slide out from underneath his hands. And she almost made it, would have made it, except that she was wearing high heels, and there was a pothole in the alley, and when she stepped back her left foot landed in it, splashing in the water collected there.

Which made her quickly twist herself to look down at her new shoe, which had just been ruined. Which put her even more off balance.

Which had her clutching at Alex's lapels as she felt herself begin to topple.

Which, because she'd managed to grab one lapel and his breast pocket, resulted in his pocket being quite loudly torn half-off his suit jacket.

"Oh, look what I did! Your beautiful suit, and I ruined

it," she exclaimed, trying to pat the ripped material back into place. "Hopeless. I'm just hopeless!"

Alex grabbed at her fluttering hands, squeezed them in his own as he stepped backward, so that she had to move with him, away from the pothole. "Hannah. Hannah—stop it. Please stop," he said several times, as she began to cry.

"Do...do you think I don't want to? Stop it, that is," she said, sniffling. "I—I thought I had it licked. Really. The longer I was away from...from here, the less I was making a total ass of myself. Tripping over things, knocking things over, colliding with things. I even tried it—and I *could* walk and chew gum at the same time. I was cured, damn it. And now? Look at me. I'm a mess! I wish I'd never come back here."

Alex held her hands and waited for her to finish. When she began to sniffle, he handed her his handkerchief, then stood by as she wiped at her eyes, blew her nose. "Feel better now?" he asked, then shook his head to decline her offer to return his handkerchief. "Consider it a present."

Hannah looked at the soggy, crumpled handkerchief in her hand and finally saw the humor in the situation. "Oh, Alex, I'm sorry," she said, caught between more sobs and what could easily become hysterical laughter. "But I did warn you."

"Thermonuclear. I remember," he said, motioning for her to turn with him and head back toward the building. He shrugged out of the suit jacket, folded it over his arm. "I'm going to have to take this to the tailor without anyone seeing it, or else I'll be answering questions into my old age. Although it might be fun to tell Cade that you were trying to rip my clothes off me. He thinks he has that market cornered."

"With me? He thinks he has the market cornered with me? That's ridiculous."

"Cade thinks he has the market cornered with every woman he meets, Hannah. And, mostly, he does. There's nothing like knowing the guy has no heart to make a woman want to not only find it, but trap it, cage it and take it home."

"I'm not after Cade's heart, Alex. I'm not after any man's heart."

"Leaving me to say exactly what it is you *are* after—which I won't do," Alex said, stopping just outside the door to the stairs leading to the apartment Hannah shared with her father.

"I—I wish you'd just forget about the whole thing," Hannah told him, trying very hard not to look at him. "And I thank you again for taking me to the club this evening. I had a very nice time."

"Yes, you said that earlier. We've come full circle now, haven't we? Very well. I suppose it's time I let you go upstairs."

"It is getting colder," Hannah agreed, hugging herself to keep from shivering. Not from the cold, but from apprehension, and anticipation. Would he just say good-night? Would he feel it necessary to kiss her? "So, um...good night."

He let her go, let her turn away from him, gave her time to pull out her key, fiddle with it for endless moments, trying to get it into the lock.

"Damn," she muttered under her breath just before Alex's hand closed around hers, helping her guide the key home so that the door swung open on the dark hallway. She turned her head to look up at him, feeling him standing behind her, so close behind her, their bodies touching. "Thanks again."

"I'd like to kiss you good-night, Hannah, if you don't mind," Alex said softly. "Do you mind?"

"I...um...no. No, I don't—"

That was as far as she got before Alex turned her in his arms, tipped up her chin and lowered his mouth to hers. Softly, gently.

Her eyelids fluttered closed as she sighed against his lips, surrendered against his hard chest, her arms so boneless she forgot she had arms at all. Arms, or legs, or a brain that should be screaming, *He's only being nice. Don't read too much into this.*

But her brain was numb and nonfunctioning, so that Hannah listened only with her senses, and her senses were purring, *Ah, yes. More.*

She sort of hung there, against Alex's strong body, breathing in the scent of him, yielding as his arms slid around her, held her close. A tightness grew in her chest and throat; a warmth in her lower belly flared into fire as Alex laid a hand on her lower spine and dragged her even closer. Her lips parted slightly, and he took up her unspoken invitation.

The outdoor overhead light went on just above their heads, and before Hannah's fogged brain could realize that she wasn't seeing stars, her father's voice said, "Putting on shows for the neighborhood, Coleman? Not with my daughter, you're not. Hannah, come inside, *now.*"

Hannah tried to get away from Alex's arms, but he still held her, probably believing she'd fall down if he let her go. And he might have been right.

"Hugo," Alex said quietly. "I'm sorry if we woke you. We were just saying good-night."

"I know what you were doing," Hugo shot back, grabbing Hannah at the elbow and pulling her toward him. "I like you, Coleman, so I'm going to give you fair warning. She's her mother's child. You don't want anything to do with her."

Hannah wanted to pull her arm free. She wanted to run away, pretend her father wasn't standing here making a scene, ruining the only good thing she'd had in her life in a very, very long time.

But she didn't. She just stood there, looking at her father, then looking at Alex. Alex looked angry, very angry. But her father looked frightened. Angry, yes, and blustering, but also frightened half out of his mind. His fear shocked her. "Good night, Alex," she said at last. "You really should go now. Please," she added, when he appeared ready to say something she knew he'd regret.

"I'll see you tomorrow, at the ranch," he said at last, then turned and walked back to his car.

Once Alex's car had pulled away, Hugo turned to glare down at his daughter. "Trash," he ground out. "You and your mother both. Trash."

Hannah didn't know where the words came from, but suddenly they were in her head, and moments later they were on her tongue. "Don't push me, Dad," she said, blocking the doorway to the stairs. "Remember, I'm pretty much the only friend you've got."

And then she turned on her heels and headed upstairs.

Chapter Nine

Vi Coleman carried two mugs of hot coffee to the kitchen table and plunked one of them down in front of Alex. It was Sunday, Ella's day off, and Vi took her one-day-a-week job as cook and housekeeper very seriously. But not as seriously as she took her role of surrogate mother to Alex and his brothers.

Sliding onto a chair on the other side of the table, she placed her own mug in the center of the linen place mat and rested her elbows on the tabletop. "So? Are you going to tell me, or do I have to connive it out of you somehow?"

Alex looked at his aunt, at her still youthful face framed with red hair just beginning to fade and filled with huge green eyes that were as young as the morning. "I have no secrets from you, Vi. God knows I've tried, but I've never been able to pull it off."

Vi lifted the mug with both hands and held it to her mouth, looking at Alex over the rim. "Really? I'm that good? Well, that's reassuring. I wish I could say the same about Jessica. That girl hasn't confided in me for years. I don't have the faintest notion what she wants to do now, besides sleep late and drive Ella nuts when she decides she absolutely must bake cookies."

"Give Jess some time, Vi. She just graduated and wants

some down time. She knows what you and Randy want, and it's what she wants, too. She just doesn't want it right now.''

"I know," Vi said, sighing as she set the mug down once more. "I think she regrets taking that extra semester of electives, and not finishing up last May. It just doesn't seem as official, or something, graduating in December. I suppose Coleman-Grayson can wait a few more months for her.''

"I think it's going to have to," Alex said, aware that he had only delayed the inevitable. Vi had wanted to talk about Jessica—she always had her only child on her mind—but that didn't mean he was off the hook.

"Have I given you enough time to figure out how you're going to tell me?" she asked, proving his point.

"What I'm going to tell you about what, Vi? Really, you've lost me.''

"I suppose that could be true," she agreed after a moment. "You might be thinking that I want to hear what you think about Randy's news. About your mother. I never met her, you know, but I wish I could have known her. She must have been—must be—quite an extraordinary woman. Brave, loyal, willing to do anything at all to protect her children. Even leave them, within a week of losing her husband to an assassin's bullet. I can't imagine the extent of her heartache the day she handed you three over to Randy, then watched you walk out of her life.''

"Mac and Cade don't know," Alex said. "Randy did tell you that, didn't he?"

Vi nodded, wiping at a tear that threatened to spill onto her cheek. "Yes, he told me. That's probably wise. It might have been wise not to say anything to you, either, but we decided that, as the oldest, you had a right to know. Do you…do you remember her at all, Alex? You never speak of her."

Alex turned the mug around on the table, keeping his eyes on it as he spoke. "I remember a great love, both from my mother and my father. Feelings, Vi, not actual memories, at least no more than snatches of memories. But the love? Yes, I remember that very well."

"I know I was never more than a poor substitute," Vi said, and Alex leaned across the table, squeezed her hand in his.

"You and Randy saved us, Vi. Randy gave up his career and his home to move here, to keep us safe. You married Randy, knowing he came with three small and not always wonderful young boys, and you never flinched. You were never a substitute, Vi. You were our salvation."

Vi's watery smile shone across the table. "Thank you, Alex. And now I pray every night that Rose will be coming home. It's so difficult to be here, so far from wherever she is, and just waiting. How are you handling it?"

"Not as well as I could be, I suppose," Alex said. "But we have no choice. I don't like being forced to trust my father's brother, but King Zakariyya seems to have his own reasons to make sure she remains safe. There's intrigue in this, Vi, things we don't understand, but it seems very important to my uncle and King Zakariyya both that my mother be alive."

"Yes, Randy said much the same thing. If he thought it could help, he would have been on a plane to Sorajhee last week, but he knows his presence would only alert the press that something is going on over there. He's barely slept these past days, you know, and you look almost as tired as he does. Is all this lost sleep over Rose, or is there another reason?"

Alex grinned. "Man, you slipped that in so effortlessly

that I really didn't see it coming. You're talking about Hannah now, aren't you?''

"Me?" Vi pressed her hands to her chest. "I'm not talking about anything...or anyone. Jessica, however..."

"I thought Jessica didn't confide in you anymore."

"She doesn't.. Not about herself. But she's a veritable fountain of information about everything and everyone else. So? What are you going to do, Alex? Let Cade and Mac make a fool of you?"

"It's not me they'd be making a fool of, Vi," Alex told her, frowning. "And it's not both of them, by the way. I overheard them last night, out on the balcony at the club. Cade got the short straw, which he considers a win, and he gets to pretend to romance Hannah. Mac gets to rub my face in it and make sure I'm jealous."

Vi shook her head and tried to look stern, but her smile betrayed her. "Oh, those three. I don't know who is the worst—Jessica for thinking up the plan, or those terrible twins for agreeing to play the game."

"It's a toss-up," Alex said, finishing his coffee and rising to take the mug to the sink.

"But you think Hannah's serious about this...this quest of hers?"

Alex returned to the table, sat down once more. "No," he said at last. "I don't think she is, even if she thinks she is. Does that make sense?"

"It seems to make sense to you, Alex," Vi pointed out. "I imagine that's all that counts. It does not, however, tell me what you plan to do now that Cade is set to play the great romancer. Girls are always going gaga over that brother of yours. I wouldn't want to see Hannah hurt, even if she does know Cade is only pretending to chase her."

Alex tipped his head to one side, looked at his aunt. "Come again? Hannah *knows*?"

Vi slapped a hand to her mouth. "Whoops! I think that part of what Jessica said could have been the part I wasn't to repeat."

"Part of it? What's the rest of it?"

"Now, Alex, you know I can't—"

"Vi, I've got enough going on right now. Tell me what I need to know. Please."

Vi sighed, lifting her slim shoulders and letting them drop. "No wonder Jessica doesn't confide in me. I've got such a big mouth. Oh, very well. In a weak moment, Hannah told Jessica that you said you'd do anything for her and she said, fine, then help her stop being the LLTV— that's Last Living Texas Virgin, or something like that. Jessica set about turning Hannah into a femme fatale, and then decided that if Cade and Mac made a dead set at Hannah, and Hannah seemed to be responding, then you'd get all huffy and jealous and cut them out and fall in love with Hannah. Hannah knows about the plan, but she only learned about it last night, and Jessica says she wasn't thrilled. But you know how it is, Alex, when Jessica gets the bit between her teeth. I don't think Hannah had a choice. Where are you going?"

Alex opened the cabinet door and took out a small white plastic bottle. "I'm taking some aspirin, Vi. I have a headache. Man, do I have a headache."

"Yes, I can understand that," Vi said as Alex got himself a glass of water to wash down the aspirin. "However, since Hannah knows, there's no chance that Cade will hurt her. Unless, of course, he decides to be particularly charming, in which case all bets are off."

She was silent for a few moments, then looked at Alex worriedly. "Do you suppose Hannah will…I mean, if she's really serious about this, what's to keep her from… Oh, boy. I'll take two of those before you put the bottle away, Alex, if you don't mind.''

HANNAH HAD BEEN DISAPPOINTED that Alex wasn't in the stable yard when she drove up at precisely one o'clock, wearing her oldest jeans and her newest burgundy shirt and a black leather vest that had once belonged to her mother.

She looked pretty good, if she had to say so herself. She knew that she looked good, because her father had taken one look at her and headed for his bedroom, slamming the door behind him, opening it again only to gruffly remind her to take the office's cell phone with her in case there was an emergency.

Considering the fact that she was pretty sure her father would rather eat dirt than ask for her help, Hannah decided that she'd get a call only because that way Hugo could throw a monkey wrench into her free afternoon.

Cade had been as good as his word, and two prime mounts were saddled and waiting, along with a picnic basket that he'd tied to the saddle of his own mount. Within minutes they were off, heading past the main house and following the path around the small lake that bounded the property on one side.

As they passed the short, wooden dock where a canoe and two rowboats were tied up, Hannah asked Cade if he and Mac still went swimming in the lake on Christmas day.

''Our yearly tradition,'' Cade said, pretending to shiver. ''I don't know whose idea it was, but, yes, we still do it. Sometimes we get lucky, and sometimes I swear we barely hit the water before we're out again, icicles forming on our ears. This was an icicle year.''

''That lake's still cold in May,'' Hannah said. ''And I should know, because I fell in it when I was about fifteen. You pushed me, so I'm pretty sure you remember.''

"*I* pushed you?" Cade asked, his eyes wide. "No, couldn't have been me. It had to be Mac. I was a good boy."

"Nice try," Hannah said, laughing. "Although you didn't exactly push me in. You just made sure I *went* in. Let's see if I can jog your memory. I came down to the lake to watch Alex practice his canoeing and generally moon over him and make a fool of myself—"

"Keep going. It's coming back to me now," Cade interrupted, smiling over his shoulder at her as the path narrowed so that the horses had to move along single file.

"Well, there I was, mooning over Alex, and there you were, putting a worm on a hook because, as you said, you were going to catch dinner that night. I winced when I saw what you were doing. You saw the wince and started backing me along the dock, holding up a worm in one hand and a hook in the other, grinning as you threatened to do it again."

"I was a worm," Cade said, reining in his horse so that Hannah could bring her mount up beside his. "Actually, I was a night crawler. Bigger worm, you understand."

"I didn't care what you called it. I just didn't want you to kill it. I was very protective of animals in those days. Still am, actually."

"You were screeching like a barn owl," Cade said, continuing the story. "You were screeching, I was coming at you, you were backing up. Screech, wiggle the worm. Back up another step. Screech, wiggle the worm. Back up another step. Screech—*whoops!* And you were treading water."

"You still don't sound very repentant," Hannah pointed out as they took another path leading away from the pond and out onto the open range. "I think I owe you a dunking."

"Actually, I think you owe me an apology. You mean to say you were at the dock that day to moon over Alex, and not me? I'm crushed, Hannah. Really, I am. I mean, even at seventeen or eighteen—whichever I was—I considered myself quite the ladies' man."

"You did? I guess that was a little hard to tell. I think I was too busy looking at the worm. Is this field clear enough for a good run? I've seen the last broken leg I want to see on a horse for a while."

Cade nodded. "No holes, no half-buried rocks, no dead branches. Believe me, we check it out every week. Just let me untie the basket and leave it here, and I'll race you to that line of trees and back."

Hannah's mount was a fine chestnut mare, larger than Cade's Arabian, with longer legs and a strong heart. She and her horse pretty easily outdistanced Cade and his Arabian for the first half of the race, as she'd expected, but by the time they'd made the turn the mare was tiring, and the Arabian had only just begun to ease into its stride.

She reined the mare to a canter and watched in awe as Cade and his splendid Arabian danced away across the meadow, man and horse seeming to have become a single, beautifully fluid unit. All the Colemans rode well, with an almost instinctive grace that had won them all many awards in the ring. But seeing man and horse here, with no rules, no restrictions, did something to Hannah's heart; something elemental that had first touched her as a child and still thrilled her today. All animals held her heart, but Arabians touched her soul.

Cade had dismounted by the time Hannah reached him, and was spreading a thick plaid blanket on the already greening grass of the meadow. "We'll probably both catch pneumonia, eating on the ground, but there's nothing quite like the first picnic of the year, is there?'' he asked, helping her dismount.

He held on to her waist for a few moments, looking rather soulfully into her eyes as he kept her inches above the ground, then suddenly grinned and carefully set her down. ''Nope, can't do it,'' he said, taking her hand and leading her to the blanket. ''I only like to think I'm a heartless bastard. Actually, I'm a pussycat. I'll break the news to Jessica when we get back, okay?''

''What news?'' Hannah said, remembering that she wasn't supposed to know about Jessica's little plot. ''Am I missing something here?''

Cade opened the basket and pulled out two cans of soda, handing one to Hannah. ''You mean you haven't guessed?'' he asked, digging into the basket and unearthing a plastic dish containing pieces of fried chicken. ''I'm supposed to romance you until Alex wakes up and tells me to back off. I know Jessica said you weren't in on the plan, but I know my cousin. She either had to tell you how brilliant she is, or burst. Since I didn't see pieces of my cousin splattered all over the house, I figure she told you. So, am I right?''

''She told me,'' Hannah said, trying to look anywhere other than at Cade. Soon the whole world was going to know that she'd asked Alex to make her a woman. This was worse than those dreams about being out in public totally naked. ''She was just trying to be nice.''

''Nice?'' Cade said, spitting a spray of soda. ''Oh, I don't think so. But Mac and I did agree, because we think it's time Alex settled down, and he'll never get around to it on his own. Not unless we point the way for him, maybe even put up signs. Jessica says you're in love with him. Is she right?''

''I never said that,'' Hannah said, carefully opening the

plastic container. She had a quick vision of the top popping off and pieces of fried chicken exploding into the air, so she was extra careful, and quite proud of herself when she completed the task without making a mess. Better. She was getting better. Gaining back ground she'd seemed to lose upon returning to Bridle, to her father's house.

"You've been mooning around him—your words, Hannah, not mine—ever since any of us can remember. Not that Alex ever noticed. And now, believe it or not, he seems to be mooning around you. At least he sure has been in a fog these past days. Well, Mac and I say more power to you, and we'll do what we can to help. Other than pretend to seduce you, that is. I think that could get me bent in half by big brother. Jessica wouldn't think about that, but I have."

Hannah put down the chicken wing she'd been gnawing on and wiped her hands on the front of her jeans. "Man. Deliver one foal, make one unguarded statement, and here I am, up to my neck in intrigue. How did this happen?"

"Can we all say 'Jessica'?" Cade teased, grinning. "But, okay. I think we're settled now. You know, I know you know, you know I know you know—and Alex doesn't know diddly. That works for me. So, short of bragging that I've taken you to my bed—saying something like that could get a fella hurt, you understand—I say we just be friends, Hannah. I'd like to be your friend. If you can forgive the night crawler, that is."

"The night crawler, the way you laughed when I fell in the manure pile, chasing me and calling me Hannah Slip-on-a-banana, pulling my pigtails, promising me crabapples wouldn't give me a bellyache, offering me a ride on your horse and then loosening the cinch before I got on so that I fell right off. You know, Cade, now that I think about it, you're probably one of my best friends."

"I couldn't have done all that," Cade protested half-heartedly. "Some of that had to be Mac's doing. Wasn't it?"

"It doesn't matter either way," Hannah told him honestly. "Coming out to The Desert Rose with my father was just about the only time I was ever around other kids, except at school, and school is *not* one of my fondest memories. It didn't matter how you teased me, I still loved coming here." She looked around at the sweep of scenery and sighed. "I still love coming here."

"And you love my big brother?" Cade asked, then ducked as Hannah threw a chicken bone at him.

THEY DIDN'T LINGER too long over the picnic lunch. The ground still held the winter cold and damp, and the sun, which had helped warm the air, began to disappear behind a bank of clouds. They kept the horses to a slow walk, riding back toward the stable yard by following the split-rail fence that marked the boundary of main pasture, and Cade kept up a running account of Coleman family activities.

"Nick Grayson, Jared's son, is supposed to be taking Jessica under his wing now that she's finished grad school and that extra semester she took to postpone her return here a while longer," he told her. "Jessica did tell you that, didn't she?"

"No, she didn't. She hasn't said a word to me about Nick Grayson."

"Really? Interesting. Because Jessica talks about everything—unless it's really, really important to her. It was Randy's idea that Nick be Jessica's mentor, or whatever, as she gets more involved with Coleman-Grayson, and from that day on, Jessica's been finding excuse after excuse not to join the firm. Don't you think that's strange? Somebody should probably ask her about that, don't you think, Hannah?''

Hannah shook her head. "Oh, no. You're not going to get me to go prying into Jessica's private life."

"Why not? She's knee-deep in yours."

"Good point," Hannah said, nodding. "But I think you and Mac would be better at questioning her. Sort of tag-team her, you know?"

"Good cop, bad cop would be another way to say it, I suppose," Cade agreed. "And I would, except that Mac has been more than his usual stick-in-the-mud self ever since we all came back from Jessica's graduation. He went off by himself one night, and didn't come back to the hotel until the next morning, refusing to say a word about where he'd been or what he'd done. I asked, but since asking nearly got me socked in the mouth, I didn't ask twice. You know, Hannah, we used to have a lot of fun, growing up here at The Desert Rose. But, now that we're all grown-up, it seems staying on The Desert Rose doesn't keep us from having grown-up problems.''

Hannah nodded, knowing what he meant, thinking about her father, and how their roles were undergoing changes even as each stuck to the old ways: Hugo yelling and domineering, Hannah nervous and doing her best to please. But they couldn't stay trapped in the old roles, because the world around them was changing, reshaping those roles. Soon she might be the parent, and Hugo the child, dependent on her.

"I hate grown-up problems," she said as they neared the stable yard. "But I think it's wonderful that all three of you are staying with The Desert Rose. I can't imagine any of you anywhere else. Just as I can't imagine myself anywhere else but here in Texas."

"It's true that we're all still involved with The Desert

Rose, although we've also taken on some of the management of other Coleman holdings, like Coleman-Grayson. But our first love has always been the horses. Always. Still, now that the property next door is up for sale, I'd like to see us buy it and expand into raising cattle."

"Really? I always knew you were less the playboy than you pretend. A new business? What does everyone else think about that?"

Cade smiled. "I'll let you know after I tell them. Right now, Hannah, it's our secret, just between you and me. So, do you want to be our vet for the cattle ranch? They wouldn't be Arabians, but they'd still have four legs and a tail. And I can pretty much guarantee we'd keep you busy."

"Sounds great," Hannah said, and they rode back into the stable yard, very much in charity with each other, Hannah laughing as Cade told her an old joke about a cattle farmer and a three-legged cow.

ALEX STOOD LEANING on the bottom half of the stall door while the young stable hand, Olivia Smith, brushed Khalid and crooned softly to the foal.

"Oh, look at you," she was saying in a singsong voice. "So handsome, and knowing just how handsome you are. So proud of yourself. You just know you're a champion, don't you? Well, even champions seem to step in their own messes now and then, don't they. Come on, my prince, lift that leg for me and I'll clean you up. That's my boy, my fine Arabian prince."

Alex shook his head as Khalid lifted his foreleg, allowing Olivia to clean his hoof, then nuzzling against her shoulder as if to thank her. In the days since Khalid's birth, Olivia had rarely been far from the stall, taking care of both mother and baby, and foal and stable hand had seemed to bond in a way Alex had seen before yet still found amazing. Almost mystical.

He'd decided that Olivia would be assigned to Khalid, and said as much to Mac, who shared the job of training The Desert Rose horses.

Mac joined him now, polishing a bit of bridle ornamentation with a soft rag. "We'll let them out of here tomorrow for a little bit, I think. Khalahari needs to stretch her legs."

"He has the look of Jabbar, doesn't he?" Alex said as Olivia pulled a flat brush from her back pocket and began working on Khalid's mane. "Something about the way he holds his head. Proud."

"Arrogant," Mac said. "He knows who he is, and I have a feeling he'll never let any of us forget it. Oh, Cade's coming in. I thought you might want to know, just in case you want to check him over for grass stains."

"Very funny," Alex said, pushing himself away from the stall door. "I think Cade has passed beyond rolling around in the grass with his latest conquest, at least at this time of the year. A picnic. Only Cade would plan a picnic this time of year."

Still Alex didn't waste any time walking out of the stable, watching as Cade helped Hannah down from her mount, his jaw tightening as a groom came up to take the horses and Cade slipped an arm around Hannah's waist, guiding her toward the main house.

Not that it was any of his business, not any of it.

Funny. It sure *felt* like his business.

Chapter Ten

Hannah, sipping at a cup of hot tea that had at last begun to chase the chill from her body, watched as Vi Coleman stuffed the turkey that would be part of the Sunday evening meal.

It was nice to sit in the Coleman kitchen. The room was warm, fragrant with the aroma of the cherry pies cooling on top of the big ranch stove. Checked gingham curtains, a matching tablecloth, soft cushions on the wooden chairs, two huge, large-pawed dogs curled up in front of the open fireplace. This was a room for family, a room that welcomed everyone who entered.

"Are you sure you don't want a slice of pie, Hannah? I think they're cool enough to eat."

"No, thank you, Mrs. Coleman," Hannah said, cupping the mug with her rapidly warming hands. "I'm still digesting the chicken, which was fabulous. Did you make it?"

"Me? No, that was Ella. I keep trying to get the recipe for the breading out of her, but so far she's been closed as a clam about it, and most of her recipes. She calls it built-in job security, even though she knows we'd never want to survive without her. Oh," Vi ended, smiling, "and please call me Vi. Mrs. Coleman makes me feel ancient now that you're all grown-up.''

"Yes, thank you," Hannah said, turning as she heard a noise in the hallway. "Hi, Mac," she said, trying to keep the disappointment out of her voice. It wasn't that she wasn't happy to see the man, but she'd much rather see his brother. Even if she had no idea what she'd say to him after last night.

"Hi, yourself, Hannah," Mac said, making a beeline for the pies. "These ready yet, Vi?"

"Touch them before dinner and die," Vi said, winking at Hannah. "Does that answer your question?"

Mac backed away from the stove, his hands up as if Vi held him at gunpoint. "In that case, I'll settle for a cold soda. Hannah, you want one? Or maybe you'd like a beer?"

She shook her head. "Thanks, but I'm sort of on call. Last thing a sick animal needs is a tipsy vet."

"You're right there," Mac said, pulling out a chair, turning it around and straddling it as he laid the can of soda on the tabletop. "So, how was the picnic? You have to say one thing for Cade, he picked a time when you could be pretty sure there wouldn't be any ants around to get into the food."

"No, just polar bears," Hannah said, and Mac and Vi laughed. Hannah smiled, put at ease by their laughter, by the way she was being allowed to relax, feel comfortable here in the very heart of the Coleman home.

In fact, she thought, sobering momentarily, the only thing that could make her feel uneasy would be if Alex walked into the room and looked at her with those deep, dark eyes of his.

"Will you be able to stay for dinner, Hannah?" Vi asked as she opened the oven door and slid the turkey inside.

"We won't eat until this bird is done, and that won't be until about seven. We always eat late on Sundays."

"I'm afraid not. I've got to make dinner for my father," Hannah said, reluctantly pushing back her chair and standing up.

Now that she'd given it more thought, escaping The Desert Rose without seeing Alex had its own appeal. He might be avoiding her, but avoiding him as well seemed increasingly like a good idea. After all, what do you say to a man who kissed you, just to have your father show up and denounce you as a tramp, even while you were still held in that man's embrace? Not a lot. At least, Hannah couldn't think of what she'd say to him.

Vi said something about inviting Hannah another time, and Mac seconded the idea. "You know, Hannah," he added, "Alex told me what a great job you did with Khalid. That foal is the future of The Desert Rose. We're all very lucky you were available, and could come save the day."

"I was just happy to be able to help," Hannah said, feeling her cheeks grow hot. She wasn't used to compliments and wasn't quite sure how to deal with them. "Dad would have handled it easily."

"Yes, but he wasn't here, was he? I've said for a while that having only one vet was cutting it too thin, with all the ranches around here. I know I'll sleep easier knowing there are now two great vets in Bridle."

Hannah smiled again, cleared her throat and looked at Mac. "You can't know how nice it is to hear you say that. Thank you again." She picked up the riding gloves that she'd nearly forgotten on the table, and said, "Well, I should be going. Please tell Cade that I thank him for a lovely afternoon. I don't want to interrupt his business call."

"Business calls on a Sunday afternoon," Vi said, attacking a cucumber with a vegetable peeler. "More than twenty-five years of them, and I still can't get used to it. Some people just don't know what it means to carve out a day of rest for themselves."

At that, and as if on cue, the cell phone in Hannah's pocket began to ring and she quickly answered it. She'd barely said hello when her father's voice barked at her, then left her holding the phone to her ear, with nothing to say goodbye to but the dial tone.

"That...that was my father," she said as Mac and Vi exchanged looks, then tried to pretend that they hadn't just witnessed Hugo Clark's rudeness secondhand. "Rafe Collins has a mare down. It could be colic. I have to get right over there."

"Colic?" Mac repeated. "That could be really bad news. Is Hugo meeting you at the Collins ranch?"

"No," Hannah said, tucking the cell phone back into her jeans pocket. "He says he thinks I can handle it."

What she didn't say was that Hugo's words had been slurred, so that she was fairly certain he'd drunk his way through the afternoon. She'd seen him drunk a time or two over the years, not very often, but he'd had a beer bottle in his hand when she'd left for The Desert Rose, and she'd worried that he might decide to make a day of it today. She had been pretty hard on him last night, and she knew it, both before her date with Alex, and afterward.

She'd have to be more compassionate, more caring. The man only did what he'd been doing for years. Having her call him on his verbal abuse now was about twenty years too late, and he didn't know how to cope with a grown-up Hannah. No more than he knew how to cope with his possible blindness. He had to be overwhelmed. How could she have been so cruel to him?

Because he was cruel to you, a small voice said inside

her head. *Being old and sick and scared does not mean that
he can continue to use you as his whipping post. If you're
going to stay, you've got to lay the ground rules, and number one on that list is that you're not going to put up with
any more of his cutting remarks, period.*

"Hannah? Are you all right?"

She blinked, then looked at Mac, who was watching her
curiously.

"Oh. Oh, yes, yes. I'm fine. I...I was just mentally reviewing the contents of my medical bag. I'm pretty sure I
can leave for the Collins ranch straight from here, without
returning to the office. Well...thank you for everything, Vi.
I have to go now."

"Go where?"

Hannah shut her eyes, waiting for the figurative fist to
slam into her gut. Bam! There it was, following the sound
of Alex's voice by no more than a split second. She turned,
slowly, to face him, but then realized she couldn't raise her
head, couldn't bear to look into his face.

"Oh, there you are, Alex," Vi said, wiping her hands
on a towel as she came across the room, to slide an arm
around Hannah's waist, protecting her, or so Hannah believed. "Hannah just got a call to go over to Rafe Collins's
place. Something about a mare down with colic."

Hannah knew Vi could feel her trembling, and the older
woman gave her a quick squeeze before letting go, saying
she was sure Hannah could wait long enough for her to fill
a thermos with more hot tea, to keep her warm while she
worked.

"Good idea, Vi," Alex said as Hannah stared at the toes
of his boots, wondering how she would ever get her tongue
unstuck from the roof of her mouth. "And put in an extra
cup, if you would, because I might want some myself.
Okay, Hannah?"

"You…you're going with me?" she asked, at last daring to look up at him. What she saw made her sharply draw in her breath. No wonder Vi had come to her, tried to comfort her. Alex Coleman was looking at her exactly the same way as he had last night, just before he'd kissed her. With an intensity that made her tremble.

"Wrong. I'm taking you. If that's all right?" he asked, accepting the thermos and extra cup from Vi. "Ready?"

"Um…" Hannah swallowed, then nodded. What was she doing, standing here like some dope? There was a mare in trouble, and she wasn't helping the animal by standing here wondering why Alex kept looking at her as if he might just be thinking about taking a few small bites out of her. Love bites? She shivered again. "Sure. Sure, okay. We'd better get moving."

Her mind ripped clean of Alex, Hannah put it in gear and took off through the house, heading back to the stable yard to get her medical bag. She was not aware that Alex had backed up quickly to let her pass, tripped over his own feet and ended up slamming his shoulder against the door frame.

"Nice, bro," Mac said, laughing as Alex rubbed at his sore shoulder. "I didn't know clumsiness was contagious."

HANNAH WAS OUT OF THE CAR almost before it stopped, her bag in her hand as she raced, surefooted, toward the Collins stables, leaving Alex to follow after her, still trying to figure out how he'd not only slammed his shoulder against the door frame in the Coleman kitchen, but had also dropped his car keys twice, and then stepped in a puddle as he finally made it to the car, where an impatient Hannah was waiting for him.

He'd never been clumsy. Never. But, as he told himself during their swift drive to the Collins ranch, he'd never been nervous, either. Not until Hannah Clark had asked him to please, pretty please, relieve her of her virginity.

Not until that outlandish request had begun to make sense to him, at least. Not until he'd found himself going to sleep thinking of Hannah, waking to thoughts of Hannah.

He should be thinking about his mother and what Sorajhee and Balahar suddenly had to do with him, with his brothers. And he was, in one part of his mind. In another part of his mind, however, his thoughts were all of Hannah. Her smile. Her unaffected laughter once she forgot to take herself and life so seriously. The way she fit against him when they danced. The way their mouths had fit together last night.

"Get a grip, Coleman," he told himself as he slammed the car door and took off in the same direction Hannah had taken, catching up to her just as she was ordering the stricken mare be walked back inside the stable and put in the largest stall.

"But we always walk colicky horses, Miz Clark," the Collins ranch hand was saying, holding his ground.

"Yes," Hannah told him, "I'm sure you have. But it really isn't all that helpful. You might think you're helping because she won't show as many outward signs of colic, but that's only because you're walking her, and not really allowing her to behave as she really wants, which would be to roll, among other things. But you have kept her from kicking herself or otherwise hurting herself, and that's good. Now we have to treat her."

"Mr. Coleman?" The ranch hand looked at Alex for help. "What do you think?"

"I think, Barry, we ought to listen to the doctor. Come on, I'll help you get her back inside."

"What's she been doing?" Hannah asked Barry once the mare was tied up inside a large stall. "Pawing? Rolling? I can see she's sweating. Whoops, there she goes. Back off, Barry, and let her lie down. What's her name?''

"Jamilah," Barry said, "but we call her Lally. She's one of Mr. Collins's favorites. He left this morning for a few days in Houston. If anything happens to her..."

"We're not going to let anything happen to her," Hannah told him calmly, already examining the horse, running her hands along the mare's belly. "Ah, Lally, Lally, what have you been eating, you beautiful girl?"

"She wasn't feeding too well, not yesterday or today," Barry said as Lally kicked out her legs, regained her feet. The mare stood, shifting her weight from one leg to another, and the stable hand unconsciously imitated the movement. "So we gave her some sweet corn, just to tempt her. She gobbled it all up, too."

Alex saw Hannah's frown. "I'll just bet she did, Barry," Hannah said, reaching into her bag. "Unfortunately, sweet feed or corn puts an animal at a higher risk for colic, and it sounds as if she was already halfway there on her own. Still, I don't think it's too serious. I don't feel any really alarming distention or twisting in the intestines. In short, Barry, what this poor baby needs most right now is a good, strong physic."

Within moments, Hannah had administered both the physic and an injectable painkiller, then told Barry she wanted to see Lally's regular stall. "This water's pretty cold," she said, sticking her finger in Lally's water. "Lally should have warmer water. She'll drink more that way, and that cuts down the chance of colic all by itself. Now, don't feed her again until the physic works, and then keep down the proportion of grain in her feed." She patted Barry's arm. "We can kill a horse with kindness, you know."

"I always thought we should keep a colicky horse moving until the vet arrives," Alex said as they walked outside the stable, prepared to stay at the ranch until the mare showed signs of ridding herself of the impaction.

"To keep her from hurting herself, kicking herself, sure. But walking a horse never cured colic. If you see a horse pawing at the ground, rolling, sweating, trying to look at her own flank area, even trying to kick herself in the belly, don't wait, and don't think you can fix the problem by walking her. Oh, and although Lally was showing the typical signs, some horses with colic just stand there, like my professor said, looking anxious and depressed, just like people do with a bellyache."

"Colic is a killer," Alex said, using the top of a long metal water trough for a leg up, climbing up on the split rail fence, then holding out a hand so that Hannah could climb up herself, join him on the top rail.

"It can be," Hannah agreed. "But I think Lally's going to be fine. It's Barry who's going to be knee-deep in…well, you know what he's going to be knee-deep in, once that physic works. I'm pretty sure Lally has eaten her last sweet corn."

"Once again, you handled the situation beautifully, Hannah," Alex said, then winced. "I'm sorry. I shouldn't keep saying that. Of course you handled it well. You're a good vet. Between veterinary school and working with your father as you grew up, how could you be anything else?"

"But it still surprises you," Hannah said, looking toward the barn as Lally became rather vocal.

"It's working!" Barry yelled from the door of the stables. "Man! What did you give her?" he asked, then he ran back inside.

"Glad I'm going to miss this part," Hannah said, laughing. "I would be lying if I said I wanted to be in there right now."

Alex watched as Hannah took a deep breath, letting it

out in a contented sigh, obviously happy at a job well-done. She looked so fragile, with her honey-blond hair drawn back into a ponytail, her blue eyes as clear and wide as a child's. Yet there was determination in her chin, and her small hands had performed competently as she examined the huge animal, soothed that sick animal.

"You know," he said after a few moments of shared silence, "last night was the first time I've ever kissed a veterinarian."

"And?" Hannah asked, looking at him, finally looking at him. He'd been wondering if she'd ever really *look* at him again.

"And, I'm thankful you didn't first insist on checking me for hoof-and-mouth disease, I guess," he said, then waited for her response.

She laughed and gave him a push on the shoulder. His sore shoulder. He winced involuntarily, lifted his hands from the fence rail...and suddenly found himself lying on his back inside the walking ring, the water trough blocking any sight of him from the stable.

"Alex! Are you all right?" Hannah asked, climbing down from the fence and kneeling beside him. "I didn't push you that hard, for pity's sake. Why did you let go? You shouldn't have let go."

"You're blaming me, Hannah?" he asked, looking up at her from the ground. He'd stay on the ground for a while. It seemed safer, and he wouldn't have so far to fall.

"Well, you don't think I'm going to blame myself, do you?"

Alex smiled, a slow, easy smile that grew into a grin. "God, Hannah, that's great," he said, reaching up to take hold of her arms, pull her down to him. "And it's about damn time."

"Time?" Hannah repeated, trying to move away from him, but he wouldn't let her. "Time for what?"

"Time you didn't blame yourself for everything that might go wrong. Time you stopped being so nervous that you end up being Hannah Slip-on-a-banana, that's what. I take it to mean that you're finally, finally able to feel a little bit more comfortable around me."

Hannah tipped her head to one side, considering his words as she looked at him. "Really. You know, I think you're right. I *am* feeling more comfortable around you, which is pretty difficult to believe after my father did his little stunt last night. But—Alex? If I'm not clumsy, what are you? I mean, don't look now, Alex, but you're lying on your back on the ground."

"What am I?" Alex considered the question as he drew her closer, closer. "A romantic might say I'm falling for you, Hannah. Literally."

"Oh."

"Yes, *oh*. And now I think I'd like to kiss you, just to be sure. It's Sunday, this place is all but deserted. We've got the water trough as cover, and the ground is relatively soft. It doesn't get much better than this. Or, at the very least, here we don't have to worry about your father interrupting us."

"There is that," Hannah said, a smile teasing at the corners of her mouth. "All right. You may kiss me."

"I didn't really ask permission," he said quietly as he moved his hands to her shoulders and pulled her all the way down to him.

This time she not only allowed the kiss, she actually participated in it. Last night her arms had remained at her sides as she let him take all the initiative, but today her hands went to his cheeks, cupping them, as she moved her mouth against his, as she slid her body lower, until she was half lying across him.

"Oh, Hannah," he breathed into her mouth, wrapping his arms tighter around her, rolling her over onto her back, crushing her body with his own in the slowly awakening grass edging the walking ring. He kissed her again and again, punctuating each kiss with "Hannah...sweet Hannah..."

"Miz Clark? *Miz Clark!* Where are you, Miz Clark? You want to come check on Lally now?"

Alex rolled onto his back and drew Hannah's head against his chest. "No, Barry, Miz Clark damn well doesn't want to come check on Lally now," he muttered as Hannah held a hand over her mouth, trying not to giggle. "Stop laughing, woman, he'll hear you."

She lifted her head slightly, her blue eyes dancing with mischief. She looked so young, so free, with not a sign of the clouds that so often obscured the real sunshine that lived inside her. "Well, what do you suggest? That we stay here?"

"It's one plan," Alex said, then dropped his head against the ground. "Oh, all right. Wait until he goes back inside, and then go check on the mare. I'll wait here for a few minutes, then follow you."

"You don't want to come with me now?" Hannah asked, showing him very clearly that she might have learned about the birds and the bees at her veterinary college, but she still had a lot to learn about certain two-legged male animals.

"Hannah, I can't come with you now, okay?" He looked at her, his eyebrows lifted, and waited until she figured out what he meant.

"Oh," she said after a moment, and he watched in

delight as a soft, flattering pink stole into her cheeks. "Well...in that case..."

How long had he known this woman? All of her life? So he should have known better. He shouldn't have done it. He shouldn't have said anything. With Hannah, doing was one thing. Kissing was one thing. She didn't, thank God, seem to get all nervous and flustered anymore when he kissed her. But talking about kissing her had definitely been a mistake.

How did he know he'd goofed? Well, that was easy enough.

Hannah and her pink cheeks and the flustered rest of herself quickly scrambled away from him, using hands and knees to push against him in order to distance herself. Alex would never be sure if it had been her hand or her knee, but he did know that his amorous thoughts were suddenly quite quickly banished, although he still wasn't going to be moving for a while.

So he just laid there as she headed back toward the stable, looking up at the sky, breathing very carefully, and wondered how a nice guy like him had gotten into a mess like this.

And smiling, because, this particular moment being the exception, he rather liked the mess he was in.

HANNAH STOOD at the narrow window in her darkened bedroom, her arms wrapped around her as she tipped her head so that she could see the moon that was only visible if she leaned right, so that she could see around the building next door.

What a day she'd had. What a *few* days she'd had.

She couldn't remember another time in her life when she'd been so stressed yet so happy.

Even her father couldn't make it rain on her parade, and

that alone was a herculean accomplishment, one she'd hopefully learn from and enlarge upon as she learned to deal with the always difficult man.

He'd been drunk when she finally got home, a bag of fast-food chicken riding on the seat beside her, as the time spent at the Collins ranch had run to their regular dinner hour, and beyond.

Saying goodbye to Alex beside her car, back at The Desert Rose, had taken another fifteen minutes, not that she was complaining about that. Far from it! She was still having enough trouble simply believing that she'd spent those fifteen minutes being very thoroughly kissed, very gently touched, stroked, reduced to a near-whimpering puddle of never-before-felt emotions.

Hannah was pretty sure that Alex knew her passion had been liberally mixed in with some apprehension, a dash of nerves, a spoonful of maidenly reticence...that whole mix of emotions leavened with a heaping cupful of "if you're sure, I'm sure, but I'm not sure you're sure."

And she wasn't sure, not about how Alex really felt. Was he only being kind? Or perhaps she had intrigued him in some way, admitting that she was still a virgin. Was that the right word? *Admitting* it? It wasn't as if virginity was a crime, was it?

In this day and age, she supposed a grown man might never take a virgin to his bed. Oh, some had probably fumbled in the back seat of their father's car with a girl just as ignorant as himself, but that wasn't anything like taking a virgin to your bed if you were already a man of the world. Was it?

She didn't think so. Alex was so tender with her, so careful. He treated her like some fragile flower he wanted to enjoy without bruising her, hurting her in any way.

So she had kissed him. Hannah smiled now, reliving that

first kiss at the Collins ranch, and the way Alex might have begun the kiss, but she had finished it. Grabbing onto his face with both hands, opening her mouth over his, sliding her body onto his.

"Shame, shame on me," she said into the quiet darkness, feeling pretty darn good about herself, fairly smug and maybe even sophisticated.

And then she frowned, sighed. How much better it would be if she hadn't said a word to Alex, if he had "discovered" her on his own, without her waving the flag of her virginity—and definite availability—under his nose.

How could she be sure what Alex felt for her was anything but curiosity? Plus, he might even think he was saving her from some imagined heartbreak delivered by his brother Cade, although that danger had been pretty well passed, as she and Cade had agreed to drop Jessica's outlandish plan.

"Could he really be falling in love with me?" she asked the moon and the stars, who both refused to answer her.

The pounding knock on her door ripped Hannah away from her questions, and she crossed the room and opened the door, to see her father standing there, weaving from side to side.

"Dad, you belong in bed," she told him, taking his arm and trying to steer him back to his bedroom at the opposite end of the living room. "Unless you're hungry? I brought home some chicken, but you were asleep when I came in and I decided not to wake you."

"You decided? *You* decided? Where do you come off deciding things for me, girlie-girl? *I* make the decisions around here, and don't you forget it. Always have, always will."

Hannah bit down on her anger as she looked at Hugo, realizing that the man's anger, the man's bluster, were only pitiful attempts to cover up his insecurities, and quite possibly his fears. Why had she never realized that before? He was just a man, a lonely man, a man deserted by the woman he loved, left to raise their daughter alone.

It couldn't have been easy for him, but he could have made it easier, easier for himself, and for Hannah. But he hadn't reached out to her. He'd shoved her away, daring her to leave as her mother had done. He was still daring her to leave, pushing her away, even as he needed her now more than he had needed anyone in his life.

Hannah slipped an arm around Hugo's waist and pressed her head against his shoulder. He smelled of beer and sweat and something almost intangible that she believed could be fear. "It's all right, Dad," she crooned, slowly walking him back to his bed. "I'm here. I won't leave you. I promise. I won't leave you."

Hugo subsided into his bed and Hannah lifted his feet, sliding them onto the bed, then pulling the covers up to his chin. "You sleep now, all right?"

She turned to leave, but his hand shot out and grabbed her wrist, holding her in place. "The Collins mare. How is she?"

"She's fine, Dad. You were right, it was colic, but we caught it early. Sweet corn. The stable hand fed her sweet corn because she wasn't eating. She was probably already starting the colic, and the sweet corn just added fuel to the fire."

"What did you do?"

"I went with the simplest treatment. A shot of painkiller and a physic," Hannah said, trying, unsuccessfully, to pry her father's fingers from her wrist, as his grip was strong and he was hurting her. "Please, Dad, go to sleep."

His grip only tightened. "You don't need me," he said at last, his eyes tightly closed, his face pale in the moonlight streaming across the bed. "She didn't need me, and now you don't need me. I'm like an old, broken-down horse, ready for the glue factory.''

Hannah sat down on the side of the bed, finally able to loosen Hugo's grip so that she could hold his hand. ''Dad, that's not true. Everything I know I learned from you. And I'll always need your advice, your help. You're the best vet in the whole world.''

''A blind vet,'' he said, lifting his free hand, covering his eyes. ''Nobody needs a blind vet. I should just take the pistol out of my bag and put myself down. I'd do it for any dumb animal in pain, why not for myself?''

Hannah's gut clenched. ''That's the beer talking, Dad,'' she told him, trying to convince herself. ''Please...please just go to sleep. We'll talk about this tomorrow.''

But he didn't hear her. The beer had caught up with him again, and he was snoring before she'd finished speaking.

Hannah left him to sleep it off, knowing that tomorrow Hugo would say nothing about what had just happened, if he even remembered it. Because a sober Hugo Clark never admitted to any weakness, and Hannah knew that as well as she knew her own name.

She also knew Hugo kept his pistol in his medical bag, and she turned on the light in the stairwell and walked down to the office, to remove that pistol and hide it in her room.

Chapter Eleven

For the next five days, Alex barely found time to eat and sleep, let alone phone Hannah.

Cade had departed The Desert Rose early Monday morning, for some unexpected but urgent business meetings in Dallas, leaving Alex to act as host to four prospective clients lined up to arrive at the ranch, one each day, through Thursday. That kept Mac busy at the stables, making sure everything was in tip-top shape there, with both the stables and the horses.

Alex found himself wishing he could sell the selected stock to the first client and be done with it, but he knew that was impossible. Each client had made an appointment, and each client had to be given an equal opportunity to inspect the horses for sale and make a bid.

Randy had agreed to do the wine-and-dine part of each client's visit, but Alex found himself being asked along each night, so that by Wednesday he believed he never wanted to see another restaurant menu again.

But it was all part of the job, and the worst part of it, truthfully, remained the idea that any of the fine stock would be leaving The Desert Rose. These horses were, in many ways, Alex's children, and proud as he was of them, he longed to keep them all, every last one of them.

Desert Rose stock was in nearly every state now, and in several foreign countries, Jabbar's offspring considered some of the best in Arabian horse circles. Jabbar was The Desert Rose, and now that rose bloomed all over the world.

Friday morning, as Alex hung up the phone after calling the highest bidder and congratulating him, Randy walked into the office, Vi with him.

"A good week, Alex. A very good week," Randy said, waiting until Vi sat down, then sitting beside her on the leather couch. "Can you stick around for a few minutes? Jessica, Cade and Mac will join us as soon as they've had their coffee."

"Cade's back?" Alex asked. "I didn't know that. What's up, Randy? It has been a while since we've had a full family conference." He sat up in his chair. "Is this about my mother? Has she been located?"

Randy shook his head. "No, and it's killing me, both the waiting, and knowing we're keeping what little news we have from Cade and Mac. This is, well, this is something else," he said as Vi reached over and squeezed his hand.

"You're not...ill, are you?" Alex asked, blindly reaching for a reason behind the family meeting.

"Oh, Randy, would you please stop frowning—you're frightening Alex," Vi exclaimed, reaching over to ruffle his fair hair. "This is *good* news. At least for us."

Jessica slipped into the room at that moment and took up a folded-arm, rather belligerent stance in front of one of the windows. "If this is going to be some sort of intervention meant to make me bow down and beg the high-and-mighty Nick Grayson to teach me all about the family business—well, I might just jump out this window."

"We're on the ground floor, darling," Vi pointed out as Randy gave out a low growl. "You'll have to threaten something at least marginally more dramatic."

Jessica shrugged, grinned at Alex. "Hey, I tried. Do you know what this is all about?"

"Not a clue," Alex said, pushing away from the desk and coming around to sit on one corner of it as Mac and Cade entered the room, each holding a coffee mug. "Ah, all accounted for. Randy? You want to get us started?"

"And a big hello to you, too, Alex," Cade said, propping himself against the other front corner of the desk. "Yes, yes, it was a good trip. I fixed all the problems—all two of them—and rewarded myself with a pair of tickets to a new musical being tried out in Dallas. Do you want to know who the other ticket was for? Can you say 'green eyes, coal-black hair, and legs up to here'?"

"Somebody ought to pour cold water on you," Mac said, dropping into a chair on the other side of the room. "I hereby volunteer. Besides, I thought you were romancing our lovely young vet."

Alex clenched his teeth while trying to look unconcerned as he waited for Cade's answer.

"Hannah?" He shook his head. "Nope. We decided to be friends. Didn't I tell you that?"

"No, you didn't tell me that," Jessica said hotly, stepping away from the window, then quickly backing up, pretending an interest in the scenery outside the window. "Yeah, well, it's none of my business."

"That never stopped you before," Mac said, looking at Cade as if for further explanation. "Okay, okay, I'll talk to you later. But, you know, it would be nice if you guys gave me an update every once in a while."

"Randy and Vi have something to tell us," Alex said as Cade opened his mouth, probably to say something that would have either Alex or Jessica jumping right down his throat.

"Thank you, Alex," Randy said, getting to his feet. "I'll

keep it short and simple. This week, I believe, was the clincher—problems in Dallas, the ranch all but overrun with clients—although I've been thinking about this for a while now. I'm retiring."

"When?" Alex asked, pretty much in shock.

"He's *semi*-retiring," Vi said, standing up as well, slipping her arm through her husband's. "We all know he could never just turn his back, walk away. And as of today, actually. It's time."

Cade raked a hand through his dark hair. "Wow, you guys sure know how to drop a bomb, don't you? So what now?"

"So now," Randy said, "you boys continue to do what you've been doing, except you won't feel the need, if you ever do, to come asking me for permission to do what you already all do extremely well. You know I never interfered here at the ranch, not in the actual day-to-day running of The Desert Rose. Now all of it is yours, soup to nuts, to divide up any way you want. At the same time, I'm asking you all to take more of an interest in all of Coleman-Grayson. That means you, too, Jessica."

"Blackmail," Jessica said, glaring at her father. "That's what this is, isn't it? You and mom deserve to take it easy, I'm not saying you don't. But you're only doing this now so that I'll roll over and play dead for Nick Grayson. That's low, Dad, that's really low."

Mac walked over and put his arm around his cousin. "Feel better now? Good. Now apologize."

Jessica sighed, looked at Randy. "I'm sorry, Dad, Mom. I just wanted some more time, that's all. Is that a crime?"

Vi held out her arms and Jessica walked into them. "Randy?" she asked, looking over her daughter's shoulder. "Is she asking so much? She's been in school for so long, away from the ranch for so long. Does Coleman-Grayson really depend on our daughter showing up in Dallas immediately?''

"No," Randy said, touching a hand to Jessica's hair, "I suppose not. Okay, bunny-bear, you can have a few more months off, to unwind, or whatever it is you want to do. Now what do you say the three of us go talk about where we want to have dinner tonight?''

Mac watched as Vi, Randy and Jessica left the room together.

"Now she's going to get all weepy, five seconds after exploding," Mac said to Alex. "But you know what? Both Randy and Jessica get what they want now. He knows she'll join the company as planned, if a little later than planned, and she knows she's a person in her own right, and allowed to make her own plans. I love this family."

"It's a good one, all right," Alex agreed, moving back behind the desk and picking up the papers he'd been working on earlier. "Makes you want to have one of your own."

"Speak for yourself, big brother," Mac said, holding out his hands and backing away from the desk. "Speak for yourself. You couldn't get me within fifty miles of an altar."

"You got a little closer a while ago," Cade put in. Then he quickly added, "Sorry, Mac. That was low. But I know what you mean. I'm sure not looking to hear wedding bells in my future, either. We'll leave that to Alex for now. Are you hearing wedding bells, Alex?''

Alex looked at his brothers. "You know what? You *both* need some cold water dumped over your heads. Now, if you'll excuse me, I've had a long week. For the next two days, pretend I'm out of town, I'm on the moon. Anything at all. Just remember that this Coleman is off duty."

"Going to call Hannah?" Cade called after him. "You won't have to call too loud. It's Friday, remember? Our regular vet day. She's down at the stables, checking on Khalid.''

Alex stopped, turned, glared at his brothers, who were both grinning at him. "Oh, what the hell," he said, and grinned back at them before heading for the stables.

HANNAH WATCHED as Olivia stroked Khalid's soft velvet muzzle, smiling as the young stable hand told her all about the foal, how smart he was, how steady on his feet, how eager he was to experience life.

"You forgot to mention that Khalid seems to have quite a crush on you," Hannah said, then laughed as Olivia blushed.

She didn't know much about Olivia, or Livy, as she preferred to be called. Not much more than that Livy was about five years her junior, an orphan who showed up at The Desert Rose one day and proved within a few more days that she had a rare affinity for horses. Livy was about as shy and retiring as a steamroller when she saw something she wanted, and had more than enough fight in her for a regiment. Hannah liked her a lot, and admired her even more.

"Khalid's special," Livy said as she walked out of the stall behind Hannah and latched the bottom of the split door. "Not just because Jabbar is his sire, although that's a large part of it. I'm just lucky to get to work with him."

"I'd say Khalid's lucky, too," Hannah said as she pushed back the sleeve of her flannel shirt and checked her watch. Office hours began in two hours, and she'd be taking them on her own again today, just as she had every day this week, along with all the calls she had to make at ranches in the area.

Hugo Clark had quit, just sat himself down in his old chair in the living room of the apartment, and quit. Given up. He hadn't gone near another beer, probably because he'd lost control Sunday night and didn't want to risk having that happen again. Oh, no, that would be terrible— losing control, actually talking to Hannah, admitting to his fears.

Hannah hadn't had enough hours in the day this week, not to do the office hours, ranch visits and take care of her father, who may have starved himself if she didn't make sure he had hot food to eat three times a day.

She didn't know what to do with him, how to handle this new, defeated Hugo. She knew to hide from his sharp tongue, steer clear of things that made him angry. She'd learned all of that many years ago. But nothing had prepared her to deal with a withdrawn Hugo Clark, a self-pitying old man who had just plain given up.

Hannah had thought about Alex, about talking to him, but as he hadn't phoned her a single time since Sunday, she knew too much time had passed for her to make the next move. That next move had to be up to him, and it didn't appear he was going to make it.

She'd thought…hoped…but Sunday must have been an aberration. Everything that had happened between them since the day of Khalid's birth had been an aberration, and she knew it.

Hannah wasn't even angry, although she was most definitely hurt. She had never really believed Alex Coleman could see her as anything more than a temporary diversion, an oddity, a piece of unfinished childhood business that he might want to take care of somehow.

And that "business" must have been completed, at least to his mind, on Sunday afternoon, at the Collins ranch and as he'd lingered over his goodbye to her back at The Desert Rose. He'd paid attention to poor Hannah Slip-on-a-banana, shown her a good time, romanced her a little, and now they were even. She had convinced herself that Alex saw it that way.

So she hadn't come to The Desert Rose to see Alex. Definitely not. She'd come on her regular Friday rounds, to check on Khalid and Khalahari, and hopefully to talk to Vi Coleman. She felt she could trust the older woman, confide in her about Hugo, ask her advice.

"You've got the ointment I gave you for Dakar's eyes?" Hannah asked as she and Livy stepped out into the morning sun. "Three times a day, in both eyes even though only the one is affected now. He should be showing improvement by tomorrow. If not—"

"I'll call you. Yes, I remember," Livy said, sticking her hands in the front pockets of her jeans. "Well, I'm out of here, seeing that it looks like your boyfriend is making a beeline in this direction."

"My boy—" Hannah turned in time to see Alex striding toward the stables. "Oh, no—no. He's not my—"

"Anything you say, Doc. Except I have to tell you that I saw you from the stables on Sunday, saying goodbye to each other for about an hour," Livy said, winking at her before retreating to the stable.

"Hannah!" Alex called out while he was still more than thirty yards away from her. "I've been meaning to call you."

Hannah hadn't had much in the way of opportunity when it came to recognizing male come-on lines, but she was pretty sure she'd just heard one. "Really?" she said, her smile weak as Alex came up to her, kissed her cheek. "But all the phone lines were down, right?"

"Ouch!" Alex said, straightening, looking into her face. "What did you do with my Hannah, the woman without feminine wiles? I think I miss her."

Hannah felt heat invading her cheeks and bowed her

head. "I'm sorry," she said almost automatically, then something deep inside her rallied, said *hey, wait a minute, bub!* and she lifted her head again, stared right into his eyes. "Scratch that, I'm not sorry. You didn't call me. Why didn't you call me?"

"Oh, Hannah," Alex said, laughing as he took her hand, turned back toward the house. "Please don't ever try to be coy. You're much better being your very innocently blunt self. I didn't call you for a couple of reasons. One, I was up to my neck in work all week."

"And two?" Hannah asked, grateful he was holding her hand, because he stumbled over a rock in the path and might have fallen if she hadn't had a grip on him.

"Damn," he said, stopping, turning to look at the stone. "Weren't you the one who was supposed to trip over that? Have you noticed, Hannah, that the more sure of yourself you get, the clumsier *I* get?"

"I'm sor—man, I've got to stop saying that," Hannah said as Alex hooked an arm around her waist and they set off again. "And if it makes you feel any better, I dropped the car keys down the floor heat register this morning because I was so nervous about coming out here. It took me ten minutes, fishing through the grate with a bent coat hanger with some sticky wood putty stuck to the end, to retrieve them."

"Very inventive."

"You have to be very inventive, when you screw up as much as I do," Hannah told him, and they both laughed. They laughed, and any remaining awkwardness between them vanished.

"Do you want to know the second reason I didn't call?" Alex asked as they stopped at the front door to the house.

"If you want to tell me, yes."

"I was afraid to call you. Or do you truly believe I don't

spend damn near every waking moment remembering that favor you asked me for last week?''

"Oh…that.''

"Yes, Hannah. Oh…*that*. And before you say anything else, I know about Cade and Mac and Jessica, so it isn't that I'm worried you're looking elsewhere for that help you wanted. This is strictly between you and me, the way it should have been since the beginning.''

"Is it? Between you and me, I mean. Standing between you and me, sort of like an elephant in the living room, a problem everyone knows is there but nobody wants to talk about? I know a lot about those elephants.''

"It could be,'' Alex said. "Maybe. But I don't think we have any way of knowing. Not unless we face down the elephant. Maybe then we can move on, figure out where things go next, if there's anywhere else for them to go.''

Hannah looked up at him for long moments, looked at the face that had invaded her dreams ever since she could remember, the man who had intrigued her as long as she could remember. "Are you…are you saying that we should do something about that favor I asked you? Just to get it out of the way, off the table or whatever, so that then we'd know if there's anything more between us than just thinking about that favor?''

"There might be an easier way to say that, but I don't know it. So, yes, Hannah, that is what I'm saying. And it took me all week to find the courage to say it.''

"I wish I'd never told you,'' Hannah said as he trailed a fingertip down her cheek, as she felt her belly go all soft and warm.

"And I'm very glad you did,'' Alex countered. "Otherwise, I might be stupid enough to still be looking at you as little Hannah-banana, the pigtailed girl who trailed after me everywhere when we were just kids.''

"Long after we were just kids, Alex, although you grew up a lot faster than I ever did. I was crazy about you, even as you ignored me, right up until I left for college and learned to hide better when I was at home, helping Dad. I even got smart enough to stay away from The Desert Rose the past few years. But that doesn't mean you owe me anything."

Alex's hand left her face, rested against her shoulder, squeezed her lightly. "Maybe we both owe each other something, Hannah. I won't lie to you and say I'm in love with you because you wouldn't believe me anyway. And I won't tell you that you have my undivided attention right now, because you don't. We've…we've got a lot going on at The Desert Rose at this time, so I'm feeling more than a little conflicted. Hell, my other problems might even make me more drawn to you. I don't know. I just know we can't stay as we are, and we can't go back to where we were. The only thing left, Hannah, is to move on, take the next step."

He dropped his hand, shook his head. "Well, hell, that has to rank as one of the worst seduction sales pitches of all time, doesn't it? Would you consider a night in this man's bed? I sure as hell wouldn't."

"I would," Hannah said quietly, her voice cracking. "I would," she repeated more loudly, lifting her chin to show that she meant what she said. "Like you told me, Alex, we can't go back. I don't want to go back. And where we are right now isn't a whole lot of fun for either of us. We really don't have any choice but to go on, take that next step. Do we?"

Alex rubbed a hand over his jaw, as if considering her words. "Are you free tonight?" he asked at last.

Brave was brave, and daring might be daring, but Hannah suddenly realized that if she opened her mouth to speak again, all that would come out would be a nervous croak. So she nodded.

"I'll pick you up at eight?"

One more nod, and Hannah turned, opened the front door and stepped inside, nearly running across the wide living room as she spied Vi Coleman standing just outside the French doors, in the slowly waking gardens.

"YOU KNOW, HANNAH, I really don't know your father all that well," Vi said as she laid a plate of homemade cookies on the small table in the living room. "It's sad, but once your mother was gone, well, he pretty much kept to himself. Not that he and your mom were ever very social. Your dad worked some very long hours in those days, establishing his practice."

Hannah nodded. "I think that's one of the reasons Mom left. Every minute of the day was spent with the practice, every spare penny went into the practice. I don't remember much about my mother, but I do remember waking up one night to hear her yelling 'One new dress, Hugo! Would one new dress kill you?'"

"Do you know where she is now?"

"Vaguely. The last time I could get Dad to say anything, she was living in New Jersey with her third husband. I'd be lying if I said I missed her. I just wish she hadn't broken my dad's heart when she left. It was as if I'd lost both of them, you know? I don't know if he blames me because she left, or if I just remind him of her too much. We look very much alike, you know."

"Hugo Clark is an idiot," Vi said, then pressed a hand to her mouth for a moment. "Oh, Hannah, honey, I'm sorry. That just slipped out."

Hannah laid down her napkin. "That's all right. I know how it all looks from the outside." She smiled ruefully.

"Actually, it's pretty much the same way it looks from the inside. Except that he does love me. I know he does. He just doesn't know how to show it...or he's afraid I'll leave him, too."

"Oh, I never thought of that," Vi said. "You know, that's just possible. How did he react when you went away to college?"

"Not well," Hannah said. "About as well as he did to my announcement that I was coming back to help at the practice. That was my first real step as an adult, you know, Vi? I didn't ask to be part of the practice. I *told* him."

"Well, good for you," Vi said, reaching over to pat Hannah's hand. "So things are getting better between the two of you? Easier?"

"In some ways," Hannah agreed. "But I've got a problem, and I don't know what to do about it. That's when I thought about you, Vi. What I want to tell you has to remain a secret, but I really believe I need help. Will you help me?"

"I'd be flattered," Vi said sincerely.

Taking a deep breath, Hannah proceeded to tell the older woman about her father's failing eyesight and the depression that had knocked him nearly to his knees this past week.

"Macular degeneration. I've heard of that," Vi said when Hannah was finished. "Does he have it in both eyes?"

"No. Not yet, and hopefully never, but Dr. Gillman told me it is possible. His left eye is pretty heavily affected now, so that the center of his vision is badly compromised, although his peripheral vision is fine. He's still cleared to drive, although Dr. Gillman advised that he not drive in bad weather or at night. But, even if it never gets worse, or if the other eye is never affected, he still is limited in the work he can do at the office.''

Vi nodded. ''And then here you come, little Hannah to the rescue, the ink still wet on your degree, with two good eyes. Yes, knowing Hugo even as little as I do, I can see where he's caught between relief and feeling that you're taking over, pushing him to one side, the useless old man. You say he's not working at all?''

''Not this week, no. And he *can* work. He just can't do the really delicate things, operations of course, and anything that takes really clear sight. Not to brag, but my dad can tell more just by feeling an animal than most vets can tell with X rays and a battery of blood tests. Anyway, at first, Dad tried to treat me as he always has—sort of the bully, you know? But I started giving him some of his own back, and then finally told him I knew about his sight. Ever since then, well, he still blusters, but mostly he's just…he just…''

''I don't know what to tell you, Hannah,'' Vi said. ''But I do think you're on the right track. You aren't a lonely little girl anymore. You're a grown woman who has made a conscious decision to come back here, help your father. Now he has to see you as his equal, whether he wants to or not. He should be proud of you, and grateful to you, but if he can't be either of those things, then at the very least he should respect you as an adult.''

Vi and Hannah stood, headed for the door, as Hannah had to get back to the office for walk-in hours. ''I guess there's only one way to wake him up, shake him out of this. Tell him, Hannah. Tell the man you love him, and that you're asking for his respect in return, and that you hope for his love as well.'' She wrapped Hannah in a motherly hug. ''And tell him that if he can't accept your love, well, then it's his loss, not yours. And it would be, Hannah. It truly would be his loss.''

Hannah wiped at the tears that ran down her cheeks, then returned Vi's hug. "Thank you, Vi. Thank you so much."

"No, Hannah, thank you. Thank you for coming to me. Now don't be a stranger, all right? I want to see more of you around here."

Hannah drove back to Bridle half in tears and yet smiling. What an eventful week this had been…and it wasn't over yet.

Chapter Twelve

Alex watched as Hannah pushed her food around her plate, pretending to eat.

He wondered if she had any idea how beautiful she looked in candlelight, her soft hair catching every bit of light, her smooth, flawless skin glowing.

She'd been waiting downstairs when he picked her up, a tan trench coat over her emerald-green slacks and pale yellow sweater, as it had begun to rain, so that the whole impact of her very simple outfit hadn't really hit him until they'd gotten inside the restaurant.

And that outfit had been "hitting him" ever since. As he'd walked behind her to their table, he'd been amazed yet again by her long legs, how well proportioned she was for a woman barely tall enough to rest her head against his shoulder.

But the sweater was the best, definitely. His hands itched to touch, to stroke the palest yellow softness while Hannah still wore it. The sweater was fairly short, and nipped Hannah's tiny waist, accentuating her smallness, and the soft swell of her hips.

Alex looked across the table as Hannah finally took a bite of baked potato. Did she have any idea what that collar did to him? Did she realize what a perfect frame it made for her face, or know that the slim column of her throat and the demure exposure of her remarkably straight collarbones and creamy skin had him caught between just wanting to look at her and longing to slide that wide collar off her shoulder, right here and now, and have her for dessert?

No, she probably didn't have a clue. She was too busy pushing at her food, not eating much of it, and avoiding his gaze.

"This was a bad idea," he said, putting down his own fork, realizing with some shock that more than half his steak remained on his plate. Obviously Hannah wasn't the only one who had no appetite. For food, that is.

Hannah looked at him from beneath lowered lashes, the innocent temptress with no idea how well she tempted. "It was?" she asked, her voice low, just a little bit shaky.

"The dinner," Alex added hastily, reaching his hand across the table and taking hold of hers. "Dinner was probably a mistake."

"That's all right. Really. And…and I had a peanut butter and jelly sandwich at home, earlier. That's probably why I'm not hungry."

When he kissed her, would she taste of peanut butter and jelly? What an odd aphrodisiac, but for some reason, it seemed to be working for him. "I brought you here because of the band. I thought we could dance."

Hannah looked across the small dance floor to where a trio of musicians were almost set up, ready to go. "Not the same ones as at the country club," she said, then smiled. "That's a good thing, right?"

"Definitely a good thing," Alex said, relaxing because Hannah now seemed to be relaxing. "I've heard this group before, and they're very professional. Piano, drums, vocalist—and enough electronic equipment to make it seem like there's a twenty-piece orchestra up there. One dance, Hannah, and then we'll go, all right?''

She nodded, then sat back and allowed the waiter to take her nearly full plate. ''Sorry,'' she said to the man. ''I guess I wasn't really all that hungry.''

The waiter, obviously a man with two good eyes in his head, smiled and replied, ''That's quite all right, miss. I won't ask if you'd like any of our larger desserts, but if I might recommend a small dish of lemon sherbet? It would match that lovely sweater.''

Down boy, she's taken, Alex thought, and then realized what he'd thought. She's taken? No she wasn't. This was one night, one night that had to happen. That's all. That's it.

That *was* it, wasn't it?

''Alex? Would you like some dessert?'' Hannah asked, bringing him back to the moment.

''Just coffee,'' Alex said to the waiter without looking at him. He couldn't look at him, because the waiter had to know, had to sense that all Alex really wanted to do was strangle the guy with his own bow tie. ''Thank you,'' he added, trying to remember he was a gentleman. And sane.

Nobody danced for any of the first two songs, which were fairly upbeat, so that Hannah had finished her sherbet before the third song began, a slow, dreamy love song the female vocalist performed in a nearly dead-on impersonation of the artist who had made it a number one hit several years earlier.

''Shall we?'' Alex suggested, getting to his feet and holding out his hand to Hannah. *Shall we? Shall we get this over with, and then get the hell out of here?*

Hannah nodded and rose, the napkin spread across her lap sliding to the floor unnoticed.

And Alex fell in love.

He didn't know why. He didn't know how. He just watched Hannah-banana being delightfully unaware of her small slip into klutziness because she was so busy looking at him, smiling at him, and something inside him went *twang.*

It felt good. It felt damn good.

She stepped into his arms, already holding up her own arms like a young girl fresh from dancing class who was still a little unsure as to which arm went where.

He'd show her.

Alex pulled her close, cradling her with his left arm as he folded her right hand in his and held both against his chest. He smiled as she put her left hand on his shoulder, then felt her fingertips against the side of his neck, sending a shiver down his spine.

Innocent seduction. Her, not him. And, bless her, she wasn't even trying. All she was doing was nestling herself against him in complete trust, intoxicating him with the smell of everyday soap and, yes, the lingering scent of peanut butter and grape jelly. He probably only imagined the peanut butter and jelly, but his imagination had gone into overdrive the moment Hannah had gotten up from the table, smiled at him as if he was the only man, the only other person, in the world.

He could feel the soft warmth of her hair against his chin and bent his head slightly to press his cheek against her head. His eyes closed and the world fell away as they moved together, as the singer told of people who need people, of how they were definitely the luckiest people in this world.

Halfway through the dance, Alex stepped away from Hannah, still holding on to her hand as he walked them back to the table. He threw down three fifty-dollar bills, handed Hannah her purse and, without a word, led her to the foyer. He collected their coats, gave the valet the ticket for his car, and maneuvered Hannah outside and into a dark corner of the covered porch that extended out over the driveway.

He stood there, Hannah's back against the wall, and watched the rapid rise and fall of her breasts, nearly groaned when she nervously licked her lips.

Behind him, lightning flashed, followed by a wild clap of thunder and a sudden downpour that came down nearly sideways in the rapidly rising wind.

A wild night in Texas. Yes, a wild night in Texas in so many ways.

"Your car, sir," the valet said just as Alex wondered how much longer he could hold off kissing Hannah, loving Hannah.

He fished a loose bill from his pocket, hoping it was a five, but the highly impressed "*Thank* you, sir!" from the valet told him he'd probably guessed wrong. But he didn't care. He just wanted out of here. Out of here, now. "Big storm warnings tonight, sir. Dangerous lightning, hail, maybe even straight-line winds or a tornado. Drive carefully."

"Definitely," Alex said, leading Hannah around to the passenger door. "I'm carrying precious cargo."

"Where are we going?" Hannah asked once they were inside the car, Alex's attention now very necessarily on the road in front of them as the rain pounded down so solidly that the windshield wipers could barely keep up.

"The Desert Rose," he told her, turning on his signal and easing his way onto the highway.

"The...the ranch? I had thought a motel...something like that."

Alex took his eyes off the road long enough to turn and grin at Hannah. "If by 'something like that' you thought, even briefly, about the back seat of this car, let me tell you that it never entered the equation. Although I did think about a motel. This is better.''

He didn't add that the thought of a motel, so reasonable a few hours ago, had been abandoned back at the restaurant, the moment that he knew Hannah belonged in his bed. His bed. Tonight. Tomorrow night. Forever. He didn't tell her that because she wouldn't believe him, for one, and because she might just run screaming into the night.

She hadn't, after all, asked for "ever after." She had asked for one night, one act, one favor. It might be that would be all she'd ever ask, her childhood crush forgotten once she felt free to be a woman, to go out and live life the way she wanted, the way her upbringing and her father would never allow.

He had to take it slow. Here, on this rain-swept highway, and again once they were in his room at The Desert Rose. Even if it killed him.

Hannah was silent for the rest of the drive, both of them listening to the radio Alex had tuned to the national weather station. It was always wise to pay attention to the weather, especially when an alert had already been put out. Alex fought the urge to press harder on the pedal. He wanted them at the ranch, out of the storm, caught up in a storm of their own.

A RAIN SCARF SHE'D FOUND in her raincoat pocket tied tight to her head, Hannah kept her head bent and held tightly to Alex's hand as he led her through the kitchen and toward a back staircase he told her went directly up to the wing holding his, Mac's and Cade's bedrooms.

Hannah had been upstairs before, in Jessica's room in the other wing, but she'd followed her new friend up the wide, sweeping staircase that led from the center of the house. She'd walked openly, not furtively, as she was doing now, trying to be quiet, trying not to stumble in the dark, holding tight to Alex's hand, hoping the stairs didn't squeak when she stepped on them.

It was fun. Sort of. If her teeth would just stop chattering.

Alex opened the door to his room and motioned for Hannah to precede him inside, which she did, a sense of *this is it, no turning back now* crossing the threshold with her. Crossing the threshold from wishful virgin to woman.

She stood still as he turned on a single light, illuminating the L-shaped room that had its own large sitting area, his bed—his very large bed—tucked into an alcove that was, when she thought about it, still twice the size of her own bedroom.

She watched as he slid out of his coat and walked over to a small bar that held a miniature refrigerator and opened the door. "Would you like something to drink? Soda? Bottled water?"

"Wa-water. Please," she answered after pulling off her rain bonnet, but still holding her raincoat tightly around her even though she knew she was dripping all over his fine Oriental carpet. She just couldn't bring herself to remove the raincoat. Not yet. Maybe in a couple of minutes, or an hour. But not yet. Definitely not yet.

"Why don't you take off your coat and throw it over the chair where mine is?" Alex asked as he walked toward her, carrying two clear plastic bottles of water.

"Sure. Fine," Hannah responded quickly, probably too quickly, and shrugged free of the damp coat. She took the bottle he'd opened for her. "Just what we both need. More water. It's really raining out there, isn't it?"

Oh, that's good, she thought, inwardly shrinking into herself. *Why not neatly segue into a discussion of animals standing in the damp too long, and the evils of hoof rot. That ought to get him right in the mood.*

Alex took her hand and led her, not to his bed, but to the comfortable-looking old couch that had been moved up here when Vi had redecorated the main living room. Not that the couch was shabby, that any of the furniture was shabby, but it all looked very lived-in. The main rooms of The Desert Rose, the living room, host room, and office had all definitely been decorated to impress prospective buyers, breeders and those who would board their horses at The Desert Rose, have them trained there. But the kitchen had been purely down-home comfortable—warm and inviting.

Alex's bedroom was warm and inviting. Probably too warm and inviting, especially when he switched on the small gas fireplace that sat in one corner of the room, built into the inside corner of the L, so that it had an opening on both the sitting room and bedroom sides.

With the light from one single bulb, the fireplace, and the frequent flashes of lightning shining in through the windows, Hannah felt certain Alex couldn't have laid a better scene for seduction if he'd tried.

Had he tried? She'd like to think so. She'd like to believe he wasn't just trying to settle a problem, get it over and behind him, so that he could get on with his life, hope she would be content to get on with hers.

"This…this is nice," she said, turning the sweating bottle around and around in her hands.

"The bottle?" Alex teased, moving closer to her so that she believed she might soon need a refresher course in how to breathe.

"No! No," she repeated quietly, belatedly remembering that somewhere on this vast second floor, several other people were either tucked in their beds or reading, or something. No matter what they were doing, there were several pair of ears out there, able to hear her if she wasn't careful. "I mean the room. You're part of the house, yet you have some privacy. It's...it's nice."

"You're scared to death of me right now, aren't you, Hannah?" he asked, so close now that she could feel his warm breath on the side of her neck. "Don't be afraid of me. I won't hurt you. I would never hurt you."

She turned to look at him, reassure him...and the bottle tipped, spilling cold water right in his lap. "Oh! Oh, God! Alex, I'm so sorry!"

She opened her purse, pulled out a small white handkerchief and began dabbing at his slacks...then suddenly realized what she was doing, and how Alex was just sitting there, chuckling low in his throat.

"That's got to be the most interesting turn-down, turn-on combination in the history of the world, Hannah," he said when she looked at him, her eyes wide, her heart in her throat. "Cold water on my plans, followed by...well, we both know what it was followed by, don't we?"

If Hannah's cheeks got any hotter, she'd have to pour the rest of the bottled water over her head, before her hair ignited. "Oh, Alex, I'm such a klutz! Just take me home, okay? We'll forget all about this."

She started to rise, although it was difficult, as the couch was old, and the cushions were very soft. Alex took hold of her arm, pulled her back down beside him. "No, really, Alex. It would be better if you took me home now."

He lifted a hand to her cheek, stroked her flaming skin from cheekbone to the place where her cowl collar rolled over, exposing her upper chest. With one finger, he lightly tugged on the wide collar, easing it to one side, exposing her shoulder. "Not for me, Hannah-banana. It wouldn't be better for me."

Alex bent his head, lightly touched her cheek with his lips, then his mouth followed the path his fingers had taken, planting small, soft kisses along the side of her neck, across her collarbone, to the tip of her shoulder. "Would it really be better for you?"

Hannah had closed her eyes the moment his lips had touched her, and now she could only shake her head as her spine seemed to liquefy and she sank lower into the cushions. "No..." she breathed at last. "No...it wouldn't."

He brought up his head, looked at her for long moments as if drinking in her every feature, committing her to memory, before he pressed his mouth to hers. Gently, oh, so gently. Slow kisses, one following upon the other. Advancing, retreating, so that she felt herself raising her head, following after him as he left her, reluctant to feel him go even though by now she was certain he would be back with another kiss, another bit of gentle persuasion that warmed her, soothed her...and began building a fire she hadn't known had been laid, ready for the match of his desire.

She felt her arms sliding around his neck, only faintly shocked that she was now making moves of her own. His body was warm beneath the knit of his shirt, his muscles hard and rippling as he moved with her, adjusting his body so that he could cup her breasts in his hands.

"Even better than I'd imagined," he whispered against her mouth as he held her, cupped her, stroked her through the material of her sweater. One hand slipped to the hem of the sweater, lifted it, slid beneath, to travel upward again, deftly releasing the front clasp of her bra.

She couldn't breathe, feeling a slight rush of cool air on her exposed skin as the bra fell away, as the sweater somehow disappeared, and she lay half-reclined on the couch, covered only by Alex's hands.

"So small, so perfect," he was saying, and she heard

him through the rushing roar in her ears, above the banging, cracking fury of the storm outside, over the loud beating of her own heart. She felt her nipples harden as he lightly grazed them with his work-roughened thumbs, heard her own soft moan as his tongue touched her, his mouth closed over her.

And then she was floating, flying, held high in his arms as he made his way toward the bed, turning down the covers with one hand as he held her so effortlessly, laid her on the cool, crisp sheets, followed her down.

A small part of her mind remembered that she'd sometimes wondered about the logistics of the thing, how difficult, awkward, it could be to remove clothing, discard hose and shoes and the rest. But it wasn't awkward, not as Alex undressed her, his mouth following his hands as he opened the button at her waist, slid down her zipper, skimmed her slacks past her knees, freed her from them entirely. He kissed her belly, her thighs, even her knees, setting even more small fires that threatened to consume her as they burned away the last of her reticence, her fears.

He moved away from her for a few moments, and she heard the rasp of his zipper, the slight clunk of his shoes as they hit the floor, moments after her own shoes had found it.

With a daring she wouldn't have believed possible even a half hour earlier, Hannah released her stockings from the lacy garter belt Jessica had insisted she buy, shed her panties, and she was entirely naked…although she had quickly slid beneath the covers. She was getting better, but she knew she was still a long way from liberated. She needed those covers.

But she didn't need them for long.

Alex rejoined her under the covers, his hand reaching out to capture her waist, pull her onto her side so that they lay facing each other, looking at each other as the lightning flashed and the thunder rolled and the very house shook under the onslaught of the wind.

"I...I—"

"Shh. It's all right, Hannah." He pressed a finger against her lips, stopping whatever she had wanted to say, which was a good thing, because she really didn't know what she wanted to say. "Be kind" seemed so very lame at a moment like this. After all, if she didn't trust him, trust him implicitly, she wouldn't have come here in the first place.

And it was all right. As if he'd sensed her fear, fear that had banished the passion she'd felt before, he started again from the beginning. Kissing her. Holding her. Touching her. Soothing and gentling her as he would soothe a horse he was breaking to the saddle.

She shuddered involuntarily when his hand slipped between her thighs, found the heart of her, the very center of her. Stroked her, relaxed her until she opened for him like a flower opens to the sun.

And then it began. Hannah didn't know what it was, what she felt, but she knew it was good. So good.

He rolled her onto her back, half-covering her with his strong body, so that she could feel his warmth, his strength, the solidity of him. He kissed her again and again, whispering things she couldn't understand, so that she just responded to the sounds, the tone.

She felt a hunger grow within her, a hunger that had her lifting her hips to Alex's touch, had her whimpering low in her throat, had her whispering his name over and over again as he held her entire being in his hand, as that world exploded around her, a pulsating explosion that went on and on and on....

Hannah held him, held on to him as tightly as she could, needing him to anchor her here in this world, so that she wouldn't go spinning off into space. She kissed his neck, his face, his shoulder, his chest, unable to get close enough, hold him hard enough, taste him, touch him, feel him enough.

There was a moment of pain, somewhere off to one side of her consciousness, but it was gone almost before she could register it. All she could feel now was a wonderful fullness, a pressure deep inside her that somehow calmed her even as she felt herself being lifted to a new level, the same in some ways as before, but more complete, more satisfying.

"Lift your legs, Hannah," she heard Alex breathe against her ear. "Lift them, wrap them around me. Don't let me go."

She swallowed down hard, hearing the words, trying to do as he said, her eyes tightly closed as she felt each new sensation, marveled at the way her body was singing, nearly shouting with an ecstasy previously unknown to her.

But she did as he said, and he began to move inside her, slowly at first, and then more urgently. She moved with him, actually began urging him on as the world narrowed to the two of them, to this bed, to this moment...and the unspoken promise of the final piece of the mysterious puzzle finally being fit into place, the final bridge crossed, the last secret known.

Hot. She felt so hot. Almost tortured, but it was a good torture, a spiraling desire that frustrated her even as she reached for more, more. Please. More.

And then, there it was. A knowing. An awakening so complete, so all-encompassing, that she could do no more than lie there, her arms and legs wrapped around this man she loved, and let the waves overtake her, send her over the precipice that had her falling, falling, even as she soared.

Alex stilled for a moment, holding her, whispering to her, and then he began to move once more. Deeply, powerfully, beginning a rhythm that increased in speed as she held him, gave him all of her body, all of her soul, gifted him with herself as he gave a final deep lunge of his body, totally became a part of her. His muscles tensed, his body became rock hard, and then she felt him gain his release, saying her name over and over again...finally collapsing against her, allowing her to gently stroke his back, soothe him as he regained his breath.

ALEX LAY ON HIS SIDE, his elbow bent and his head propped on his hand, watching Hannah sleep.

His innocent temptress, not so innocent anymore, but still tempting, always tempting, with her halo of honey-blond hair splashed against the pillow, the slight pink in her cheeks, the way her full bottom lip relaxed in sleep so that it was nearly impossible not to lean over, press his mouth against hers, taste her yet again.

They hadn't talked much last night, partly because Alex sensed that Hannah didn't want to talk, and partly because if he did talk to her he'd say something dumb, like "I love you, Hannah-banana. Marry me."

She wouldn't believe him. She had every right not to believe him.

So Alex had decided that what he had to do was go at this whole thing backward. First the lovemaking...then the declaration of love. He would have to court her, seriously court her, until the moment she realized that he had every intention of being with her, sleeping beside her, loving her, into eternity.

He should wake her, he supposed, now that the storm had finally moved on and the dawn had come, lighting the sky with that special sun that only shone right after a rain.

In a few minutes. He'd wake her in a few minutes. With a kiss. After he'd looked at her just a little while longer…

"Alex?" Mac's voice came through the door, followed quickly by Mac himself. "Problem, Alex. A tree fell on the stables, knocking straight into a stall. It's Jabbar, Alex. He's cut up pretty bad. I called Doc Clark, and he's here, but I think you ought to—*whoa!*"

Alex pushed Hannah back down on the bed, but not before Mac saw her naked shoulders above the covers and came to his own conclusions. "Stay here, Hannah."

"No," she said, although she didn't move, and Alex knew she wouldn't until Mac got the hell out of the room. "I've got to help Dad. He can't— I have to help him."

Alex was already pulling on jeans and a University of Texas sweatshirt, pulling boots from the closet. "All right. I'll see you at the stables. Damn it, Mac, why didn't you wake me right away?"

"Because I'm a big boy now, and I know how to react, what to do without first asking big brother's advice," Mac suggested, following Alex out of the bedroom. Once they were in the hallway, he grabbed his brother's arm, grinning at him. "I know we don't have time right now, but, in the immortal words of Ricky Ricardo, 'Lucy—you've got some 'splaining to do!'"

Alex shook off his brother's arm, curtly told him to wake Cade and headed for the stables, his heart still with Hannah, but his mind fully concentrated on Jabbar, his parents' horse, the gift he wanted waiting for his mother if she really was alive, if she really would one day soon be here with them, at The Desert Rose.

Chapter Thirteen

Hannah had no room inside her for embarrassment as she struggled into the clothes she'd worn to dinner, the clothes that lay scattered all across the floor of Alex's room. The clothes Mac had seen scattered all over the floor.

She had to admit to herself, though, that it would be a long time before she forgot the startled, almost bug-eyed look on Mac's face as he first saw her in Alex's bed.

She heard noises elsewhere in the house as she opened the door and ran into the hall, and had only made it to the top of the main staircase before Jessica joined her, still buttoning her blouse.

"Oh, thank God you're here," Jessica said as the two of them ran down the stairs. "It's Jabbar, Hannah. I'd hate it to be any of them. But Jabbar? That just can't happen. It can't!"

Hannah didn't answer her. She just kept moving, silently cursing her high heels but still managing to break into a run once they were outside the house.

Jessica ran beside her, then suddenly stopped, grabbed her arm. "Look! That big old tree snapped off right at the root."

Hannah, who had kept her eyes focused on the ground so that she wouldn't trip in her heels, lifted her head and

stared. "Good God," she breathed, able to see that the roof
of the far corner of the main stables had been crushed under
the weight of the top half of the tree. Everywhere she
looked, people were either running or pointing or shouting.

Two of the ranch hands were already on the roof, working with a huge power saw, cutting away the branches in
order to relieve some of the pressure on the roof.

"I can't believe we didn't hear anything," she said,
thinking she was talking to herself, then winced when she
felt Jessica's eyes on her.

"Yeah...about that. You're weren't coming upstairs
when I saw you—you were heading downstairs. Weren't
you? Now why would you—aha! Details, Hannah, I want
details. But later," she added, as Hannah was already running toward the stables again, and she had to run to catch
up. "We *are* going to talk about this later."

"No, we're not," Hannah said, seeing her father's vehicle pulled into the stable yard, abandoned more than
parked. She opened the back door and began rummaging
around inside, coming out with one bag she might need,
and another she prayed she wouldn't, because the small
locked box bolted to the floor of the SUV had contained
the leather bag holding her pistol.

Alex met her at the entrance to the stables. "We were
lucky. The tree only damaged the roof, none of the animals," he said as he walked with her toward the small knot
of people standing outside one of the stalls. "But the damage was mostly over Jabbar's head, with some wood coming down from the rafters. He must have been frightened
out of his mind, spooked, and tried to break down the stall,
get out of there."

"How badly is he cut?" Hannah asked as Alex pushed
at shoulders and elbowed the way clear for him and Hannah

to enter the stall they'd moved Jabbar to as soon as they'd found him.

"Some scrapes on his forelegs, one on his side. Pretty minor, and Hugo checked, said there was no internal injury that he could detect just by feeling him. He said we might think about getting some X rays later, although he doubts it. But Jabbar's got a hell of a gash in his neck. Your father—"

Hannah stepped to the middle of the stall, taking in the sight of her father on his knees beside the already sedated stallion. Everything was just as it ought to be, the stall set up as a portable operating room. But there was one thing— one person—out of place. "Dad, you can't do that," she said quietly. "Step back now, and I'll take over."

"Hannah…?" Alex questioned quietly. "What are you doing? Hugo's just going to stitch him up."

"No, Alex, he is not going to stitch the wound. Are you, Dad?" Hannah said, knowing her voice was quavering, just as her knees were shaking. But she stood her ground, returned her father's angry stare until the man put down the instrument he'd been holding and stood up to face her. She saw the anger in his eyes. And something else. Could it be relief? He'd never admit to it, but Hannah felt certain Hugo was relieved to see her.

"Well, well, look who finally showed up," her father said, each word a slap. "Doesn't come home all night, catting around, just like her mother before her. Go away, girlie-girl. This horse needs a doctor, not a tramp. Can't be clearer than that."

"Hugo—" Alex began, but Hannah waved him off, took another step forward.

She knew there were people everywhere, hearing every word, taking in the sight of her in clothes never meant to be inside a stable. And she didn't care. She just damn well didn't care. There was an animal in trouble, and that's all she could think about now. Everything else would just have to wait.

"Not right now, Dad. You can yell at me later. Right now, you're going to tell me what you've done so far, and then I'm taking over. Is that clear? Now, step aside. I have to work while Jabbar's still sedated."

"The hell I'll step aside!" Hugo yelled in a voice that had always had the power to turn Hannah into a little girl trying so very hard to please. But not today.

"Hugo, step aside," Alex said, standing behind Hannah, his hand on her shoulder. "I don't know what's going on here, but if Hannah says you're to step aside, then you damn well do it. Unless you want some help?"

"Alex, don't threaten him," Hannah said, lifting her hand and resting it on his, willing his strength into her own body. "Dad knows what he has to do. Don't you, Dad? You haven't started the stitching. You wouldn't do that to an animal. You were waiting for me, weren't you? Hoping I'd come?"

Hugo stood his ground for another few seconds, then slowly began to walk out of the stall, his eyes on Alex the whole way. "Son of a bitch. You no-good son of a bitch. I won't forget this," he warned, then slammed out of the stables.

Hannah didn't watch her father go. She was already on her knees beside Jabbar, issuing orders. More light. Another blanket. Someone to kneel at the stallion's head, just in case he woke earlier than expected.

Using a prepacked antiseptic wash on her hands, she visually checked the supplies her father had laid out on a sterile cloth, running her own mental checklist and finding everything in order. Of course everything was in order. Her dad was a great vet, the best.

Alex knelt by Jabbar's head, his eyes on Hannah, but she really didn't see him. She was glad he was there, but that was it. Pulling on a pair of sterile gloves, she picked up a probe and began checking the deep, ragged tear on the stallion's neck.

Her father had already shaved the area and cleansed the wound, and had been about to start on the first deep row of stitches, but Hannah didn't pick up the needle. Instead, she tersely told Alex to bring the light closer and continued to probe the wound.

"What are you doing?" Mac asked from somewhere above and behind her. "Your dad already did that. He says it's clean."

"I know," Hannah said, reaching for long tweezers, inserting it and withdrawing a thin sliver of wood. "Now, if you'll please step back? You're blocking my light."

She probed for another five minutes, extracting two more evil-looking wooden splinters before disinfecting the wound again and finally starting on the stitches.

Nobody talked, and nobody left the stall. They all just stood there, watching Hannah work.

Only when she was done, and Jabbar's neck was bandaged, did she sit back on her haunches and realize that she'd had an audience. She stripped off her gloves and smiled at Alex. "He'll be fine. Would somebody please find my dad and ask him if he's already injected antibiotics?"

Three stable hands besides Livy, and Mac, all turned as one and left the stables to do as Hannah had asked.

Which left Jessica still standing there, shaking her head. "I don't get it, Hannah. Why didn't your dad see those splinters? If he had closed Jabbar up that way the poor baby would have gotten an infection and—"

"We'll talk about this later, Jessica," Alex said, helping Hannah pack equipment away. "Okay?"

"But I want to… Oh, all right. Nobody has to hit me over the head with a brick. Or a tree. I'm going." As she turned to leave, Mac entered the stall. "Don't bother," she told him. "They want to be alone."

Mac looked at his cousin for a moment, shook his head and then said to Hannah, "Your dad's gone. I don't know if he gave Jabbar the antibiotic or not. Now what?"

Hannah picked up an empty medicine vial and read the label. "It's okay, Mac. He gave Jabbar the shot. Do you think you could stay here for a while, until Jabbar wakes up? I need to go back to the office and…I need to go back to the office."

Alex took her arm. "I'll take you," he said as Mac stepped aside, giving them room to get out of the stall. "Mac, we'll be back shortly, but you can reach me on my cell phone if you need me."

"Yeah, sure, all right," Mac said, scratching the side of his head. "But I sure wish I knew why Hugo—"

"Later, Mac. We'll all talk later."

"About everything?" his brother asked, giving him a lopsided smile Hannah found it very easy to interpret.

Putting her head down, she aimed herself at the doorway and left the stables, stopping just outside in the morning sun to take a few deep, steadying breaths.

"Are you all right?" Alex asked her, taking her hand, rubbing his thumb against her palm. "Do you want to go somewhere and sit down for a while? I know there's coffee ready in the kitchen."

Hannah looked up at him, tears stinging her eyes. "Thank you, Alex, but no. I…I've got to get back to the office."

"To talk to Hugo," Alex said, walking with her toward

his car. "I'd like to talk to him myself. Unless you're going to tell me what the hell is going on?"

Hannah waited until they were on the road, heading away from The Desert Rose, then began to speak. "It's not my secret, Alex, but I guess it's not going to be anybody's secret after this morning. Dad..." She sighed, closed her eyes, then said the rest of what she had to say quickly. "Dad's got macular degeneration in one eye. Pretty bad, too. So far, his other eye is clear, but he simply can't do close, delicate work anymore. He didn't get those splinters out, Alex, because he couldn't *see* those splinters."

"He couldn't see them? Then what was he doing? That was my horse, Hannah, and—"

"And," she interrupted, "before you start calling him names, I'm pretty sure he was stalling, waiting for me to show up, and only put on that show, yelling the way he did, to protect himself. I don't think he would have sewn up Jabbar's wound. I really don't. He just did the prep work, and was waiting for me."

Alex was silent for some time. "How long? How long have you known about this?"

Hannah looked out the window, not really seeing the scenery as it went by. "About a year before I graduated. Doc Gillman let me know. He said it could stay the same, get worse in the affected eye, even ruin both eyes so that all Dad had left was peripheral vision, no center vision at all. He's really lost ground this past month or so, according to Doc Gillman. Nobody knows exactly what will happen, although Dad's convinced now that he's going blind."

Alex pulled over to the side of the road, turned off the ignition. He took Hannah's hand in his, looked deeply into her eyes. "You weren't going to come back, were you? You'd finally gotten out, gotten away, and you weren't going to come back. Not until Doc Gillman told you about

Hugo. That's why you're here, isn't it? You came back to help your father, even knowing he'd hate you for it.''

Still Hannah avoided his eyes. "I might have come back anyway. I really didn't have anywhere else to go." She turned her head at last, looked at him. "I think I always wanted to come back."

Alex squeezed her fingers. "Because of me?" He let go of her hand, stabbed his fingers through his still uncombed hair. "Damn, that was arrogant, wasn't it? Don't answer me, Hannah. I don't deserve an answer."

She pressed a hand to her mouth, squeezed her eyes shut, trying to imagine herself somewhere else, anywhere else. She couldn't do it. She was where she belonged. Here, in Bridle. With her father, who refused to love her. With Alex, who suddenly sounded as if he felt he had some duty to her.

How did everything get so complicated?

"Hannah?"

She opened her eyes, looked at him and shook her head. Her hand dropped back into her lap as she sniffled once, then said, "I need to see my dad, Alex. Please, let's get moving again."

"There's going to be one hell of a confrontation when you do see him, you know. A confrontation that's about a dozen or more years late in coming. Another ten minutes isn't going to matter."

Hannah kept her head down, picked at some straw that stuck to her emerald-green slacks, then couldn't quite figure out what to do with the pieces once she had them in her hand. "You want to talk about last night," she said quietly. "But I don't. I really, really don't."

"Okay," Alex said, starting the car once more, pulling out onto the highway. "We won't talk about last night. I don't think we have to, as we were both there and we both know what happened. But I think we do have to talk about this morning. About Jessica, Mac, and everyone else who was at the stables, and about the fact that before lunchtime today there won't be anyone within fifty miles of here who doesn't know at least a little something about last night.''

Hannah looked at him curiously. ''And that embarrasses you?''

Alex nearly ran off the road as he whipped his head around to glare at her. ''No, Hannah, that does not embarrass me. Damn it, do you ever listen to yourself? I'm not worried about me— I'm worried about you. Or did you like hearing your father call you a tramp?''

She shrugged. ''It wasn't the first time. I'll survive.''

''Will you, Hannah? Will the no-longer longest living virgin in Texas really be able to survive Hugo's nasty, sarcastic, hurtful tongue this time? Because this time, Hannah, Hugo is going to have an audience that listens to him.''

''I don't care,'' Hannah said, her voice trembling, because she did care. She cared that something so very special was about to become the latest gossip. ''I mean, what are we supposed to do to stop it? Get married, for crying out loud?''

Alex was silent as they pulled into the parking space beside Hugo's SUV. He didn't turn off the car, he didn't move, he didn't say anything.

Hannah turned and looked at him. ''What?'' she exclaimed as he sat there, returning her gaze. She shrank toward the door, her hand on the handle. ''Oh, no. Oh, no, no, *no.* I'm no charity case, Alex. Don't even think about it.''

He smiled. Oh, so slowly, he smiled, even as he reached for her. ''Marry me, Hannah-banana. Marry me.''

She opened the door, nearly falling out of the car, then stuck her head back, pointed a finger in Alex's direction.

"You know what, Alex Coleman?" she asked, tears streaming down her face, even though she was unaware of them. "You know what? You're a jackass. A walking, talking jackass. And…and I should know, damn it—I'm a vet!"

His laughter followed her all the way to the door leading to the office.

HANNAH FLIPPED the Open sign on the front door to Closed, and went in search of her father, calling for him as she walked through the empty waiting room and headed toward the examining rooms at the rear of the building.

She wouldn't think about Alex and his stupid solution. She wouldn't think about last night, and how that one night would have to sustain her through a lifetime of loneliness.

All she could think about now was her father. How she would find him. What she would say to him.

She opened the door to his small private office. "Dad? Dad, where are you?"

And then she heard it. Upstairs. Strange noises upstairs. She looked up at the ceiling, realizing that her bedroom was just above the office, and that the noise was coming from just above her.

"Dad?" she called out, heading back through the waiting room, slamming open the door, heading outside, racing around to the side door that led to the apartment.

Alex caught her in his arms as she all but barreled into him, her eyes focused upward, to the open window above her.

"What's going on?" she asked as he pulled her away from the building. "Why are you still here?"

He pointed to his car, and the pile of jeans and shirts, complete with hangers, scattered on the hood. "I was about to leave when he threw out the first load," Alex told her as another pile of her clothing, underwear this time, came sailing out of the window.

"Here!" Hugo shouted, leaning out the window. "Take her, take this—take it all. I won't let that tramp back in my house!"

"Oh, God," Hannah said quietly, staggering where she stood. "Dad. Dad! Don't do this!"

Hugo's head and shoulders disappeared, and within moments Hannah's riding boots were on their way to the ground. Alex pulled her over to the far side of the car, out of the way.

There was a small crash, the sound of breaking glass, and Hannah looked across the hood of the car, to see the only picture she had of her mother lying on the cement, the frame and glass shattered.

"Oh, that's it," Hannah said, feeling her hands draw up into fists. "That...is...it!"

Alex tried to stop her, but only ended up following after her as Hannah stormed toward the door leading up to the apartment. "I'm coming with you," he said as she bounded up the stairs, two at a time.

"I don't care," Hannah muttered, her heart pounding hurtfully in her chest. "But just stay out of my way. This is *my* fight."

She banged open the door at the head of the stairs, so that it slammed against the far wall, recoiling nearly hard enough to knock Alex back down the steps. Hannah didn't notice.

"Stop! Stop right there!" she ordered her father, who was coming out of her room and heading, arms loaded, to the window once more.

Hugo dropped the clothing and turned on his daughter. "You! You're even worse than your mother. She just left me. But not you. Oh, no, not you. You had to destroy me first!''

''I found three splinters in Jabbar's neck, Dad. Three! If the animal had died, that wouldn't have destroyed you? You wouldn't have been able to live with yourself if you knew you'd killed that horse. I had to step in. You didn't leave me any other choice. Besides, I know you. You wouldn't have stitched that wound. You were waiting for me. Admit it, Dad. You were waiting for me, even as you hated having to wait for me.''

Hugo backed up a step. ''You weren't here! I needed you, damn it, and you weren't here!'' he challenged, picking up the argument, looking at it another way. His way. ''You were going to help me,'' he said, his tone almost singsong, mocking her. ''My little girl was going to help me. That's what she said when she came home, the brand-spanking-new doctor. Well, where were you when I needed you, girlie-girl? I'll tell you where you were. You were rolling in the sack like the tramp you are. That's where you were. How do you think I felt when I saw you? Even half-blind, I knew what you'd been doing. Anyone could see what you'd been doing.''

''Hugo—''

''Shut up, Alex,'' Hannah said, stepping in front of him. ''I can handle this.''

''I want you out,'' Hugo continued, picking up the bundle of clothes once more, throwing it out the window before anyone could stop him. ''Is that clear enough for you? I want you out of my house, out of my practice—out of my *life*.''

Hannah felt Alex's hand on her shoulder and longed to turn into his arms, cry until there were no more tears. But she resisted the urge and walked across the small room to stand directly in front of her father.

"I feel sorry for you, Dad," she said quietly, refusing to quake as she looked at this man who had always towered over her, both physically and emotionally. "Oh, not because of your eyes. You can still practice. You're still the best vet I know, even if you can't operate anymore, even if there are things you can't do now that you did so well for so many years. That's not why I feel sorry for you, although I did want to help you. I never asked anything else from you, Dad, except to help you, to love you, to have you—just once—say you loved me."

Hugo didn't answer and Hannah said the rest of it before she lost her nerve. "But you know what, Dad? You never saw me. You looked at me, and saw Mom. Well, I'm not my mother, and I never was. I'm Hugo Clark's daughter, and I'm a vet because my father made me see that being a vet is the best thing in the world to be. I had hoped, Dad— Oh, God, how I had hoped. Hoped that we could be friends, that we could work together, that you'd finally look at me and see me, Hannah Clark, Hugo Clark's daughter."

She shook her head, swiped at the tears on her cheeks. "But you know what? You can't see me, can you? And it has nothing to do with macular degeneration. You can't see me because you refuse to see me. Well, Dad, a very wise woman told me that's your loss, not mine. *Yours.* Because *I* have seen me, and I'm worth looking at."

"Hannah—" Alex said, holding out his arms to her, but she shook her head, headed for her room, surefooted, head held high, Alex close behind her.

"There's not much more," she said with what she knew was a false calm before a storm of weeping she wouldn't allow. Not yet. "I'll finish packing this up and you can get some plastic garbage bags out from under the kitchen sink and load up the stuff that's already outside. Okay?"

"Okay," Alex said softly, touching her cheeks with one

finger, wiping at her tears. "I'll meet you downstairs, and we can go back to The Desert Rose."

"A hotel," Hannah said. "You can take me to a hotel."

"Tomorrow, Hannah," Alex told her firmly but gently. "Today, we go to The Desert Rose. I want you with Vi and Jessica. And I need you with me."

Hannah bit her bottom lip, nodded. She couldn't fight anymore. There wasn't anything left inside her to fight with, no strength left. She flinched as she heard her father's bedroom door slam, then got a shoe box out of the closet and began loading her few toiletries in it as Alex walked out of the room.

She was done in less than five minutes, faintly amazed that twenty-eight years of her life could be packed up so easily, so quickly. But, then, packing didn't usually include having half her wardrobe tossed out of an upstairs window.

Hannah smiled at the thought, then started to laugh. She sat down on the edge of her bed and laughed out loud, until she began to cry. She cried as if she might never be able to stop.

Alex found her there, half lifted her in his arms and helped her downstairs, into his car.

"I phoned ahead, and Vi is getting one of the guest rooms ready for you. Mac says Jabbar is up and eating, and doesn't seem much the worse for wear. And it isn't even noon yet. I wonder what the rest of this day is going to bring, don't you?"

Hannah turned to him, gave him a watery smile. "Not another proposal, I hope, because you're starting to look like a real good port in this storm, Alex. I might just take you up on your offer."

"I've always wanted to be a port in a storm. Ask anyone," he said, reaching over to ruffle her hair. "So, what do say about a week from Saturday? I mean, you don't want anything elaborate, do you? Unless you do want the works? I'm amenable either way, as long as the wedding's a week from Saturday.''

"You're a—"

"Jackass. Yes, we've already covered that. But you have to admit one thing, Hannah. I made you smile."

Hannah sniffled, then laughed. "You're right. You did. I didn't think that was possible."

"Anything's possible, Hannah," Alex said quietly, reaching over and taking her hand. "You wouldn't believe everything I've found possible in the past two weeks."

Chapter Fourteen

Randy and Vi looked up as Alex entered the living room and sat down on one of the couches. "How is she?" Vi asked, concerned.

"Magnificent," Alex said, smiling as he leaned back on the couch, dropped his head against the cushions. "She was, and is, magnificent. You should have seen her, heard her. Hugo looked to be in shock, the big bully somebody finally stood up to, knocked down. I don't think he knew what hit him."

"We've been talking about Hannah, Randy and I," Vi said, "and we're both feeling rather ashamed. We all knew Hannah was growing up with only Hugo, with her mother gone. But nobody did anything about it. I should have done something about it."

"Vi, you had three boys and a daughter to raise," Randy pointed out. "She was always clean, well fed, and she seemed to tag along after Hugo happily enough whenever they came out here to the ranch. The older she got, the more she became his helper, his assistant."

"Yes, but she wasn't happy, was she? I just thought she was shy, quiet—and, yes, clumsy. Poor thing. It never occurred to me that she was lonely."

"Well," Alex said, slapping his hands against his thighs

as he stood up, "she's not going to be lonely anymore. She's still fighting it, doesn't quite believe me, but Hannah and I are getting married a week from Saturday. I'd like to have the wedding here, if that's all right?"

Vi was in his arms before he'd finished speaking. "Married! Oh, Alex, that's wonderful! Jessica said—but I didn't—oh! Do your brothers know?"

"More than they should, Vi. They know more than they should, as does half the world by now, I'm sure. Or didn't Randy tell you?"

"Tell me?" Vi asked, stepping back to look at Alex. "Tell me what? Am I missing something again? I'm always missing something."

Alex leaned over and kissed his aunt's cheek. "Hannah spent the night with me, Vi. We spent the night together, upstairs, in my room, and Mac found us there this morning. But that's not why we're getting married. We're not getting married because Hugo threw her out and she has no other place to go. We're not even getting married because I think she's just about the bravest, most wonderful person I've ever known."

"So why *are* you getting married?" Vi asked, grinning.

"Because I love her so much I can't imagine spending another day of my life without her," Alex responded, grinning right back at his aunt. "Not that she knows that, of course."

Randy had also gotten to his feet. "You want to run that by me one more time, Alex?" he asked, looking confused. "Are you or are you not getting married?"

"Oh, I'm getting married, just as soon as I can get Hannah to stop exercising all her newfound independence and remember that she's loved me since we were kids. At least I hope she has."

Mac came into the living room just as Vi opened her

mouth to say something—Alex was pretty sure she didn't know exactly what—holding a cordless telephone.

"Randy? It's for you. Long-distance from someone from someplace called Balahar. Whoever it is says he'll only speak directly to you."

Alex shot a quick look at his uncle, seeing the tic beginning in his cheek. "Should I take it?" he asked, remembering that King Zakariyya had spoken to him on the last call and might realize that Randy's voice was different.

"No, I'll take it," Randy said as Vi slipped her hand in his.

"What's going on?" Mac asked, looking from his brother to his uncle. "Something *is* going on, isn't it? Cade!" he called toward the kitchen. "Get in here, okay? Something's up."

"Look, Mac," Alex began, "there's nothing going on. You and Cade can just take off and— Oh, hell. Randy?"

"Let them stay. They've got to know sooner or later." He took the phone, took the caller off Hold and lifted it to his ear. "Hello? Randy Coleman here, to whom am I speaking, please?"

Randy was silent for a few moments, his expression unreadable, and then he collapsed onto the couch. "Rose? Oh, sweet God in heaven, Rose, it *is* you. It is!"

EVERYONE WAS TALKING at once, until at last Vi stood up and clapped her hands, an old trick but one that had worked for years. Mac and Cade found chairs at the kitchen table along with Vi and Randy, and Alex stopped pacing and took up a position in front of the refrigerator.

"Then it's true?" Cade asked in the tense silence. "Our mother is alive?" He turned in his chair, glared at Alex. "And you knew? You knew all along and didn't tell us?"

"I've known for close to two weeks, Cade," Alex said,

"but only that she might be alive. If you and Mac had thought she might be out there—out there somewhere—I don't think Randy or I would have been able to stop you from charging off to Sorajhee to wring answers out of our uncle."

"True enough, Cade," Mac said reasonably. "Besides, that's not important now. What's important now is our mother—where she is, how she is, when we can go to her."

"She's coming here," Randy said, his voice still rather hollow with shock. "She's already traveled as far as Paris, and will be flying here in King Zakariyya's private jet in the next few days, as soon as they can get papers in order, passports, things like that. They'll try to keep it all quiet, but we have to be ready for the press if word gets out. Vi?" He reached out his hand to his wife.

"It's all right, Randy," Vi said, still wiping tears from her eyes. "Your sister is coming home. Everything else is secondary."

Alex wandered out of the kitchen, walking across the living room, looking up the curved staircase, knowing Hannah was up there in the guest room, sleeping.

Everything else was secondary?

No. Not everything else.

Definitely not everything else.

He was overjoyed that his mother had been found, that he would see her again after all these years spent without her. Would Rose become the mother Hannah had never had, had longed for all of her life? Could they be that lucky?

Alex would like to think so, but he also knew that there were no certainties anymore. His world had been turned upside down today, and upside down again. Happiness on top of happiness, even with Hannah still not believing he wanted to marry her, that he loved her.

A few days. His mother would be at The Desert Rose, flying straight to the ranch by helicopter after landing in Houston and going through customs there. In a few days, mother and sons would be reunited—strangers who loved—after decades apart.

A few days. Alex knew he had only a few days to convince Hannah that he loved her, before his life was picked up, given another shake and Hannah slipped away from him.

He walked up the stairs.

HANNAH WAS AWAKE, lying on the wide bed, trying to clear her head. The short sleep had left her feeling muzzy, shaky.

Had her father really done that—thrown her clothes out the window? Had she really said what she said? Been so blunt, so honest, yes—but also so blunt?

He'd looked so old when she'd finished speaking. So defeated. How could she have been so cruel?

"No," she said out loud, hunting for the strength she had somehow found to say what had to be said. "No, *he* was cruel. Don't try to tell yourself he was only scared, much as he has a right to be scared. The man could go blind, lose his livelihood, his only real love. But that doesn't give him the right to be cruel, so judgmental. I'm not a doormat, damn it, and nobody is going to walk on me again."

There was a knock at the door just as Hannah finished her pep talk, and she immediately sat up, swung her legs over the edge of the bed. What could it be? News of her father? Alex had promised to leave her alone for a few hours, and it hadn't been more than an hour since he'd deposited her here, kissed her forehead and left her.

Her father's pistol. Had that been in her baggage? She'd hidden it, but had he found it as he emptied her closet?

And, if he had? She had to ask Alex to bring all the bags upstairs so she could go through them, check for the pistol.

"Who is it?" she called, heading for the door, her legs unsteady beneath her as she opened the door. "Alex," she said as he just stood there, looking at her. Looking very solemn. Panic gripped her. "What? What's wrong? Dad? Alex, is it my dad?"

"Your dad?" Alex looked confused for a moment, then shook his head. "No, not your dad. You didn't really expect him to come out here, did you?"

"No. No, I didn't. But, then, what's wrong? You look like you've seen a ghost."

Alex walked into the room, sat down on the side of the bed. Hannah joined him. "Alex?"

He took a deep breath, let it out slowly. Looked at her. "It's a long story, Hannah. A very long story. And it can wait," he added, smiling, although his eyes didn't smile, only his mouth. "First, I think we need to talk about us. Because there is an *us,* you know. Well, *I* know. I'm not so sure you do. Not yet."

"You know, the last thing I want or need right now is charity." Hannah tried to get off the bed, but Alex shot out his hand, grabbed her forearm. "And if you think you have to say all this because I spent the night in your bed and then Dad tossed me out on my ear—forget it. I was in your bed because I wanted to be in your bed."

"And you were there because I wanted you there," Alex reminded her. "Hannah, this doesn't have anything to do with your father. What he said this morning in the stables, what he did later back at your apartment. This has to do with last night, and how we got to last night. Or do you think what happened between us last night wasn't something very, very special?"

"We...we got to last night because I was stupid enough to ask you, and you...and you..."

"Yes? And I what, Hannah? I took advantage of you?"

"No!" Hannah exclaimed. "You'd never take advantage of me, of anyone."

"Well, then if I didn't take you to my bed to take advantage of you, why did I?"

Hannah twisted her hands in her lap. "Curiosity?" she said at last, wincing.

Alex released a bark of laughter. "Curiosity? Oh, God, Hannah—I should be saying that to you, and not the other way around."

She pulled away from him again, this time succeeding in getting off the bed, then turned and glared at him. "Don't you make fun of me, Alex Coleman. Don't you dare make fun of me. And if you tell me one more time that you're in love with me, I'll...I'll..."

"I'm in love with you, Hannah-banana," he said as she subsided into soft splutters of nothing. "I am madly, wildly, deeply, and most eternally in love with you."

She said the stupidest, most juvenile words she'd ever spoken. "Are not!"

Alex stood up, took hold of her shoulders. "I love the way you look at me when you think I don't notice. I love the way you get a little fumbly when you're nervous. I love your pure heart, your unselfishness, your courage and determination, and the way you finally stood up to your father, told him things he needed to hear."

He pulled her closer, and Hannah was too numb to resist. "And I most especially love the way you sort of purr, deep in your throat, when I kiss you here...and here...and here."

Hannah closed her eyes as Alex's mouth touched against her throat, her cheek and finally her mouth.

Her arms lifted of their own volition, encircling his neck

as he stepped back, eased them onto the bed. "I love you, Hannah-banana. I love you, and I need you. I need you so much right now it hurts."

He wasn't as gentle as he'd been the night before, and Hannah didn't want him to be gentle. She needed to feel. To feel alive…to feel wanted. To feel loved.

He spoke to her as he undressed her, as she fumbled with his clothes, partly embarrassed, but mostly because she trembled so with need that she couldn't manage the buttons, the snap.

"Love you," Alex breathed against her mouth, her ear. "How I love you. I'm going to spend the rest of my life proving to you just how much. Sweet Hannah. My sweet, darling Hannah…"

She sighed as his hands found her breasts, as his mouth followed his hands, ministering to her, arousing her, taking her back to new yet strangely familiar territory, but taking her there faster, with more urgency.

He raised himself over her and looked down at her. He closed his eyes as she lifted her hands, cupped his face and lifted her head for his kiss. "Love me, Alex," she heard herself say, then grinned at the quick rush of freedom that sang through her, a release of any last fear or inhibition she had brought with her into this room. "Oh, yes, Alex, please. Love me. Love me as I love you. I love you…I love you…I love you…"

IT WAS AFTER MIDNIGHT when Alex finally told Hannah what had to be said. After an intimate dinner for two at a local restaurant, as far from his family as he could get her. After they'd danced, and talked and kissed. After the ride home, and after Hannah had insisted on checking on Jabbar and changing his bandage.

It had been Jabbar who had given him the opening he

needed. "He comes from Sorajhee, you know," he said as Hannah stroked the stallion's velvety nose, told him what a fine old man he was. "I think it's time you found out how he got here. How we all got here."

Hannah looked at him curiously, still lovingly. How he hoped she would continue to look at him lovingly after he told her everything she had to know.

He held out his hand, and she slipped hers into it. They walked out of the stables and sat down on a wooden bench near the fence. "I don't know where to start," he said after a few moments. "Everything has been a secret for so long, and everything was so long ago—sometimes it seems like a dream. Like it all happened to someone else. But it didn't. It's true, and it happened to us. To my parents, to Mac and Cade. To me."

"Alex, you're frightening me," Hannah said, leaning into him as he slipped his arm around her shoulder, as they sat together in the dark, out of the light of the lamps that burned on high poles all through the night. "Whatever it is, can it be all that bad?"

"Oh, not bad, Hannah," he said, rubbing her arm. "Just sad, sad and secret, and finally with some sort of happy ending." He sighed, continuing to rub her arm. "I guess the best thing to do is start at the beginning. Hannah, my name is Alex Coleman, here in Texas. But in Sorajhee, I was Alim, oldest son of Ibrahim Bin Habib El Jeved, king of Sorajhee."

He waited, feeling Hannah stiffen under his arm. "Go on," she said after a few moments, her voice small, her hand beginning to rub lightly against his chest.

"There's so much to tell, and yet so little. Most of it can wait, but there are some things you have to know. My...my father was assassinated a long time ago, when I was about four, and my mother believed that his brother, my uncle, arranged for my father's death, planned the deaths of Mac and Cade and me as well.''

Hannah pushed herself away from him and looked at him closely. "Your own uncle? Why?"

"For the throne, of course," Alex said. "My father wanted an alliance with Balahar, a neighboring country, but Azzam—that's my uncle—was very much against it. My father had gone to the people, to make an announcement of the details of the alliance when he was shot and killed. Azzam took power immediately and closed our borders, with no more talk of any alliance with Balahar. Within a week, our mother had secretly slipped us out of Sorajhee—along with Jabbar, who was only a foal at the time—handed us over to Randy in England, and returned to Sorajhee to fight for our rights as our father's heirs."

"She left you? She took you to England, and then she left you?"

"Not willingly, Hannah. I can still remember how she looked, how fiercely she held us. How she cried. I wanted to go with her. I can remember begging to go with her." Alex pressed his fingers against his eyes, which had begun to sting. "But she wouldn't let me, of course. She told me I had to take care of Mac and Cade, be the big boy for her until she returned—you know how mothers talk."

"Actually, no, I don't," Hannah said, then squeezed his hand. "We both lost our mothers, Alex. Long, long ago. What happened to her? Because she never came back for you, did she? Otherwise, you wouldn't be here. You wouldn't be Alex Coleman. You'd be…Alim? How strange to even hear myself saying this. It's like you've just told me a story."

"If she had succeeded, yes, my mother would have come back, and there would be a happy ending to my story. But she died, Hannah. Word came to Randy that she'd died trying to kill my uncle in his bed. We'd already been living in Boston under assumed names, and Randy moved us here, to Texas, to continue our lives, hopefully never to be discovered by my uncle, who'd been told we had been victims of a boating accident. Lots of people telling other people that people were dead.''

"But you're not dead," Hannah said, then drew in her breath sharply. "And your mother? Alex—are you saying that your mother—"

"That she's alive? That, after all these years, she's alive? Yes, Hannah, that's exactly what I'm saying. We just found out for sure today, although I've known she might be. I've known for nearly two weeks. But today Randy talked to her."

"You've known?" Hannah asked, her tone questioning and thoughtful. "For nearly two weeks? Since...since the day Khalid was born? Then, Alex? *Before* then?"

"Around that time, yes," Alex said, wondering why Hannah needed to know.

"So...so when you were walking around in a daze...it was because your mother might be alive? Not because of me, Alex. Because your mother might be alive?"

"I don't understand what you mean, Hannah," Alex said, truly confused. "And if I was, what of it?"

"I don't know," Hannah said slowly, getting up, beginning to pace. "I don't know. It's just that Jessica said...and I thought...I hoped." She stopped pacing, looked at Alex. "Are you sure, Alex? Are you sure you love me? Or was I just a very good diversion, keeping your mind off the question of whether or not your mother was alive?"

"That's nuts, Hannah," Alex said, standing up as well, holding out his arms to her. "Oh, all right, so maybe in the beginning a diversion was just what I needed. Randy and I had agreed not to tell Mac and Cade, not until we were sure, and I was sort of walking around in a daze. Sure I was. I didn't know where my mother was, if she was sick, well, in prison—I knew nothing, Hannah, less than nothing. Spending time with you was just what I needed. But that wasn't all it was, all that it became. Hannah, I love you. I want to marry you. In two weeks, as we planned, or tonight, tomorrow. I love you.''

"Oh, Alex," Hannah said, moving into his arms. "I'm sorry. I guess I still can't believe in my own happiness. You tell me about your mother, you tell me you're an Arab prince, and I just think about me, how it affects—Alex!'' She pushed herself out of his arms, looked up at him. "You're a prince! Does your uncle know about you now? Does he know about your mother? Are you...are you in any danger?''

Alex pulled her against his chest, stroked her hair. "You know, Hannah, that's a good question, and one I hadn't yet asked myself. I've been Alex Coleman for as long as I can remember. Sorajhee was another time, another life. I do know that my Uncle Azzam has no sons, but that doesn't affect me. I won't let it affect me. My life is here.''

He pushed her slightly away from him, looked down into her face, smiled into her face. "My life is with you, Hannah. Always and forever, with you.''

Hannah smiled at him, but tears swam in her eyes even as unease took up residence deep in Alex's gut. His mother was coming to The Desert Rose. The whole world was coming to The Desert Rose.

Coming to Alex. *Alim.* Coming to Cade. *Kadar.* Coming to Mac. *Makin.* The past was alive, and coming to them all.

How could he promise anything, know anything?

"DID YOU KNOW?'' Hannah asked Jessica as they sat across a small table from each other, finishing the last of two huge chocolate, marshmallow and peanut sundaes. "About Sora-jhee, I mean."

She and Jessica had been shopping, rather successfully, too, because Hannah had been easy to please and Jessica had a great eye for just what looked best on the woman soon to become Alex's bride.

There was a simple wedding gown in a plastic bag hanging over the back of another chair. It was hardly more than a slip—sleeveless, with a scoop neck and back, and a barely flared skirt, with no train. Hannah had wondered if it might be too plain, although she hadn't wanted anything fancy, but Jessica had assured her it was "perfect."

Other bags held shoes, several sets of new underwear fit for a bride, some toiletries, and an ivory silk peignoir Jessica had insisted Hannah buy at a shop in the mall called Darla's Delectables.

Hannah hadn't wanted to go shopping, but Jessica had offered and Alex had insisted. There was going to be a wedding, he kept telling her there was going to be a wedding, and he wanted her to be ready for it.

He also, she was sure, wanted her out of the way, so he could stay closeted with Randy and his brothers, planning for his mother's arrival.

Rose Coleman Jeved would occupy the housekeeper's suite of rooms on the first floor, because Ella lived in the carriage house with her husband, Hal. That much was settled.

But that was about all that had been settled.

The world still knew nothing about Queen Rose Jeved, about her reemergence as the widow of the king of Sora-jhee, and even less about Alex and his brothers.

The Desert Rose had, almost overnight, turned into an armed camp, with all the gates closed and manned, with new faces, hard faces, showing up, walking the grounds, patrolling the paddocks on horseback and in Jeeps. If the world wanted to come, it would have to do more than merely knock and ask for entrance.

Which was another reason Alex wanted Hannah to finish her shopping now, before it might become difficult for her to leave the ranch. Jessica had been thrilled right from the beginning, but Hannah had been upset, frightened. Everything was happening so quickly. Maybe too quickly.

"Jessica, stop licking that spoon and answer me. Did you know about Sorajhee?" Hannah persisted. "Besides, there's a guy over there watching you, and I think he's going to drool if you don't soon put your tongue back in your mouth."

"Where?" Jessica asked, putting down the spoon and casting her gaze around the restaurant. "Oh, I get it. Nobody's really looking at me, are they? You just want me to answer your question. And here I thought you'd already figured out the answer yourself. Think about it, Hannah. If you had a secret, would you tell me? At least the me I was until I grew up and became so sensible?"

"Not a chance. Sorry," Hannah said, smiling. "Well, then, aren't you angry that nobody told you? Your cousins are royal princes, for crying out loud."

"Not to me, they're not," Jessica answered, taking the check when the waitress put it on the table. "My treat," she said, digging in her purse as she spoke. "I mean— Cade and Mac? Princes? These would be the same two princes who used to hide under my bed at night, then jump out and make faces at me, flashlights held under their chins so that they looked like the twin monsters they were. No, Hannah. They're Mac and Cade, no matter how grown-up they are now. Although I have to tell you, all three of them *look* like princes, don't they?"

"Excuse me. Ms. Coleman?"

Hannah looked up at the same time Jessica did, to see a fairly rumpled looking man in a tan ill-fitting suit standing beside the table. "You *are* Ms. Jessica Coleman, aren't you? Cousin to the heirs to the throne of Sorajhee? My name is Bud Hampton, and I work as a stringer for several national newspapers. May I have a word?"

"Sora-*who?*" Jessica asked, wrinkling up her nose. She and Hannah then exchanged quick looks, both of them rising at the same time, quickly gathering up their packages. "I'm sorry, Mr. Hampton," Jessica said smoothly, "but, no, I'm not Jessica Coleman. Although she *is* here, because I saw her a few minutes ago, in the ladies' room." She looked around the restaurant, then pointed toward the exit. "Why, there she goes now. You'll have to hurry if you want to catch her. Now, if you'll excuse us?"

"But—but—"

Hannah and Jessica threaded their way through the tables, walking slowly toward a second exit that led straight out of the mall and into the parking lot, then broke into a run once they were safely outside the restaurant, not stopping until they were inside Jessica's car, the doors locked.

"Whew! That was close," Jessica said, her hand shaking as she slipped the key into the ignition. "I guess you'd better phone ahead to the ranch and tell my dad it's starting. Damn, and I wanted to go to the movies in Bridle tonight. Well, I guess that's out."

"Yes," Hannah said as they pulled out of the parking lot and headed for the highway. "I suppose it is. I imagine a lot of plans are going to be changing soon."

"Maybe, Hannah, but not one of them," Jessica told her, handing her the cell phone. "You're getting married, lady. You *are* getting married, whether my aunt shows up or not, whether or not the whole world is camping outside our gates. I know Alex, and it would take a whole lot more than this to change his plans.''

''I hope you're right, Jessica,'' Hannah said. ''I just wish this feeling I have would go away.''

''What feeling would that be?''

''The one that tells me I'm entirely too happy and that something is bound to happen to change all of it. *That* feeling…''

Chapter Fifteen

Two days later, Hannah stood on the front porch, shielding her eyes as a helicopter approached, blowing dust everywhere as it slowly came to earth about one hundred yards from the main house.

Just that morning a press release issued in Sorajhee told the world that Queen Jeved and her sons, who had been living in seclusion in Europe and America, had decided to reenter the world. Already the press had found its way to the gates of The Desert Rose, but Alex assured her that within days, when no new announcements were forthcoming, they'd all go away again. After all, it wasn't as if Ibrahim's widow and sons were more than an old curiosity.

"Come with me!" Alex shouted above the noise of the rotors, but Hannah shook her head and motioned for him to go without her, follow his aunt and uncle and brothers, who were already heading toward the helicopter.

Alex looked at her, pleading with her without saying a word, then finally shook his head, gave her a quick kiss and ran after his brothers, at last seeming to believe what she'd told him, that this was a moment for mother and sons. A private moment in which she didn't want to interfere.

"Look at him, running like a child, fairly flying across the ground, he's so eager. He's probably forgotten me already,'' she said as the rotors slowly died, so that Jessica heard her.

"You know, Hannah, you've been doing pretty well,'' Jessica said, "but I think you still have a ways to go, trying to build that ego of yours. He hasn't forgotten you. He loves you.''

"I know,'' Hannah said, still watching Alex, "and every day I believe it more. But right now, Jessica, all Alex can think about is his mother. How she'll look. If he'll remember her. Will she be proud of him. And that's how it should be.''

"Because that's how you'd feel, if it were your mother on that helicopter?''

Hannah shook her head and smiled. "No. Not at all. My mother made her choices. She left me, without so much as a goodbye. A few years ago, I finally figured out that I was probably better off with her gone. But this is different, Jess. Alex's mother didn't want to leave him.'' She leaned forward slightly as the door opened on the side of the helicopter. "And now, at last, they're all going to be together again. It's beautiful, Jessica. Just beautiful.''

"Here she comes,'' Jessica said, then shook her head. "No. It's a man. Look at him, Hannah. He's wearing Arab costume, just like my cousins do for some of their shows. Oh, isn't he magnificent! Who do you think he is?''

"King Zakariyya of Balahar,'' Hannah said, watching as the tall, older man bowed his head ever so slightly to everyone, then turned back to the doorway, holding up his hand to help the other passenger disembark. "He insisted on personally escorting Queen Rose. Alex still isn't sure if he's happy about that, but he wouldn't say why. Just that he didn't like picking at old wounds. Ah, there she is!''

Hannah jumped up, trying to see the small woman who had been so quickly surrounded by so many tall men. All she had seen was a small, slim form and the flash of soft blond hair in the Texas sun. "Come on, Jessica. Let's go inside and make sure Ella has all the refreshments ready."

"Chicken," Jessica said, looking over her shoulder at the group beside the helicopter, even as she followed Hannah inside the house.

Hannah stayed there for a few minutes, pretending to help Ella set out coffee cups, but then left the kitchen, mumbling an excuse, and headed out the back door and toward the stables. Nobody would think to look for her there and she could prolong the inevitable. Besides, this was a time for family. She wasn't family, not yet.

ALEX COULD BARELY SPEAK. He was four years old again, and his mother was smiling at him. Touching his hair, although this time she didn't bend down to him, but reached up to him. Saying his name in that same never-to-be-forgotten voice. "Alim. My dear baby, my brave warrior. Alim. So like your father."

"Mother," Alex heard himself say over the rushing in his ears that had nothing to do with the now quiet helicopter rotors. "Welcome to The Desert Rose," he said, then gathered her in his arms, felt her small, fragile body as he breathed in the smell of jasmine, traveled back in time to days not clearly remembered, and a love never forgotten.

"Mother?"

Alex reluctantly released his mother at the sound of Mac's voice. "Mother, this is Mac—*Makin*. Your baby."

"You're all my babies," Rose said, stepping forward to kiss Mac, to kiss Cade. "Kadar, do you still suck your thumb?" she asked, smiling as Cade kissed her cheek. And then she put her hands to her mouth, as if trying to hold back whole storms of emotions, and turned to her brother, swaying where she stood. "Oh, this is hard. So hard. I thought I was ready, that I could be strong. Randy," she said on a sob. "It hurts. It hurts so much. My boys. All the wasted years."

Randy quickly lifted her into his arms, and she rested her head on his shoulder while he carried her to the house.

"Your mother is delighted to see you, my son, as I am delighted to see you all. All these ghosts, raised from the dead. She has been ill, as you already know, her body filled with drugs to dull her mind, but the doctors assure me she is daily recovering her strength. Have no fear on that head, my son. A word, if I might," King Zakariyya said as Alex made to follow after his mother, his brothers.

"Your Highness," he said, turning back to the man who stood very much at his ease, very much aware of his own power, even here, far from his homeland of Balahar. A true prince of the desert. Alex saw much of his own father in the man, but that didn't mean he trusted him or his motives. "Perhaps you'd like to go somewhere private, where we might talk?"

"A suggestion hovering on my own lips, dear prince," King Zakariyya said, motioning for the two male servants who had also disembarked to stay where they were. "I must return to the airport within the hour for my flight home. Your mother and I have spoken on the way from Paris, and she knows what is required. But that is not the same as speaking to the crown prince, now is it?"

"My uncle usurped the throne, Your Highness, long ago. I have no burning desire to try to wrest it from him."

"Perhaps not, but since when has personal desire taken precedence over the duty of a prince? The duty of a son to his martyred father?"

Alex had no answer for that and merely turned, leading the way to the stables, where they kept a small refrigerator stocked with bottled water and soft drinks. He didn't ask if the king wanted to follow everyone else into the house, because he knew this was to be a highly private conversation.

And it might not be all that diplomatic a conversation.

"I have heard of the purity of your stock," Zakariyya said, entering the stable and walking the length of the stalls, stopping to inspect the occupants until he came to the stall with Jabbar's name visible on a small brass plaque. "Ah, the mighty sire." He held out his hand and Jabbar nuzzled it, allowing Zakariyya to lift his noble head, inspect his mouth. "Long in the tooth, as many of us are, but still strong, still proud. Your father would be pleased, Alim."

"Yes, thank you," Alex said impatiently. "Look, Your Highness, I know we could spend days being polite to each other, dancing around whatever it is you want to say, but you already told me you have to get back to the airport, and I think I already know what you're going to say. It's about that long-ago proposed alliance, isn't it? I can think of no other reason for Balahar to take such a personal interest in my mother, or her arrival here in Texas. The secret alliance between my father and you, made, then abandoned years ago. The alliance never made public because the father died and the sons of Ibrahim disappeared."

"Just as your mother was reported to have retired into seclusion," Zakariyya said, turning away from the stall, looking carefully at Alex. "How do you know? How do you know that the alliance was to hinge on the son of Sorajhee wedding the daughter of Balahar? This was never made public."

Alex's knees almost buckled. "I didn't know," he said quietly, rubbing a hand across his chin. "My God, I didn't even guess."

"Ah," Zakariyya said, looking at Alex. "Well, this has certainly saved us some valuable time, hasn't it, my son?

How very American of me, I'm sure, to have located the point so quickly and placed it on the table. I have a great affection for your mother, Alim, but I have a greater affection for my people. I never believed your mother had willingly taken you all into seclusion somewhere deep inside Sorajhee. I believed her to be dead, believed all of you dead. When I was informed that your mother might still be alive, when I began some investigations of my own and discovered you and your brothers, my hopes for my people blossomed within me.''

Alex kept shaking his head, trying to assimilate what he was hearing. ''You're going to have to go back to the beginning, Your Highness. You lost me somewhere along the way. How *did* you hear about my mother?''

King Zakariyya walked to the center of the stable and sat on a small wooden chair, arranging his robes about him, obviously prepared to hold court.

''Very well, Alim, we go back to the beginning. Sorajhee and Balahar are two independent but very vulnerable countries bordering each other on the coast of the Persian Gulf and the Gulf of Oman. A prime location for both of us, and for those who covet us. Balahar has oil, Sorajhee has excellent ports.''

''I know the geography, Your Highness,'' Alex interrupted, pulling two bottles of water from the small refrigerator and handing one to the king.

''Yes, I'm sure you do,'' Zakariyya said, tipping his head to look closely at Alex. ''So like your father, and yet with some of the impatience of your uncle, the dear Azzam. An interesting combination. You do not bend to another's will with much grace, do you?'' He lifted one hand, as if to halt his own words. ''But I digress. Shall we go on?''

''If you would, Your Highness,'' Alex said, cocking his

own head slightly, as he thought he might have heard something. Someone.

"Your father had three sons, Alim, and Balahar had none. No sons, no daughters. But great hopes, I assure you. It was one thing to pledge an alliance between our two countries, but those would be only words, on paper. So your father and I agreed to a marriage between the son of Sorajhee and the daughter of Balahar. This our people could understand. This the world outside could understand." He took a drink of water and smiled. "There is nothing very new about this sort of alliance, Alim."

"But Azzam didn't want the alliance, and had my father killed the very day it was to be announced," Alex said, preferring to concentrate on the facts and not the plan behind them. "Our mother took us away, sent us into hiding, because she feared for our lives, then returned to Sorajhee to fight for our rights as the sons of Ibrahim."

"Almost correct, my son. It would appear that King Azzam had wanted only a demonstration by the people that day, a protest of sorts, and planned for one to occur. He believed his brother died when one radical went too far, and was devastated when Ibrahim died." Zakariyya smiled. "Not that he was so brokenhearted that he did not immediately have himself declared king, holding you and your brothers and mother as near prisoners until his power was established."

Alex thought he saw a hint of movement in the shadows. Hannah? Was it Hannah? How much had she heard?

"And you believe him?"

"I do. Now," Zakariyya said. "I did not, not at first. Not for many years. But now the truth is clear. It was not Azzam, but his wife, Layla, who arranged for your father's death, your own removal from Sorajhee. Layla had once been promised to Ibrahim, before he met your mother. I doubt you know this, but perhaps it will help you to understand her envy of your mother, of your mother's sons, of your mother's place on the throne. She fed your suffering mother lies and used her to rid Sorajhee of the three princes. You must admit, Alim, her plan did work, for within a week of Ibrahim's death, all three princes were gone, hidden somewhere in America. It was only a small matter for Layla to then capture your mother upon her return, make up some story about the queen having gone mad with grief and plotting to kill Azzam.''

''She was caught in his chambers, with a knife,'' Alex said, remembering the story he'd heard from Randy.

''She was in his chambers, that's true enough,'' Zakariyya agreed. ''But she was sound asleep, the knife beside her. Drugged, my son. I believe your American movies call it being *set up?*'' He sighed. ''It was no great feat for Layla to convince Azzam that the queen was insane, even easier to convince him to let her handle the queen's removal to a suitable sanatorium. Then, a few months later, Layla reported to Azzam that the queen had died at her own hand, and that was the end of it. Rarely does a man question his own good fortune, and Azzam did not question his, even when Layla told him that Ibrahim's princes had also perished in—was it a boating accident? I believe your American uncle and Layla made up that particular story between them. To the world, you were all still in voluntary seclusion. To Azzam, you were all dead.''

''My mother has been in a sanatorium? All these years?''

''Several of them, all over Europe,'' Zakariyya confirmed, nodding. ''In truth, Layla seemed to have misplaced her this past year, when her own mind began to falter, when the bitterness in her heart invaded her mind. It was then that Layla began walking through the palace, tearing at her clothes, muttering unbelievable things. She is losing her mind, Alim, rapidly, as the punishment so unfairly heaped on her enemy becomes her own just punishment.''

"So," Alex said, pacing in front of the king, "Azzam found out and brought you into it." He stopped, looked at Zakariyya. "Why? Why did he bring you into it?"

"Because I left him no choice, of course," Zakariyya said, smiling with all the innocence of a desert fox. "We gave birth to intrigue in the Middle East, my son. I have my people inside the palace at Jeved, just as my dear friend Azzam has his people listening at the walls of my own palace." His smile faded. "Sorajhee and Balahar very much need this alliance, my son."

"The son of Sorajhee and the daughter of Balahar," Alex said, almost to himself. Was Hannah listening? What was she thinking?

"The son of Sorajhee united with the daughter of Balahar, uniting our two countries. You Americans have said it many times, Alim. United we stand, divided we fall. We have stood, these last years, but we have been staggered. It is now time to unite, to stand strong."

"And is there a daughter of Balahar, Your Highness?"

"Our dearest Serena," Zakariyya said, nodding. "My wife and I have been blessed with two adopted children, Alim, to warm our hearts, fill our lives, although my wife has been gone from me these last years. Sharif, a foundling brought to us as an infant shortly after our own child was born dead and my wife needed so badly to hold an infant in her arms. We were blessed with Sharif, and blessed twice with my good American friend's orphaned daughter who has grown to be the crown jewel of my people, loved by all."

"American? This Serena—she's American? And she knows about this alliance? Agrees to it?"

"Serena is my daughter now, and she knows where her

duty lies. She *will* marry the son of Sorajhee, Alim. Your mother has already agreed.''

"My mother," Alex said bitterly, "is still being used, isn't she? Tell me, King Zakariyya, would she still be lost somewhere in Europe, locked away from the world, if you did not believe you needed her to convince her son of his duty?''

Zakariyya shrugged. "Once I knew about you and your brothers, you mean? Who is to say? But the queen is here now, your mother is here now, and I leave it to her to convince you that your father cannot have been martyred in vain." The king stood, placed a hand to Alex's shoulder for a moment before moving toward the doorway. "You are your father's son, Alim, as are your brothers. You will do what is right. Peace to you, my son. Peace to us all.''

HANNAH WIPED AT HER WET CHEEKS as she laid the last of her clothing in one final suitcase and closed the lid.

Too good to be true. She didn't know quite how, but she'd known it all along, sensed it all along. There would be no wedding next Saturday. There couldn't be. Because her Alex was a royal prince. Because her Alex had a duty.

Alex, she knew, was a man who always did his duty. The older brother. The protective one.

He'd probably—definitely—make a fine king.

The entire Coleman family, except for Jessica, had been closeted with Rose for hours. King Zakariyya had flown away after delivering her, after dropping that terrible bomb on Alex out in the stables. She'd heard every word. Died a little with each word she'd heard.

And still Alex hadn't come to her. He couldn't, could he? He needed to be with his mother, and Hannah understood that. So many lost years, so much to say, so much to learn about each other.

Would he even tell Rose about her, about the woman he'd nearly married? And did it matter? Could anything matter more than Alex's duty to his dead father, to the country of his birth, the throne his mother had given so many years of her life to gain for her son?

At least she, Hannah, could make all of this a little easier on Alex. Having heard what she'd heard out in the stables, she could at least be gone before he had to sit her down, tell her that they could never marry.

Hannah picked up this last suitcase, then looked at the small collection that had been purchased to hold her clothing for her honeymoon, knowing she'd never be able to get all the pieces out of the house without being discovered. She'd never be able to get Livy or one of the other ranch hands to drive her into Bridle without being discovered.

Hannah subsided onto the side of the bed, stabbing her fingers through her hair. What was she going to do? Was she really just going to run away, without saying goodbye? Was she that unsure of Alex's love that she'd believe he would let her go?

Yes, she told herself as tears threatened once more. Yes, she was that unsure of him, that unsure of herself. No matter how many times Alex told her he loved her, no matter how many times he held her, kissed her, she had been unable to really, *really* believe him.

"Dad, you did your work well," she said in the empty room. "And I've still got a long way to go before I believe I'm worth more than you think I'm worth—which isn't much, is it?"

There was a knock at the door and Hannah stiffened, looked around the room at the luggage that would give away her plans. "Alex? I've got a headache," she called out. "If you don't mind, I'd rather just skip dinner and see you in the morning."

The door opened slightly, then more fully, and Rose Jeved walked into the room. "It's not Alim, Hannah," she said, her smile sweet if tired. "I've convinced him to stay downstairs with his brothers, so that you and I can talk. He didn't want to, of course, but he knows to obey his mother, or at least to indulge her. Is that all right?"

Hannah was already on her feet, looking at this small blond woman who had suffered so much, survived so much. "Alex told you about me?" she asked, then winced at her blunt question. "Your Highness," she added, knowing it wasn't enough.

"Please, not so formal. Call me Rose, and I will call you Hannah. Such a lovely name for such a lovely girl. You hold my son's heart in your hand, do you know that?"

"I—I—"

"Ah, and you blush so prettily. I wonder. Does Alim notice that we are both blond, and small? And yet we are different. You're so educated, so independent, and I married my Ibrahim while still nearly a child myself."

Rose motioned for Hannah to sit back down on the bed, and sat down beside her. "Alex knows, Hannah. He knows that you were in the stables earlier, that you heard Zakariyya talking about this second, secret alliance my husband and he had agreed to so many years ago. Zakariyya has placed great hope in that alliance. And he wishes to use me to gain Alex's agreement."

Hannah pressed her lips together, wet them with her tongue. "Alex knows?" She hung her head. "Oh, I see."

"You do? Why do I doubt that, Hannah?"

Hannah looked at her. "He is going to obey you, isn't he? He's going to go to Balahar, marry this princess?"

Rose laughed softly, almost musically. "I believe it would take an army twice that of Balahar and Sorajhee combined to move Alim a single step from your side, my dear. That's why I'm here, Hannah—to meet the young woman who is so loved by my oldest son. I'm here to welcome her to my family, to thank her for giving my son the love I see shining in his eyes. His father's shone much the same for me. I remember, Hannah, and I would never allow anything, even Ibrahim's beloved alliance, to take that light from my son's eyes.''

She looked across the room at the suitcases, and then at Hannah. ''Oh, and one more thing. I do believe I'm also here to help my new daughter unpack. Unless...'' she added, smiling. ''Yes, I do believe that knock at the door is probably Alim. I'm only surprised he was willing to obey me, and stay away from you for so long. Shall I let him in?''

At Hannah's nod, Rose crossed the room and opened the door. She tipped her head so that Alex could kiss her cheek, then stepped outside, leaving her son and Hannah alone.

''You okay?'' Alex asked, sitting down beside Hannah, just where his mother had been just moments ago. He looked at the suitcases, frowned. ''No. Guess not.''

''Your mother is going to help me unpack,'' Hannah said, her hands folded together in her lap. ''Your mother, I believe, is going to help me with a lot of things.''

Alex slipped an arm around Hannah, drew her against his shoulder. ''I love you, Hannah,'' he said, kissing the top of her head. ''I know things have changed around here, but not for us. Not if you love me.''

Hannah closed her eyes for a moment, then pushed herself away from him, looking up into his eyes. ''You know what's wrong, Alex?'' she asked. ''Do you know what's really wrong?''

''With us?''

She shook her head. ''No, not with us. With *me*. And it took listening to your mother to make me realize how stupid I was, packing my bags, thinking to make a clean get-away before you could tell me to take a hike, you're off to be a king.''

She took his hands in hers, squeezed them. ''What's wrong with me is that I didn't trust your love enough to believe you still wanted to marry me. I apologize for that, Alex, and I promise never to doubt you again. It…well, maybe it's difficult for me to believe in unconditional love. The sort your mother had for your father, the sort she has for her sons. The sort of unconditional love,'' she said, sighing, ''I have for you.''

''I'll bet you say that to all the princes,'' Alex teased, then tried to lay her back on the bed.

''No, Alex, I'm trying to be serious here,'' she said, hopping to her feet beside the bed. ''I want you to know that I trust you, as well as love you. I want to apologize for being so scared, for not believing, even for a moment, that what we have now, and what we'll have for the rest of our lives is real. It's forever.''

''You know, Hannah, there are times I want to shake both your mother and father for what they did to you. Your mother, by leaving, and Hugo for making you all but beg for his love.''

''I do love him,'' Hannah said, sitting down on the bed once more. ''I won't say it's always been easy, but when things were bad I always tried to think about the hours we spent together treating sick animals, him teaching me what he knew—and me watching him with those animals, caring for them, caring about them. There were good times, Alex. There really were.''

Alex stroked her cheek. ''You'd still forgive him, wouldn't you?''

''Oh, yes,'' Hannah said truthfully. ''He's my father,

Alex. I'd always forgive him. But I'm afraid that he'll never forgive me.''

She looked at Alex, saw a strange light in his eyes, but then he smiled and she didn't ask him what he was thinking. She still had something else to say to him. ''There's one more thing, you know, and it's terribly important.''

''You want to know if I snore?'' he asked, once more tipping her back onto the mattress, this time succeeding.

''I don't care if you snore,'' she told him, her hands planted against his chest, keeping him away until she'd said everything she needed to say. ''I told you something was wrong, but it's really two somethings. The second one is nearly as important as the first. Alex,'' she said, looking at him searchingly, ''I was so busy selfishly feeling sorry for myself and doubting your love, that I've yet to ask the most important question. Are…are you and your mother and brothers in any danger?''

Alex rolled onto his back, taking Hannah with him, so that she half lay across his chest. ''Danger?'' he repeated, frowning. ''You mean from my uncle? Do you know, Hannah, I really haven't given that much thought. We're in Texas, and we're American citizens as well as the heirs to the throne. Whatever happens from here on out is going to happen on a very public stage, with a lot of the world watching us. My uncle has already made a statement to the press proclaiming his delight in my mother's *recovery*—a word with many meanings—and the fact that Mac and Cade and I are alive and well. So, no, I don't think there's any danger. Why?'' he asked, rubbing Hannah's back as he grinned up at her. ''Are you planning to protect me?''

''Always, Alex,'' Hannah said sincerely, then relaxed slightly, needing to believe Alex was right, that a watching world would keep both him and his brothers safe. ''I do carry a pistol, you know," she reminded him, then giggled as he began tickling her and rolled her over onto her back.

If he was trying to divert her from her thoughts, he was doing a good job of it, and an even better job once he grabbed her hands, held them up over her head and bent to capture her mouth.

He kissed her once, twice, then moved slightly away from her to look down into her eyes. "Are we all done talking now?" he asked her. "No more doubts, no more questions?"

Hannah moistened her lips with the tip of her tongue, then smiled as Alex gave out with a low groan. "Only one, my prince. Are you going to just lie there, babbling away, or are you going to make love to me."

"Babbling? You know, Hannah, I should probably warn you that in Sorajhee women are not usually permitted to make fun of their husbands. Especially when that husband is a royal prince."

Hannah giggled. "Gee, I'm scared," she said, wrapping her arms around his neck once he'd released her hands. "Am I going to be punished now?"

"Definitely," Alex told her. "Punished with kisses, imprisoned by love and doomed to a life sentence with this adoring servant right by your side. Can you live with that, my Hannah-banana?"

"Oh, yes, Alex," she said as he drew her close. "I most certainly can live with that."

ALEX HELD HANNAH'S HAND as the family sat together in the living room the next day, listening to Rose's story of her missing years.

"I think Rose is getting tired," Hannah whispered as Alex's mother finished telling them about Layla and how she had believed her sister-in-law, how she had been duped by the woman. "Perhaps you should suggest we stop for the night, continue tomorrow?"

"I think she needs to say it all now, Hannah, so that it's over and we can move on."

Hannah nodded, squeezing his hand. "I think we all need it to be over, so we can move on."

"To our wedding," Alex said, leaning over and kissing her hair. "It's the perfect celebration." His smile faded and he turned his full attention back to his mother. "What did you just say?" he asked, his entire body tensing.

"I said, Alim," Rose told him, told them all, "that I was already carrying your father's last child when Ibrahim was cut down, murdered."

"My God, Rose!" Randy exclaimed. "And you knew? That day in England, when you handed the boys over to me—you knew?"

She shook her head. "No, I didn't, Randy. If I had, who is to say if these past years wouldn't have been quite different. As it was, I was more than ready to sacrifice myself to protect the children I had, keep them safe, regain their inheritance, which I'd always seen as the throne of Sorajhee. But if I'd known about the baby? No, I don't think I would have gone back, would have stepped so neatly into Layla's trap."

Vi poured more hot tea into Rose's cup and handed it to her. "The baby, Rose," she asked gently. "What happened to the baby?"

Rose's blue eyes shone with tears. "I don't know. After the birth, the baby was taken from me at once, and from that point on I was worse than just a prisoner. My heart broke when my child was taken from me, and I do believe I did go a little mad for a while. I'd lost my husband, my sons and now my baby. They even told me there had never been a pregnancy, had never been a child. There were times

I began to doubt myself—but I knew. I *knew*. They couldn't make me stop believing. I was drugged, kept half-insensible at times and then moved from place to place. Each new Sanitarium, luxurious as it might be, was given the information that I was the victim of a cruel delusion, believing that I was a queen, that my husband had been murdered and my babies ripped from my arms.''

"That's inhuman," Hannah said. "How did they get away with it?''

"The language barrier didn't help, not at first, as they kept me away from anyone who spoke English or Arabic. And then, over the years, and with the drugs, I suppose even I began to doubt what I believed. And doubting, at last I suppose I just accepted. Until I was found, until the drugs were withdrawn.''

She looked at Alex and his brothers, a frail woman whose inner strength nearly unmanned them all. "You do have a brother, or perhaps a sister. I know it. Ibrahim's child could be anywhere in Europe, anywhere in Sorajhee. I refuse to believe that the child is dead, that even Layla would have ordered an infant killed.''

She sighed, wiped at her eyes with her napkin. "Unless I just refuse to believe she was ruthless enough to have had my baby killed, the last child of Ibrahim, the last remaining threat to the throne. However,'' she ended, looking at her sons, "we all know she'd killed before.''

"We have a brother or sister,'' Mac said, looking at Cade, then at Alex. "Did you hear that? We have a brother or sister—out there somewhere. My God.''

Cade stood up, began to pace. "We start in Paris,'' he said, thinking out loud. "We start where they found Mother, and work our way back through the years, the moves from sanatorium to sanatorium. It's the only way, as Layla will just feed us more lies, if she can even separate the lies from the truth anymore.'' He stopped, looked down at his mother. ''Is she really insane?''

Rose shrugged. ''Zakariyya says she is. He told me that her mental infirmity is punishment for all the wrongs she did our family. But Azzam refuses to lock her away, blaming himself for not seeing the danger in his own wife, and for handing me over to her, leaving my well-being in her hands.''

She looked at Alex. ''Poor Azzam. How he longed for the throne, and now he has only daughters, and to hear Zakariyya tell it, he now looks longingly at Ibrahim's sons, seeing them as the future of Sorajhee.''

''Seeing Alex married to the daughter of Balahar, you mean,'' Mac said, and Alex felt Hannah inch closer to him, not in fear but in support. ''Well, that's not going to happen, now is it?''

''Not Makin, no,'' Rose said, slowly looking from one twin to the other. ''But there are more sons of Sorajhee, my children. And there is still the promise and the hope of your father, who sacrificed his life for this alliance. Zakariyya wasn't wrong to believe that I would do everything within my power to finish what my husband began, the dream of protecting his beloved Sorajhee that he gave his life to protect. Your father promised one of his sons to the daughter of Balahar. As it turns out, to Serena, the princess of Balahar. Kadar? Makin? Would you both turn your backs on that promise?''

She held out her hands, as if to say she did not wish either of them to answer her just yet. ''And now, if you'll all excuse me, I'm tired and would like to go to bed.''

There was complete silence in the room as Rose stood. Her three sons also got up. Each kissed her cheek in turn, then watched as Randy escorted her from the room, their mother leaning heavily on her brother's arm.

Once she was gone, Mac looked at his brother, saying quietly, "I don't know what you're thinking, *Kadar,* but this son of Sorajhee is thinking we'd better get on the stick and find our lost sibling, while praying like all hell that we have another brother...."

Epilogue

"It still seems so plain," Hannah said as she stood in her simple wedding gown, looking at her reflection in the long mirror. "I don't know why I let you talk me out of buying that headpiece with the orange blossoms on it."

Jessica looked at Rose and winked. "Orange blossoms, Hannah? How very *ordinary*. Alex had a much better idea."

"Alex?" Hannah turned to look at the two women in confusion just as the door opened and Vi came in carrying a long box. "Vi? What's that?"

"This, my dear," Rose said, taking the box from her sister-in-law, "is your bride present from Alim...from Alex. It was the only other thing I brought to England when I left Sorajhee, for Randy to keep safe for me. Now hurry, we don't have much time."

Hannah stood, transfixed, as Rose laid the box on the bed and removed the lid, pulling out a long, straight white robe shot through with golden threads. "My wedding clothes, Hannah," she said, stroking the soft cloth. "And now yours, if you wish."

Blinking back tears, Hannah approached the bed, touched the soft cloth. "I...I would be honored," she said quietly. "I would be truly honored."

Ten minutes later, the silk and golden robe with its slits on either side tied to her waist over her simple gown with a golden sash, Hannah stood in front of the mirror once more, bending her knees so that Rose could place the long head veil called a *khalak* on her head, arrange it over her shoulders.

"Something old," Vi said, handing Hannah the small prayer book she'd carried at her own wedding.

"Something new being the wedding gown," Jessica said, sighing in pleasure, "and the something borrowed being the most beautiful thing I've ever seen in my life. Except for you, Hannah. You're even more beautiful than that gown."

"The *khurkeh*," Rose corrected. "But you're right, Jessica. She's lovely. And now we must go downstairs and tell everyone that we're ready. Hannah?"

She nodded, trying to tear her gaze away from her reflection. "I'm ready, Rose."

"And the weather has cooperated completely," Vi said, still dabbing at her eyes with a small linen handkerchief. "Not that it won't change in the next fifteen minutes, so we'd better hurry. It may be tempting fate to plan an outdoor ceremony at this time of year."

Hannah still hesitated, watching the others proceed out of the room, head for the curved staircase.

She was so happy, and yet a small sadness clung to her as she lifted her chin and headed for the landing. An emptiness that couldn't be filled.

Hannah got as far as the landing when she sensed someone walking toward her from somewhere back down the hallway. She turned, a smile on her face, half-expecting to see Alex, who had been very vocal on the subject of not being able to see his bride before the ceremony.

"Hello, little girl," Hugo Clark said, stopping a good

five feet away from her. She stared at him, openmouthed, taking in the black tuxedo he wore, the way his hair was still wet and slicked back from his face. "Would it be all right with you if a stupid, stubborn old man walked you down the aisle? Your Alex is a damn stubborn man, and wouldn't stop coming around, pounding on my door, interrupting my office hours, until I'd talk to him."

He took another step, bowed his head. "Until I admitted that I loved my daughter. That I loved her—love her—very, very much. And that I'm proud of her, and that I want her to be a part of my life, and I want to be a part of hers."

"Oh, Daddy," Hannah cried, launching herself into his arms, hugging him, being hugged in return.

Hugo gave her one last squeeze, then pushed her away, hunted in his pocket for a huge red cotton handkerchief he used first to wipe at Hannah's tears, then at his own. "Okay, enough of that, girlie-girl," he said with some of his old bluster, and Hannah gave out with a shaky laugh. "I think I've got a daughter to give away, not that I plan to ever let you go again."

Hannah bit her lips together to try to hold back her tears, then smiled as she slipped her arm through Hugo's. "I love you, Daddy," she said, kissing his cheek.

"Good. I don't know why you do, but good, good," Hugo said, clearing his throat. "Now, let's go get you married. I don't want that man of yours camping on my doorstep anymore."

Caught between tears and laughter, Hannah floated down the stairway and across the room, to where Randy held the door open for her, winking at her as she and Hugo walked through the doorway and out into the sunshine.

She stood just outside the door for a few seconds, taking in the sight of the small gathering, seeing Mac and Cade, but there was no sign of Alex.

And then, from the direction of the stables, a tall figure clad all in white approached on horseback. Jabbar, black as night and fitted out in his dress bridle and beribboned saddle, with Alex riding him, a true prince in his flowing white *tobe* and *kihr,* his head covered by a *kaffiyeh* of purest white banded with a twisted *agal* of golden ropes.

Jabbar stepped high, dancing daintily, with all the fire and spirit of a young colt, his head high, his tail a flag in the soft breeze, proud to carry this prince of Sorajhee, this man of Texas, this bridegroom.

Alex dismounted, handed the reins to Mac and walked toward Hannah, his arms held out to her, beckoning for her to join him.

She looked at her father, waited.

"Go to him, girlie-girl," he said, kissing her cheek, then holding her hand, offering that hand to Alex, who took it. "As I thank God I was able to see this day, see more than just this day."

"Hannah?" Alex said, his dark eyes sweeping over her. "Will you make me the happiest man in the world?"

She smiled, let him take her hand, and together they turned to walk down the path to where the minister waited, to where the future waited.

*   *   *   *   *

Will one of Alex's brothers honor the royal
agreement between Sorajhee and Balahar and
marry Princess Serena? Find out next month when
TEXAS SHEIKHS *continues with*

HIS ARRANGED MARRIAGE

by Tina Leonard, on sale for
Harlequin American Romance in May 2001.

Meet 50 loving dads in

& BACHELORS USA

Take 4 FREE BOOKS,
Plus get a FREE GIFT!

abies & Bachelors USA is a heartwarming new collection of reissued
vels featuring 50 sexy heroes from every state who experience the
s and downs of fatherhood and find time for love all the same. All
the books, hand-picked by our editors, are outstanding romances
some of the world's bestselling authors, including Stella Bagwell,
istine Rolofson, Judith Arnold and Marie Ferrarella!

**Don't delay, order today! Call customer service at
1-800-873-8635.
Or
Clip this page and mail it to The Reader Service:**

In U.S.A.	In CANADA
P.O. Box 9049	P.O. Box 616
Buffalo, NY	Fort Erie, Ontario
14269-9049	L2A 5X3

S! Please send me four FREE BOOKS and FREE GIFT along with the next four
vels on a 14-day free home preview. If I like the books and decide to keep them, I'll
y just $15.96* U.S. or $18.00* CAN., and there's no charge for shipping and
ndling. Otherwise, I'll keep the 4 FREE BOOKS and FREE GIFT and return the rest.
decide to continue, I'll receive six books each month—two of which are always
e—until I've received the entire collection. In other words, if I collect all 50 volumes,
ill have paid for 32 and received 18 absolutely free!   267 HCK 4534
                                                                      467 HCK 4535

ame	(Please Print)	
ddress		Apt. #
ty	State/Prov.	Zip/Postal Code

Terms and prices subject to change without notice.
Sales Tax applicable in N.Y. Canadian residents will be charged applicable provincial taxes
and GST. All orders are subject to approval.
RBAB01R   © 2000 Harlequin Enterprises Limited

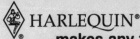

Harlequin truly does
make any time special. ...
This year we are celebrating
weddings in style!

To help us celebrate, we want you to tell us how wearing the Harlequin wedding gown will make your wedding day special. As the grand prize, Harlequin will offer one lucky bride the chance to **"Walk Down the Aisle"** in the Harlequin wedding gown!

There's more...

For her honeymoon, she and her groom will spend five nights at the **Hyatt Regency Maui.** As part of this five-night honeymoon at the hotel renowned for its romantic attractions, the couple will enjoy a candlelit dinner for two in Swan Court, a sunset sail on the hotel's catamaran, and duet spa treatments.

To enter, please write, in, 250 words or less, how wearing the Harlequin wedding gown will make your wedding day special. The entry will be judged based on its emotionally compelling nature, its originality and creativity, and its sincerity. This contest is open to Canadian and U.S. residents only and to those who are 18 years of age and older. There is no purchase necessary to enter. Void where prohibited. See further contest rules attached. Please send your entry to:

Walk Down the Aisle Contest

In Canada	In U.S.A.
P.O. Box 637	P.O. Box 9076
Fort Erie, Ontario	3010 Walden Ave.
L2A 5X3	Buffalo, NY 14269-9076

You can also enter by visiting www.eHarlequin.com
Win the Harlequin wedding gown and the vacation of a lifetime!
The deadline for entries is October 1, 2001.

PHWDACONT1

HARLEQUIN WALK DOWN THE AISLE TO MAUI CONTEST 1197
OFFICIAL RULES
NO PURCHASE NECESSARY TO ENTER

1. To enter, follow directions published in the offer to which you are responding. Contest begins April 2, 2001, and ends on October 1, 2001. Method of entry may vary. Mailed entries must be postmarked by October 1, 2001, and received by October 8, 2001.

2. Contest entry may be, at times, presented via the Internet, but will be restricted solely to residents of certain georgraphic areas that are disclosed on the Web site. To enter via the Internet, if permissible, access the Harlequin Web site (www.eHarlequin.com) and follow the directions displayed online. Online entries must be received by 11:59 p.m. E.S.T. on October 1, 2001.

   In lieu of submitting an entry online, enter by mail by hand-printing (or typing) on an 8½" x 11" plain piece of paper, your name, address (including zip code), Contest number/name and in 250 words or fewer, why winning a Harlequin wedding dress would make your wedding day special. Mail via first-class mail to: Harlequin Walk Down the Aisle Contest 1197, (in the U.S.) P.O. Box 9076, 3010 Walden Avenue, Buffalo, NY 14269-9076, (in Canada) P.O. Box 637, Fort Erie, Ontario L2A 5X3, Canada

   Limit one entry per person, household address and e-mail address. Online and/or mailed entries received from persons residing in geographic areas in which Internet entry is not permissible will be disqualified.

3. Contests will be judged by a panel of members of the Harlequin editorial, marketing and public relations staff based on the following criteria:
   - Originality and Creativity—50%
   - Emotionally Compelling—25%
   - Sincerity—25%

   In the event of a tie, duplicate prizes will be awarded. Decisions of the judges are final.

4. All entries become the property of Torstar Corp. and will not be returned. No responsibility is assumed for lost, late, illegible, incomplete, inaccurate, nondelivered or misdirected mail or misdirected e-mail, for technical, hardware or software failures of any kind, lost or unavailable network connections, or failed, incomplete, garbled or delayed computer transmission or any human error which may occur in the receipt or processing of the entries in this Contest.

5. Contest open only to residents of the U.S. (except Puerto Rico) and Canada, who are 18 years of age or older, and is void wherever prohibited by law; all applicable laws and regulations apply. Any litigation within the Province of Quebec respecting the conduct or organization of a publicity contest may be submitted to the Régie des alcools, des courses et des jeux for a ruling. Any litigation respecting the awarding of a prize may be submitted to the Régie des alcools, des courses et des jeux on for the purpose of helping the parties reach a settlement. Employees and immediate family members of Torstar Corp. and D. L. Blair, Inc., their affiliates, subsidiaries and all other agencies, entities and persons connected with the use, marketing or conduct of this Contest are not eligible to enter. Taxes on prizes are the sole responsibility of winners. Acceptance of any prize offered constitutes permission to use winner's name, photograph or other likeness for the purposes of advertising, trade and promotion on behalf of Torstar Corp., its affiliates and subsidiaries without further compensation to the winner, unless prohibited by law.

6. Winners will be determined no later than November 15, 2001, and will be notified by mail. Winners will be required to sign and return an Affidavit of Eligibility form within 15 days after winner notification. Noncompliance within that time period may result in disqualification and an alternative winner may be selected. Winners of trip must execute a Release of Liability prior to ticketing and must possess required travel documents (e.g. passport, photo ID) where applicable. Trip must be completed by November 2002. No substitution of prize permitted by winner. Torstar Corp. and D. L. Blair, Inc., their parents, affiliates, and subsidiaries are not responsible for errors in printing or electronic presentation of Contest, entries and/or game pieces. In the event of printing or other errors which may result in unintended prize values or duplication of prizes, all affected game pieces or entries shall be null and void. If for any reason the Internet portion of the Contest is not capable of running as planned, including infection by computer virus, bugs, tampering, unauthorized intervention, fraud, technical failures, or any other causes beyond the control of Torstar Corp. which corrupt or affect the administration, secrecy, fairness, integrity or proper conduct of the Contest, Torstar Corp. reserves the right, at its sole discretion, to disqualify any individual who tampers with the entry process and to cancel, terminate, modify or suspend the Contest or the Internet portion thereof. In the event of a dispute regarding an online entry, the entry will be deemed submitted by the authorized holder of the e-mail account submitted at the time of entry. Authorized account holder is defined as the natural person who is assigned to an e-mail address by an Internet access provider, online service provider or other organization that is responsible for arranging e-mail address for the domain associated with the submitted e-mail address. **Purchase or acceptance of a product offer does not improve your chances of winning.**

7. Prizes: (1) Grand Prize—A Harlequin wedding dress (approximate retail value: $3,500) and a 5-night/6-day honeymoon trip to Maui, HI, including round-trip air transportation provided by Maui Visitors Bureau from Los Angeles International Airport (winner is responsible for transportation to and from Los Angeles International Airport) and a Harlequin Romance Package, including hotel accomodations (double occupancy) at the Hyatt Regency Maui Resort and Spa, dinner for (2) two at Swan Court, a sunset sail on Kiele V and a spa treatment for the winner (approximate retail value: $4,000); (5) Five runner-up prizes of a $1000 gift certificate to selected retail outlets to be determined by Sponsor (retail value $1000 ea.). Prizes consist of only those items listed as part of the prize. Limit one prize per person. All prizes are valued in U.S. currency.

8. For a list of winners (available after December 17, 2001) send a self-addressed, stamped envelope to: Harlequin Walk Down the Aisle Contest 1197 Winners, P.O. Box 4200 Blair, NE 68009-4200 or you may access the www.eHarlequin.com Web site through January 15, 2002.

Contest sponsored by Torstar Corp., P.O. Box 9042, Buffalo, NY 14269-9042, U.S.A.

PHWDACONT2